BUSTILLO

By Kenneth Royce

Bustillo

Kenneth Royce

Coward, McCann & Geoghegan, Inc. New York

First American Edition 1976

SBN: 698-10762-4

Library of Congress Cataloging in Publication Data

Royce, Kenneth.
   Bustillo.

   I. Title.
PZ4.R8892Bu3   [PR6068.098]   823'.9'14   76-26907

Printed in the United States of America

1

BUSTILLO LEFT THE WASHROOM and went back to the darkened, empty office. He stood in the doorway viewing the reflected milkiness of the head-high glass panelling above the wood partitioning, his qualms growing. Beyond the windows to his right was the tapering column of Tokyo Tower outlined against the night sky by rows of light bulbs like strings of fluorescent pearls. He walked carefully between the desks of the larger office and stopped by Kasaka's door, telling himself that he must be mad. The central heating had been turned down and the chill was creeping up his legs.

He knew that the door was locked without trying it. Equally, he accepted that it would be no problem to open. Producing a plastic case the size of a long, fat cigar, he selected from it a thin, unusually headed key. As he crouched before the door he had an attack of nerves. He was crazy to try it. All this was behind him. Yet he owed it to Nikki. The conviction was strong. It was a duty to her.

At first he fumbled. He badly needed a drink. Wiping his mouth with the back of his hand he steadied and tried to concentrate. Once working he felt better. The lock sprang back and he went into Kasaka's office cursing himself for possessing a sharp observation, acute hearing and an ability to form a pattern from seemingly unconnected innuendoes. He couldn't help himself. It all came together in his mind uninvited; a snip of a telephone conversation he should not have heard; an action; an expression and, of course, the meticulous jottings. Only part was due to his training. The remainder arose from a natural curiosity that carried its own interpretation mechanism.

5

He reached the desk, dropped to one knee and groped under the knee hole. The button was recessed and his fingers were shaking before he found it. The click was almost inaudible. He pulled open the panel of false drawers and shone a pencil torch which he shaded with one hand as he examined the inner drawer which was really a desk safe. He worked away at the lock trying key after key. Only when he rested did the shakes move over him, and the sweat began to roll. Part of him wanted to flee, the other part was hypnotised by the challenge. He almost gave up but he had gone too far. When he finally opened the safe he was wet through.

It was a loose-leaf book, small and ordinary. There were traces of paper fibre around the coiled spring of its spine where pages had been torn out. While he sat with his back to the desk, legs out, quietly reading in the torchlight, his scalp began to prickle. There were names, a few of whom he recognised and would mean trouble. The amounts too, were considerable. Enough to demand reciprocal returns. It was not what he'd expected to find and the information startled him. His inclination to run almost bordered on panic but he read on and was then sorry that he had.

Rather breathlessly he returned the book and closed the safe. His real problems began when he tried to lock it. He could feel the bolt going so far then the tumbler stuck as the spring resisted. He calmed fraying nerves and worked away but could get no further. Finally, he had to leave it. The bolt was sufficiently across for the safe to remain locked but the tumbler had not been fully sprung.

Bustillo locked the door over the safe and sank back on his heels. It would depend on how sensitive Kasaka was. He mentally reversed their positions and he groaned. He was back to where he had started before arriving in Japan. His life was running in circles. He knew then that he would have to move on again. Oh Christ. Why had he done it? He knew why and accepted the reason as valid. Where it had gone wrong was in an anticipative sense. The favour he'd imagined himself to be performing was the opposite of expectation. It was like stabbing a friend in the back. He rose despondently, knowing that he dare not stay on here. Okay, so he was running again. That's the way it went. He'd get that drink. Several. That was part of the pattern too.

*　　*　　*

The two men stared at each other across the room. On the top floor, the panorama of a darkening Tokyo was being spiked by

6

lights beyond the picture windows. Most of what the room revealed displayed the interest of the two men and the empire they controlled. Glass, metal, furniture, bricks, plaster; the amalgamate of the building industry and its fringe concerns. The Miyoto Consortium went beyond that, into plastics and travel and freight and minor areas lost in the smaller subsidiary companies engulfed by the giant.

Below their feet, occupying a corner block, the Miyoto Building swelled out into the administrative centre of the multi-million giant, the heart of an increasing group known throughout Japan and to importers around the globe. It had offices or agents in every western capital in the world. It was one of the foundations of Japanese industry, solid, impregnable, highly profitable, still growing, swallowing others.

Many of the lights in the building were now out. Inside the massive glass doors the vestibule lights had been dimmed, the coloured fountains turned off. These were matters of minor routine and not of concern to the two men as they watched each other with worried eyes.

"We must get rid of him."

"How do you mean?"

"Father, you know dam' fine how I mean."

The older man, shaken, nervously raised a hand, then lowered it, fingers trembling. "You mean kill him?" The bloodless lips barely moved.

The son, as tense as his father but in more control of himself, nodded briefly, gaze unwavering, trying to pick up a nuance of positiveness from the deep eyes that flickered away from his.

"*No.*" The ageing face was pale.

The younger man shrugged, disgusted. "What then?"

"I don't know. Let's think." The father gestured irritably and walked to the window. He held himself easily as he looked out towards Tokyo Tower, seeing the illuminated frame as Bustillo had done the previous night. The mixed American and Japanese blood had given him height and interesting looks. He was handsome with an almost unlined face and slightly puckered eyes. From the back it was impossible to detect his concern; he did not move, yet his posture was relaxed. His gaze was uneasily probing the darkening sky, the long fingers seeking each other for reassurance. From the front it was clear that he was in a highly nervous state. As his features tautened two lines appeared down his face like calipers closing on the narrow jawline.

7

"We have thought. Over and over. Hedging is the way to disaster." The son, watching his father's back, was not fooled by the illusion of languidness. The old boy was bombed out of his mind. It was understandable but it had to be faced. All of it. The son, slightly shorter and stockier, was aggressive in almost every aspect. Not necessarily objectionably so, but his stance was eager, the power of him indicative in every move, each gesture. He knew what needed to be done and would have been far less tolerant had it not been his father who obstructed him. His jet hair was glossy, thick and brushed across; his eyes smouldered.

"Come on, Father. Come on."

"We don't yet know that he's a risk."

"Oh, Jesus." Two hands clawed towards the ceiling. "Do you have to wait until the damage is done? The guy knows. We know that he knows."

"We don't know his intent." The lights up the tower looked polished and glossed and were thankfully distracting. But not enough.

The son struck at space angrily. "Is that why he walked out? Because he had no intent?"

"We can't know what's in his mind." The father turned slowly to face his son, seemingly calmer. "If he puts on the screws we'll know soon enough. If he's been to the police, it's already too late."

"Great. So we just hang about and wait for the noose to tighten, for a colossus to fall. You realise he's been seeing Nikki." Contempt was barely concealed.

"That's one reason I think we should wait. Whatever she is she wouldn't betray her own family."

"She doesn't consider she has a family. She's a lush and a junkie and he probably used her for this purpose."

"She knows nothing."

The son was breathing evenly, eyeing his father with concern.

"I'm not prepared to wait. And you'd better get your priorities right."

"As a member of the Diet I have more to lose than you. I think I have my priorities right. I don't believe in hasty decision."

The son showed his exasperation. There was little of the oriental in his face, just the barest touch of linenfold about the lids. His mother was Virginian. His grandmother had been Bostonian and had married a wealthy Japanese. So the occidental was uppermost in him and came through in direct ways that sometimes confused his father.

8

"Father, we really aren't playing politics now. We've gotten into a mess. There's only one way out that I can see and I don't think we should hesitate—right or wrong. We stand to lose too much." He looked shrewdly at his father, saw the wavering. "You could spend the rest of your life in prison. At your age, after the luxury you've been used to, it would kill you."

The father left the window, sat wearily at his desk, deep eyes brooding, hands restless. "*Does he deserve to die?*" It was a plea.

Kenji Miyoto shrugged. Carefully he said, "I don't think that's the question. Maybe he doesn't. *Can we afford to let him live?* Isn't that what you should have asked? Isn't that what must be answered?" He smiled grimly. Always the realist, he added, "It's him or us, Father! Make up your mind."

The older man looked up, torn between self-interest and the dreadful alternative. He couldn't sit on the fence forever. It had been a mistake to take Bustillo on. He'd done it as a favour for an estranged daughter who had already ruined her life and for whom he felt a phantom conscience. As he'd got older regret had come too, but qualified and much too late. Kenji was right. Almost always was.

Seeing something of his father's torture, Kenji said softly, victory his only thought, "It's too late for scruples, Dad."

The old man nodded slowly, defeat breaking his face. "I'll have nothing to do with it. You must do as you please."

Kenji Miyoto hid his contempt. He'd got his way. It was enough. Yet he couldn't resist a barb. "There was a guy called Pontius Pilate who washed his hands like that."

The older man looked up, afraid and disillusioned. He well knew the unyielding hardness in his son. "Even so, I guess you'd better first offer a sweetener. Money may do it, it usually does. That is my order."

About to argue the futility of such a move, Kenji hesitated. He could go through the motions, might learn something.

"Okay." He started to walk towards the door then stopped, half turned. "Have you any ideas?"

"About what?" The stomach cramp was inexplicably spontaneous, fear rippling through his system.

"If he can't be bought off, who's going to hit him?"

"You find it easy to be so matter of fact about killing a man?"

"Not easy. Necessary. We'll have to find someone to do it. You don't just step out and say, Hey, feller, I want someone knocked off."

"I don't want to know."

"No. It'll be tricky. Not something that can be shoved in the personal column."

His son's perverse enjoyment of the situation appalled his father. Hardness was one thing, but this was blood lust. He said evenly, "You have to find Bustillo first."

*   *   *

They met near the Shimizudani Park and headed towards the Imperial Palace, turning left up Uchibori-Dori Avenue. She was dressed western fashion, her coat collar turned up high around her ears, her black glossed hair mostly hidden by a peaked fur cap pulled well down over her eyes. Even beneath the shadowed peak he could see the ravages in a fragile face aged long before its time. By her general steadiness, her brightness at seeing him, he guessed that her immediate needs had been attended to. Her small boned hands were at the moment out of sight in the deep pockets of the expensive coat. She wore her clothes casually, like the model she had once been.

"Aren't you cold like that?" She gave his cardigan and open-necked shirt a disapproving glance as they fell in step.

"A little. But the sun's warm."

It was true. The sky was the palest blue, clear but for a low-slung lozenge of sun which, when swallowed by the pink lip in the east, would change the temperature noticeably. The frost would fall, the water around the Palace would freeze again. Swans swam lazily below them, but nearer to the Palace itself where the sun could not reach, ducks waddled over the ice.

They leaned on the parapet with others. "Something's wrong." She didn't face him but watched the serenity of the swans as if they symbolised a past she had briefly known.

"Your old man and Kenji are up to their eyeballs in corruption. The shareholders deserve a better deal."

"Let's go to bed. I'm in the mood." She pushed into his side, putting an arm round him, the hand creeping under his cardigan.

"You're not interested in what they're up to?"

"Why must we talk about them? Come on, honey. I need a drink and I need you. Both, together."

He turned his back on the Palace and caught her hand as she was on the point of being reckless. "There are people watching, Nikki. Behave yourself."

"Behave yourself," she mimicked. "Let's go home." She meant her place.

"I can't. Not again. I walked out on the job."

"Oh, Jesus. Did you have to? You've spoiled it for us, Jimmy."

He thought she was going to cry, never really used to her sudden emotional surges that could break out in any direction. She never did things by halves. Passion of one kind or another was behind almost every move she made. But she'd provided a ready ear, until now, and a shoulder. They both needed a shoulder. The danger of tears receded as fast as it had come.

"Let's take a room in an hotel." Her mind was still anchored on bed and he despaired at getting anywhere with her other than on a mattress and that had never been a problem.

"Nikki, can you be serious for a moment?"

"About *them*? No." Her young face screwed. "Why do you think I'm like I am? I know what they're like. I don't need you to tell me. You should've stayed. It was a mistake to pry."

He took her arm, pulling her gently away from the wall and the ears of others. "I did it for you. I was trained in a certain way. I noticed small things over the course of time. I had the feeling that your family might be being swindled. That's why I did it. Once you turn one stone you have to turn others." They were walking again.

"And you found that it's *they* who are doing the swindling."

He glanced down, surprised at her indifference. "Their bribery list would rock the country."

"So it's very bad."

"Bad enough to ruin your father."

"Good."

He felt her helplessness. "It wouldn't do your government much good. Scandals like this sometimes have many tentacles."

"You mean you're going to tell someone? The police?"

Suddenly he was cautious. "I haven't thought about it. I could do without what I know."

"Blackmail him. He's loaded."

He laughed uncomfortably. "Blackmail's not my scene."

She looked up at him then, pupils pinpoints against the beautiful moist sepia of her eyes. She touched his nose with a finger. "Jimbo, you're too weak for your own good."

"Is that what it is? Weakness?" He was worried by her light-hearted assertion, recognising the truth in part. She knew she had hurt him, had an inkling why, and in one of those little sadistic moods of hers, prompted by the realisation of her own short future, she let him torture himself with doubt. Only he could find the extent of his weakness. She had tried to get him hooked but he had never gone beyond the bottle, although in her eyes he had cause to go all the way, to join her among the damned. So he had strength too, and sometimes she needed it. God how she needed it. But mostly they were complementary props, a suspect taking of weight from either side that worked for the moment.

As they wandered off slowly, in no hurry for anywhere, a European slightly separated from a group of tourists watching the Palace, pushed away from the wall. His home environment could not account for his pallor as he stared after them. He had received a shock. Worried eyes beneath a homburg followed the erratic course of the couple. From the cut of his topcoat, the quietness of his tie, and the general well-tailored image of the man, coupled with his features, he might well be English, possibly German. They were almost out of sight when he made up his mind to follow them. Not rehearsed in such a tactic, he held well back, aware that his appearance was against him. It is true that virtually all Japanese males wore western clothes, and, certainly in the cities, most of the women, but ethnically he could not be missed. Fortunately the couple were engrossed in one another, the girl noticeably more forthcoming in public than was deemed correct by her contemporaries who would blame her mixed blood and hide their shame. For if a Japanese woman has one noticeable trait, then it's dignity. If fine looks are coupled with it there is an image worth more than a second glance. Bustillo and Nikki followed by the European headed towards the dipping Japanese sun.

She took him to a good hotel north of the Ginza. They had walked aimlessly, engrossed in the need of each other. In spite of this Bustillo was disturbed. Awareness had been driven into him like a nail in wood. He was incapable of ignoring it completely and its intrusion irritated him. He was upset over his discovery the night before, accepted that he had foolishly left without warning. Running away was nearer the truth. He faced it shakily. Why was he always running? He wrongly decided that it was this that caused his uneasiness and turned back to his refuge in the girl, putting his arm round her and pulling her close.

Graham Leach saw them turn into the building and hurried forward. By the time he reached the hotel he could see them checking in at reception. No luggage. Not even a hand grip. They wouldn't be there for long, possibly not even overnight. Yet what could he do? He would be remembered if he bribed the receptionist for their names and, anyway, the names would be meaningless. Two girls went past, one in a kimono of pinks and reds with a coat over the top. Her wedge sandals clacked as she crossed the road. Both girls looked at him interestedly. He dare not stay here. He made a note of the hotel and wandered back the way he had come, angry and worried that the sight of the American had upset him so.

Following the same route he reached a busy main street and stood waiting for the flow of traffic to ease before crossing. As he stood there a group of people formed about him and he was glad then that his medium height was at least an advantage among them. It came as a shock to him to realise that he must have crossed this street on the way down, yet he had no recollection of doing so. Had he waited, gone straight across? He didn't know. With the traffic on the left-hand side of the street as in England he possessed an instinctive advantage over most foreign visitors but the possibility of his having crossed recklessly confounded him, pinpointed his distress.

At the crossing point a yellow metal holder was fixed to a lamp post. In it were small yellow flags with a black silhouette of a walking pedestrian on each one. One of the waiting Japanese pulled out a flag, held it high and started to cross the street. The traffic immediately stopped. The whole group of pedestrians followed the flag bearer, Leach among them. At the other side the flag was dropped into a complementary holder and the group went their separate ways. Leach was always impressed by the orderliness of the Japanese. He couldn't recall having jay-walked. Yet is that what he'd done? Or had he taken a flag or crossed with others? It seemed a futile matter yet it magnified in his mind. The fact was *it had happened only minutes ago and he couldn't bloody remember*. Damn the American. Damn him. Damn him. Dear God, something had to be done. Leach found he was shaking, his mind obsessed. Here of all places. And *that* he found suspect in the extreme.

*   *   *

The hotel was totally Japanese, not designed for the western tourist. Had Graham Leach been aware of the ramifications of this, he would have been more worried still, for the lack of luggage of Nikki Miyoto and Jimmy Bustillo had little meaning.

13

The room was seemingly without beds until Bustillo took two mattresses from a cupboard and laid them side by side on the floor. In the same cupboard were sealed packs of pyjamas and kimono jackets. In the bathroom leading off were hermetically sealed toothbrushes, paste and a razor.

While Bustillo attended to the bedding Nikki undressed with a weary familiarity. Her young body was still firm, though beginning to thin, the needle marks in her arms like the start of a chickenpox rash. She lay down on a mattress while he unbuttoned his cardigan, her earlier need of sex no longer evident as she watched him indifferently. She had used it as a pretext to get off a subject she detested. Yet she did need his comfort. Contact gave her brief reality, even reassurance. She clung to the meaningless mumbles of passion as she entwined the bodies that so frequently engulfed her. She could feel, hear, be excited by them. And forget, just for a short time. If sex created distraction she used it mercilessly.

They had put no blankets on the mattresses. The room was warm. A refrigerator stood in one corner, a television set in the other. Before joining her Bustillo opened the refrigerator hoping that a bottle or two may have been left by a previous occupant. He joined her on the floor and they made desultory love, afterwards realising that it was not what they wanted just then. There were problems on their minds. One at least, the same problem.

She turned to face him as he lifted himself on one elbow. She ran a hand over the curves of his shoulder down the arm that reached for her thigh. He was well built, she reflected. Not much superfluous, although that would change if he continued drinking the way he did. There was the suspicion of bulge below the hairy chest. It did not worry her. He was here. That was enough. He, or someone. But he was better than most of them. He didn't just want her body. She knew that he found a strange sort of comfort in her. Perhaps he saw in her a kind of warning. A danger signal. She didn't mind that either although she'd pull him down with her if she could. She had already tried unsuccessfully. She took his hand away from her body and held it loosely. If she could hold a hand all the way it would be easier. Much easier. She wanted to cry again and stopped.

His wide eyes were watching her. He had shaved badly; there was a patch of stubble on his chin; she had felt it against her neck while they had been erratically interlocked. Yet he had a good face, a ridiculous innocence about it years younger than he. Nice nose, lips, fair, unruly thick head of hair, not like the dark hair on his body. And eyes that were always questing, searching for something he might never find. She didn't know what. As she now stroked his face she realised how little she knew about him.

Did she want to know more? He was afraid of something. Not afraid, uncertain. There was diffidence in almost everything he did. The bottle unleashed him but only so far. In better moments, usually after she'd had a shot, she understood him more. He was escaping from something. But these moments of clarity never penetrated his secret thoughts. There were areas of his mind she felt she would never know. She was locked out from them and it seemed to her that he tried also to lock himself out. Why had he come to Japan?

If Caucasians wanted to avoid others of their kind then it was a good place. Some Americans worked here; military, navy, air force, business men. But very few Europeans. He hadn't even told her where he had come from. That he was American was obvious, but his accent was subdued, his mannerisms mixed, as if he'd spent most of his life away from his own country. He was tanned, that pale amber of the fair skinned, so he had last been somewhere where there was sun in winter. She leaned forward to kiss him and realised that the spontaneous peck had been motivated by warmth for him. He did not respond and, in any event, she did not want to rouse him again yet.

"Where did you meet Tadashi?"

His expression became veiled as she'd seen before when she'd entered protected territory.

"I want a drink."

She ordered a bottle of bourbon from room service. "Where?"

"God knows."

"Before he worked as a journalist?"

"Hasn't he always?"

"I've always thought that was only part of his job. He's away a lot."

"Journalists often are."

She pushed him with her fingers. "You don't like the subject."

He smiled ruefully, amused by her friendly tolerance. "What subject?"

"I see. You expect me to talk of my family but you don't like it back."

They slipped silk jackets on for when the drink came.

"Tadashi is not my family. You should ask *him* these things."

She rose, and he noticed the beginning of the loose flesh on the

15

thighs below the hemline. He looked up to her eyes. She was twenty-five he had discovered. Already she looked well over thirty but not in a natural way. Debauched. He felt sick, worried for her. He hadn't helped. He doubted that anyone could. Where was the waiter, for Chrissake? He was up as soon as he heard the tap on the door. Taking the tray he laid it on the floor, making a gap between the mattresses. He was drinking from the bottle as soon as he had the top off, while Nikki tried to pull it from him.

"Let go, you bastard. *Please.* I want some."

He let her have it, disgusted at his own craving but in no mood to subdue it. She poured into two tumblers and he was touched by the delicacy of her action. What a different life she might have had. She ignored the carafe of water but went to the ice box, clinking chunks into each glass until it rose nearly to the top. The bottle was already half empty. Noticing it, she rang a surprised room service for another bottle.

Squatting on her haunches she drank half her liquor before looking at him again, delicate fingers still clutching the glass.

"I think Tadashi deliberately arranged our meeting."

He buried himself in his own glass. "You know that he did."

"You know what I mean. He wanted me to get you a job."

"I needed one."

She raised her glass, the liquor already doing its damage to her empty stomach. "Listen, you bum. Stop being obtuse. He *wanted* you to work for my father. He knew you were a trained accountant."

He didn't answer because the same grave doubts had already assailed him. In fairness Tadashi hadn't asked anything of him but he had the strong feeling that he had unwittingly anticipated a request yet to come.

Nikki pointed a finger, the ice rattling in the glass. "But that's only part of what you are, isn't it? You've been spying on my father."

"No." He meant it. "At first for *his* benefit, I thought. It only happened . . ." He tailed off. How could he explain?

"Go on."

He couldn't tell her. It wasn't a new situation but the remedy was old and worked quite well. He drained his drink and poured some more. She held her glass out and he wondered what had happened to him that he hadn't served her first. "Good luck."

"Cheers. You never answer me, do you?"

And he didn't answer now. The waiter knocked again and he

16

was relieved at the interruption. He came back with a bottle, putting it beside the empty one.

Nikki's voice was becoming slurred, yet she never seemed to go beyond that stage. She entered a dulled state of euphoria and there she stayed. The only time he had seen her collapse was after taking a shot of heroin when already full of liquor. It had frightened him, particularly as he couldn't revive her and he had sat, after lifting her on to her bed, periodically ready to call a doctor if her heartbeat worsened. It had sobered him but only to make him seek further escape. When she had come to he was already half drunk again.

"You know what's going to happen to you?" she threw at him, spilling her drink, amber flowing between her breasts.

"Sure." He grinned and presented a different person. "I'm gonna get bombed."

"You sure are, lover boy."

He sensed she meant it in a different way. "What're you getting at?"

She loosened her jacket. "Come to Nikki. Please, Jimbo. Come to Nikki."

"Tell me first. What did you mean?" His hand was reaching for the bottle but he didn't move it, waiting for her to answer.

She lifted her free hand, pointed a finger with raised thumb like a cocked pistol. "Ping," she said. "Thas what's gonna happen to you."

He drank quickly. Poured. "Why do you say that?"

"Now you're worried." She was getting back at him. "If my brother finds out that you've found out, you're dead. Dead," she repeated with an effort.

"But why should he?"

" 'Cause you walked out, you dope."

"But he's in no danger from me."

She held out her glass unsteadily. "Just a teensy, Jimbo, and then you come to Nikki."

"I'm not going to tell anyone," he insisted.

She waggled a finger. "But *he* doesn't know that. Does he?"

*   *   *

Before she married, her name was Chieko Kita. Her hair went straight back from her forehead, neat about the small ears and held at the neck by a coral-studded comb. Her faint brows were delicately arched above wide, slightly tilted eyes which were

17

smiling, as were the pale, finely shaped lips. The fragility of complexion belonged to the porcelain transparency of her country. To encase this superb image was an ivory-coloured kimono of finest silk flecked delicately with woven birds of Paradise in soft reds and pinks and blues. The black band around her middle had, horizontally embroidered, a rich green double stemmed solitary flower of pale ochre. She held her arms out to Graham Leach as he entered the wide hall of their villa.

"My husband, you look tired." She took his coat and hat, hung them in the closet. Then he embraced her, keeping his head close to hers so that she shouldn't see his concern.

On the way back, he had recovered some of his poise, but the face of the man he knew as Warton would haunt him and time would be no cure. The sensation of feeling threatened would remain. It would grow in his mind and already it had become an unshakable obsession. How could he escape it? He eased away from her, doing it gently, taking her by the shoulders. He preceded her into the drawing room, a habit he had cultivated from her.

"I saw your father."

She was quick to notice a change in his voice. "And everything was all right?" Her English was clear, but her accent quaint. Sometimes he just wanted to sit and listen to her talking. At others, they would speak in Japanese at which he was proficient. But then he was at most things he tackled.

"Everything. The company has been formed. Trading should start within a few months. Your father is an astute business man."

She smiled with pleasure, her head on one side. "He says so of you, too." She knelt at his feet and he took her face between his hands marvelling, as he always did, at the softness of her skin. This part of his life, planned though it was, had turned out better than he could have hoped. It was sometimes difficult to believe his luck. He could live it out this way, with Chieko beside him, undemanding, unasking, a superb ornament.

"You would like your tea now?"

It was unbelievable. "A drink first, darling."

Chieko rose and even that simple movement was done with grace. She didn't ask him why he had broken a habit. He never drank at this time of day. "Saki. I can warm it."

"Cognac."

Now that *was* strange. She crossed the room, widely spaced with light chairs and cushions, and went to a drinks trolley which had been one of his innovations. The windows swathed some thirty feet across one wall facing south, away from the city, across the green undulations of open country. Now it was dark and only pinpricks of lights came from the blackness outside. She carried the charged goblet back to him with it cupped between her hands the same way he had held her face.

"You are not well?"

"You're too perceptive, Chieko." She had meant, what is wrong? what is on your mind? but he knew that she would never ask the direct question.

"Is there something else I can get you?" Again he wasn't misled by the apparent innocence of the question. She knew very well that something was wrong. In a way he would prefer her to be more direct, he could then cut it dead. Playing it with a smile on his face was more difficult and he did not know how to hide it from her.

"Yes," he said, looking her straight in the eye. "Tea would be nice after this." He raised his glass at her but it was a dismissal. She gave a little bow and left the room. There were times when he wished she wasn't from such a highly bred family. He went to the window, searching the darkness to find only the ghostly image of his own reflection. He sipped his drink, watching himself and the strange aura around his reflection cast by the soft room-lighting. He lifted his glass again as if to a friend who responded simultaneously.

"Graham, old boy," he said quietly to his image. "Face up to it. You've got to kill him." He saw the splendid reflection of Chieko enter with the tray as he spoke and he hoped she had not heard. He did not think she had, then was more certain. But there was nothing in the fuzzed expression in the glass to indicate either way.

2

KENJI MIYOTO BUSTLED FROM the huge office block into the cooling air. The sky was still clear, it was going to be cold again. He hailed a cab and gave the address of an expensive apartment block on the fringe of the Ginza. His father was going soft, always had been a little. As he sat restlessly in the cab he reflected that he had laid his plans too carefully to forego anything now. He always thought in English, his father in Japanese. It was one of the differences between them. But their actions had been shared. He saw no blame on either side nor anything wrong with the quick way to a lot of money. What really angered him was the way his father squandered a good deal of his on Nikki. It made him wonder. The old man was buying her a quick funeral. Maybe that was best. His thought was quite callous. He had no feeling for his sister other than contempt. She was as weak as he was strong.

As they neared the Ginza the advertising signs were springing up. He always liked the perpendicular ideographs in lights, like illuminated pennants. Apart from the signs the Ginza, the fashionable shopping centre of Tokyo, was almost entirely western-ised. The Orient lay at its fringes and further out. The exceptions were the restaurants. He thought like this, almost as if he were a foreigner himself. But most of his education had been in the United States, mainly because of the commercial advantages that had accrued later.

He began to relax as the heat of the car reached him. And he considered Bustillo. The old man must have been out of his mind to have taken him on but that was due to that useless bitch Nikki. Even so, Bustillo must have qualifications far beyond those given to the Chief Accountant. And he must have nosed. He must have nosed in a quite deliberate fashion. Unlocking a desk safe to which he had no keys. So how had he done it? It put the man in quite a different light. A snooper. Perhaps a very highly qualified one. And that was the worry. That meant the law or a shakedown.

They wouldn't have known but for the fact that the lock had stuck. It required a special key. What else had he opened? Bustillo had been seen leaving the building late and had not shown up again. He had not communicated nor could he be raised. He had apparently left his apartment two days ago and they'd been trying to find him ever since.

It was impossible to know what Bustillo had actually seen apart from the one safe which contained only half the story. The other half was tax-free cream-offs. Had Bustillo understood what he'd seen? They had to assume that he had or he wouldn't have walked out. Which made him believe that Bustillo wasn't police. They'd have been there before anything could have been moved. But the sum total of Bustillo's knowledge was unknown. Even a little could hurt. A lot could be total disaster.

Kenji Miyoto paid off the cab in a quiet side street at the foot of a towering block. As the night closed in the window pattern of blank spaces was gradually being illuminated. In the foyer he demanded the apartment key from a startled porter who recognised him. Kenji took the elevator to the top floor where the noise was less apparent. In fact Nikki had never been the party girl Kenji still envisaged. Company, yes. A succession of lovers, male and female, quiet orgies on occasion. Drugs and drink, of course. But noise had never attracted her. The nearest she had got to it was the wild laughter of abandon or the sobbing of remorse. The rhythm of music reminded her too vividly of her own frantic heartbeat as if it was pulling the very life from her.

He turned the key and stood in the open doorway as if expecting some immediate response. He had telephoned her several times to check on the whereabouts of Bustillo, and the few times she'd been in she'd disclaimed all knowledge. Which was why he had come now. The surprise visit. He closed the door and went in, wrinkling his nose. The air conditioning was switched off, the windows, high above the city, closed. The air was stale. The place was clean, but untidy, clothes carelessly thrown over chairs. The bed was roughly made. Powder flecked the dressing table, spilling on to the carpeting where a lipstick had been crushed, its case flattened.

His lips curled as he wandered further into the room, his head stuck forward pugnaciously. Locating the air conditioning in the lobby he switched it on. The small kitchen needed tidying. The crockery had not been put in the dishwasher. All she had to do was to press a button yet it had been too much for her. Empty bottles were stacked in a corner. One rolled away from him as he inadvertently kicked it. The dregs of liquor formed sticky pools over the floor. His disgust was paramount, yet, inexplicably for him, he felt suddenly sorry for her.

He could never understand the reasons for her debauchery. She could have had a slice of the cake, had one in fact, but this was what she had used it for. Self-abasement. A masochistic need to hurry the death process. It couldn't be escape. Not in terms he understood. She was too much like her mother, who was now somewhere in Florida. Nikki was a dangerous pain in the neck. Okay, they kept things from her but this sort of behaviour drew attention even if she did most of it in private.

They had tried to get her a cure earlier on. The failure rate was depressing and in her case she hadn't wanted to co-operate. She had set her sights on a short, sometimes gay, ultimately painful destiny. Part of the evidence was at his feet. He hadn't been here for some time, hadn't realised just how far downhill she had come.

His momentary sorrow was replaced by a new fear. He considered Nikki's relationship with the American. He hadn't really noticed the man; he was too far down the ladder to consider. Until now.

He searched around the apartment, confused, appalled and worried. They really had been lax. He blamed his father and then himself for not keeping an eye on the old man. They must fix Bustillo and the thought stretched to a more unsettling one of what they should do about Nikki. Suddenly everything seemed out of hand. If he didn't straighten matters quickly his life, as he knew it, would be finished.

On the way out he questioned the porter but Bustillo hadn't been seen for two days. Nikki had left earlier that day on her own. Without luggage.

*   *   *

The news of Jimmy Bustillo's disappearance reached Tadashi Fujuda late. Last evening he had telephoned Bustillo at his apartment and had then phoned Nikki, receiving no reply from either. There was nothing odd about that. What had surprised him was when he had tried to contact Bustillo at his office in the Miyoto

Building only an hour ago. With the expertise of years of journalism he had quickly learned that Jimmy Bustillo hadn't reported in for the last two days and nobody seemed to know where he was. That fact puzzled and worried him and he had immediately gone round to Nikki's apartment.

He saw Kenji Miyoto through the glass doors talking to the porter. He drew back behind the outside cornice of the huge doorway. Small, he was used to using the advantages of his size. When Miyoto came out, Tadashi saw him without being seen. He knew that aggressive head and shoulder line well but something else had been added to the usual tight expression. Worry? Concern? Kenji Miyoto being worried or concerned about anything was almost news in itself. The sighting was too brief for a conclusion; Miyoto was in and out of the light so quickly. But something was wrong.

Tadashi waited until Miyoto was well away, then leaned against the wall to think, hands in topcoat pockets. He didn't want the porter drawing conclusions that might filter back to Miyoto. He made up his mind, entered the vestibule with his bright and breezy act, thick lips drawn back in a long toothed grin.

"Tell Miss Miyoto I'm here."

The porter knew him, of course, not his profession but that he was a friend of the strange, rich girl. "She's out, sir."

"We're supposed to meet here. When did she go?"

"At least some hours ago, sir."

"Ah, then, she'll be back. I'll wait up there." Tadashi held his hand out for the key. He'd done it before.

The porter ignored him awkwardly. Tadashi guessed then that Miyoto had issued instructions.

"Come on. The key." He flipped his fingers.

"I cannot, sir. The owners have issued new instructions. I could lose my job."

As Miyoto's wallet was infinitely thicker than his own Tadashi kept his in his pocket. He would get nowhere and it might be reported back. His quick, bright eyes immediately expressed sympathy with the porter. "We don't want that to happen. Where did she go?"

"I don't know, sir."

"Was she with the tall, fair-haired American?"

The porter opened his mouth, then closed it. His expression informed Tadashi that the question had been asked before and that was ominous. Miyoto had sewn the porter up and Tadashi didn't want to push too hard. "Okay." He switched on his grin and flipped a hand. "I'll come back a little later if I don't find her."

The porter was uncomfortable, would prefer to speak to Tadashi than Miyoto but was well aware where the power lay and had felt the evil of it.

Tadashi went outside and hunched once more against the wall. He had a troubleshooter's instinct that something was drastically wrong. Kenji Miyoto never called here, and he doubted that it was Nikki he wanted. Why seal the porter's lips over trivia? Which meant that it wasn't. He must find Jimmy Bustillo. Fast.

*   *   *

Fujio Miyoto left the glass and concrete mass of the Miyoto building some time after his son. For once, he felt his age. He clutched his briefcase to his spare body like a hot-waterbottle to fend off a cold night. The Rolls-Royce drew up as though operated by the doorman, who saluted as Miyoto reached the sidewalk. The chauffeur held the car door open for him and Miyoto hesitated before stooping. "The flat," he said. The chauffeur showed no expression, never did. He had worked for Miyoto for twenty years and would have died for him.

The flat meant that he did not want to return to the villa on the outskirts of town. It meant, too, that he required solace from the concubine he kept installed there. He sat in the back of the limousine, briefcase held upright on knees, gaze hooded and unfocused. He had slipped up badly, yet on reflection it could be justified. The American had been taken on as a book-keeper. No more. And it had been done because Bustillo had given Nikki a new interest. A quick enquiry had shown that although Bustillo could hit the bottle he wasn't on the needle. That couldn't be bad for Nikki, a change from her usual crowd.

It had been obvious that Bustillo was running from something. But that was an advantage. Placed him the right side of the line if it came down to it. He had no record, not in that name. Miyoto had had it checked out. He had even had sight of his passport unknown to Bustillo. Nothing wrong with it. If it was a forgery it was perfectly adequate. So there should have been no problem at all. Nothing Bustillo had handled had any informative value. Yet he had pried. Deliberately. So why? And just who the hell was he? Fujio Miyoto caught himself out in the kind of western thought he sometimes despised. But it sufficed. Bustillo didn't add up.

Fujio Miyoto trusted no one except the diminutive chauffeur Yuzuru. He had trusted Bustillo no less than anyone else, yet had seen no danger in having him employed in such a minor post. It was now clear that Bustillo had engineered the job. And that meant that he had used Nikki. Which forced Fujio nearer to the thoughts of his son. For that matter nor did Fujio trust Kenji. As he grew older he knew that his own authority hung tenuously. He had share control, of course. Even now he had a bigger single block of shares than anyone. He could always call on some totally reliable shareholders who would back him on a vote. Reliable, that is, while they saw his interests as their interests. What he could never know with certainty was the extent of Kenji's machinations behind his back. If he ever found out it would probably be too late.

As he sat back in the luxury of the car, lights flashing past the tinted windows, he felt old and tired and let down. He made no complaint about any of this, it was a product of the life he had led. Yet given it over again he would do the same. It wasn't greed that motivated him as it did Kenji, he had given too much away for that, but the need of achievement at any cost, against all odds. And he had done it. Beaten the system, beaten everything and amassed a personal fortune. He had no monetary need to do a dishonest act again but he'd been doing them for so long. And in truth he enjoyed it. The sense of the piratical had always attracted him, always would. He had been so successful at it that it was difficult now to feel he was in any danger. It was almost impossible to believe. Yet the warnings he'd experienced in his earlier days stirred like oil in a cold motor engine. Building up a huge and respected organisation had given a false sense of security over the years. He had become unassailable. It had all been worked within the organisation, with the consent and to the great profit of Kusaka the chief accountant who was bound to them as they were to him.

But now at last they had been careless or at least unsuspecting. There's no fool like an old fool, he reflected without bitterness. The more he thought about it the more he turned from his natural view. It had to be a shakedown. What else could it be? But killing someone? Suddenly he had an unexpected insight into what he had done over the years. Suddenly it was no longer fun, a game of wits, an accumulation of wealth. An outsider was now involved. And they had to kill him. It forced home the issue as nothing else could. Everything was turned on its head. Kenji understood it and Kenji was the realist. Was what they'd been doing so bad that it necessitated murder? Now he was forced to agree with Kenji. Yes it was. It was easier to accept, away from the brashness of his son.

As the magnitude of what was involved finally got through, fear reached his loins and sickness filled his stomach. He retched, dropping his briefcase to the floor. The terrible risk they were running, the involvements, publicity, the collapse of the world he knew was suddenly in danger of exploding. The shock waves would reach the extremities of the country he loved. How could one abuse it and love it at the same time? He did not know, only that he did.

Shivering, he opened the cabinet, poured a drink, the decanter rattling against the glass. He wasn't even sure of what he was pouring, only that he needed something quick. Even now he hadn't the nerve to go through with it. He would leave it to Kenji. Kenji who would know precisely what to do. In that moment he abdicated from his throne unaware that he had become the first casualty of an affair that had barely begun and that what he'd received so far was the mildest flesh wound compared with what was to come.

When Yuzuru opened the car door he noticed the change in his master, even had to lend a hand to help him out. He didn't like the fixed expression nor the uncertain air of Fujio Miyoto who stood beside the car as if unaware of his whereabouts. The old boy made an effort, straightened and walked away without a word. Yuzuru called softly, "The usual time tomorrow, sir?"

Fujio stopped in mid-stride, turned his head and nodded. He realised he'd given something away to Yuzuru but he knew too that the impression would remain locked inside the head of the diminutive chauffeur. In the elevator he remembered that he hadn't warned Hitomi that he was coming but she had better be there. He let himself in with a key and when the lock turned she rushed forward to greet him keeping the surprise from her face.

"My sweetheart. You should have telephoned. I've nothing prepared." Hitomi flung her arms round his neck, one hand deftly removing his hat, and pressed close to him. With her face against his she was aware of the lack of response in him. His hand was patting her back as if she were a child when normally it would already be exploring her sturdy body. Instinctively she felt that it was company he wanted, no more. She cupped his face and kissed him fondly.

"I'm not hungry," he said. "Don't worry about food."

"I'll get something light. From the freezer. Let me take your coat."

He wandered into the lounge while she hung up his hat and coat. He was already seated when she returned. His gaze was searching and she tightened the sash of her Happi-coat knowing that this was not the time to loosen it even though she was naked beneath. It was warm in the apartment and she had not long finished a bath. She stood before him trying to read behind the hooded eyes and noting that a mask had been pulled over them.

It wasn't age that had suddenly subdued him. He was something over sixty but had never lacked virility to her knowledge. In fact he could teach the younger ones a thing or two, she mused as she watched him and wondered at how best to please him. To keep him satisfied was essential. An instruction. Not from him.

She sat on the arm of his chair and in spite of her attempted modesty the smooth silk of the Happi-coat slipped from the brown, curving thigh. In her thirties, Hitomi had long since realised that when her figure went so did her income and she had looked after hers by exercise, diet and by careful selection of her lovers. Fujio Miyoto was the first man to be selected *for* her but she had no complaints. He was a good lover, not yet sloppy with age, and he was generous. She caressed his face and forehead, careful not to touch his hair; he hated having his hair disturbed. After a while he began to relax, soothed by her action. His head nestled into her side as she pushed her hip further on to the chair. One hand came over to hold her leg, not moving, fingers digging lightly into the flesh. She bent forward to kiss his forehead.

"You're good for me, Hitomi. You always have been." He held no illusions about her. She did the job for which she was paid and she did it well. She could amuse, be silent, passionate and totally professional. She provided all he needed without involvement.

She squeezed the hand on her leg and smiled contentedly, still soothing his forehead. "Has something gone wrong? You seem down, my darling." She felt his slight stiffening and guessed she had asked the right question at the wrong time. Giving no sign that she had noticed anything she continued caressing until he relaxed again little by little. His very silence told her something but she needed to know more. It was never easy with someone like Fujio. The day she asked too pointed a question, something that smacked of deliberately prying, was the day he'd tell her to pack her bags. She knew it. Her tone of enquiry had to be just right.

There were times when she felt she was sitting on a powder keg. He wasn't beyond beating her if he felt himself betrayed and in danger. As she continued to stroke him she wondered if he would go beyond that. She wasn't sure. His arrogant son Kenji would. At the drop of a hat. When she thought like this she was afraid, found it difficult to keep warmth in the movement of her hand. If she had stiffened as he had she'd be in trouble.

He seemed relaxed again. Hitomi said, "Would you like me to run your bath?" and then with just the right amount of conviction, "It will remove your tensions." One day she'd get it wrong and the more she thought about it the harder it would become.

"That would be nice." He patted her thigh. "You're a good girl."

Useful, she thought, not good. That was how he'd meant it anyway. She still had her hand on his forehead but was about to move when unexpectedly he said, "We've had trouble over one of the staff. He hasn't turned up for two days."

"Perhaps he's sick." Hitomi stayed where she was with an effort.

"No. At least if he is he's not sick at home."

"Is this what's worried you?" She'd gone as far as she dared.

He reached up to catch her hand, holding it close to his lips. Drawing his head back he looked up at the moon face peering down at him. Hitomi smiled. Her eyes lit up into a soft glow. "Not especially," he replied.

She detected a warning in his tone. "Then don't talk about it. Have your bath. You'll feel better." Hitomi stood up but he still held on to her hand so she circled round to the front of the chair. "I cannot turn the taps if you don't release me." She thought he was in a strange mood. He wanted to communicate yet held himself back. He pulled her slightly towards him and started to say something, then decided against it. When he released her hand she knew that he would not return to the subject.

She went to the black glass-walled bathroom and ran the water, pouring in a liberal amount of pine essence. As the steam rose she switched on the extractor fan. Ensuring there were adequate towels on the hot rail she returned to the lounge. From the complete orderliness of the place it was clear that she was as fastidious as Nikki was untidy. It was one of the comparisons that Fujio Miyoto was always making to himself. Here was a whore with an obsession for cleanliness.

Hitomi helped him partially to undress in the bedroom then

28

turned off the taps. When she finally got him in the bath she washed his back then said, "You'll feel hungry afterwards. I'll see what I can do. Don't hurry, darling. It will take me a little time."

The bathroom was off a bedroom whose bed was canopied with gossamer silk drapes. She eyed the telephone near the bed but decided it was too close to the door she had just closed behind her. In the bright lounge she stared at the second phone. Unknowingly, her tongue darted between her full, rose-petal lips. There might not be another opportunity until morning. It had to be risked.

Pushing the door Hitomi picked up the telephone, hoping the bedroom extension wouldn't tinkle. She licked her lips again and dialled. The number rang out while she kept glancing nervously towards the bedroom door. Fujio never stayed in a bath long. On the verge of panic she was about to put the phone down when she heard a voice the other end. She whispered urgently:

"Susumu? Is that you?"

"It had better be."

A quick nervous glance towards the door, then, "He's worried about something. I don't know what. I've not seen him like this before."

"You're there to find out."

"It's impossible. Even in bed his mind is half on his business. I think it's something to do with someone leaving."

"Leaving? Leaving what?"

"One of the staff. He must mean the office."

"You've no idea who?"

"No. Someone who hasn't turned up for two days and is not at home."

"Do you know how many employees there are at the Miyoto building apart from the branches and factories?"

"I'm sorry, Susumu. I can't ask him outright."

"I don't know why we pay you to stay there. You're getting a cut both ways. You're useless."

"Then take me away. It won't be long before he finds out who I really belong to."

"All right," Susumu grated. "Hang on there. And try to do better."

Hitomi very gently replaced the receiver, glanced towards the door again then nervously went to pour him some warm saki. He always enjoyed that after a bath. She hoped he would be a few minutes longer to give her time to recover and to start the meal.

She hated telephoning from the apartment and was sure that one day he would catch her.

*　　*　　*

The advantage Tadashi had over Kenji Miyoto was in knowing Nikki's haunts. But it was a doubtful advantage for part of his knowledge was accepting her unpredictability about almost anything. Where would they go? To bed for an almost certainty. And there would have to be liquor. On these two fundamentals he started a search. Although he had numerous contacts throughout the city he was reluctant to use them. He was never against doing his own leg work if he reasoned it important enough and he was beginning to believe that he was on the point of touching a fuse that might lead to a massive bomb. Anything involving the Miyotos had to be big.

He used a good deal of money, cunning, expertise and time and it was almost midnight before he thought he might have found them. He had reasoned that without extra clothes they wouldn't go too far and then probably to a hotel. Nor would they use a tourist or international hotel. Although Nikki was no longer influenced by style, he considered they would still go to a good class place if only for comfort and good liquor. He tried the best of the central Japanese catering hotels.

The night staff was on by the time he tried the right one. As the night receptionist had not been on duty when they had checked in during the early evening, Tadashi's description was of no use. An inducement produced the register. Tadashi remembered handwriting as well as he remembered faces. There was little to go by when he finally located the entry, but no other signatures stirred his mind. The Japanese symbols were untidy but he was sure he knew the style. Nikki. And sober at that. He had to pay extra for the room number. It was becoming an expensive operation. He went to a booth and asked for the number from the night operator. After two more attempts he had almost reduced the operator to tears but there was no reply.

He took the elevator to the second floor. He knocked softly on the door. There was no reply yet when he crouched he could see a light strip under the door. If they were in there they were stoned. He knocked again, louder, more desperately. Someone moaned in the next room. He put his ear to the door but could hear nothing. He knocked again, keeping the volume down but more repetitively.

"Whosat?" It was drunken English and gave Tadashi faith. He

knocked again. Softly. "Whose there?" Japanese this time but the same voice. It was Bustillo all right.

With his lips close to the wood Tadashi said, "You ordered another bottle of bourbon, sir."

Feet shuffled uncertainly towards the door which was opened by a red-eyed Bustillo who was too slow to stop Tadashi pushing against it. When the American tried to grab him Tadashi ducked under his arm and was in the room.

"Kenji's out looking for you." Shock tactics. Anything to cut through the liquor clouds in Bustillo's head.

"So let him." Bustillo heard without fully understanding. He could barely see Tadashi and the journalist, at the moment, was hardly his favourite man. Then in English, "What the hell d'you think you're doing busting in like this in the middle of the night?" He had no idea what time it was. He guessed it to be night time because a light was on. He staggered against the wall and tried to focus on Tadashi. "For Chrissake, you'll wake Nikki."

Nikki was inelegantly sprawled under a rumpled sheet, one foot poking out. An empty bottle on its side near her foot suggested she had knocked it over. Two empty glasses and another bottle had been pushed against a wall.

Tadashi looked down at the pathetic figure of the girl and told himself that even if he had used her he had played no part in reducing her to this. He didn't quite convince himself. "Nothing will wake her. But when she does surface she'll need a fix. But quick. Get dressed, Jimmy, we're on our way."

"Go to hell." Bustillo flopped down on his mattress.

"That's where you're going if you don't move. The Miyotos'll have a contract out on you and the way you're going you're a sitting duck."

Bustillo gazed up blearily. His head was pounding and he wished that Tadashi would keep still. Through the fog in his mind he painfully saw the truth of his recent conviction about Tadashi.

"You bastard," he said, trying to move. "You've fixed me."

3

TADASHI HUNTED AROUND FOR Bustillo's clothes, dismayed at the slothfulness of two people he basically liked. Their garments were everywhere. If they could do this to a room in half a day what would it be like after a week? He threw Bustillo's clothes at him as he found them. Picking up the two empty bottles he went into the bathroom and dropped them in the trash can.

Tadashi's silent actions did more to sober Bustillo than anything else. As he dressed he was filled with self-disgust, the more so when he heeled over trying to put his socks on. It was impossible to shake off the effects of the liquor just like that but he made latent use of a strength he thought he'd long since lost. He pulled himself together to a considerable extent, not quite separating his speech nor completely defining Tadashi. But he started to think straight if painfully slowly. Tadashi had a lot to answer for.

Before putting his shirt on Bustillo pushed his head under the cold shower. God it was agonisingly icy but he kept his head there partly as punishment for his weakness and realising by this action, the contradiction in his make up. He returned to the bedroom with a towel over his head and fairly near normal. It was overwhelmingly hot in there. Nikki liked heat, had to have it. For her sake he made no adjustment to the heating. He rubbed his hair with the towel and gazed guiltily down at the helpless girl.

"We can't leave her here."

"We can't take her with us."

"What do you use for a heart, Tadashi?"

"What do you? You brought her here."

It wasn't true but it wasn't worth arguing about. "She'll think I've walked out on her."

"It's happened often enough before. If not with you, with others."

Bustillo snapped from the last dregs of alcohol angrily, his eyes narrowing. "You'd better be careful what you say."

The little Japanese shrugged, untouched by Bustillo's flare.

"Don't you like being part of the pattern? You created it, not me. I didn't put lead weights on your feet when you jumped in."

Bustillo put his shirt on, then his cardigan. "I've yet to find out what you did do. But whatever it was you were rooting for number one."

"And who were you rooting for, Jimmy?" Tadashi was kneeling by Nikki's topcoat, ferreting in the pockets.

"What on earth are you doing?"

Tadashi looked up, a big purse in his hands. He opened it and it was crammed with high denomination yen. He removed some notes. "Someone's got to pay the bill. It's cost me a small fortune finding you. Do *you* want to pay?"

Bustillo felt ashamed and helpless. He had little money on him but he had a cheque book which he produced from his hip pocket.

"Forget it," said Tadashi rising. "They won't accept a cheque from you and she has plenty. Daddy will always give her more." Seeing Bustillo's confusion, Tadashi added, "She'd have paid anyway. Right?" Then as Bustillo's jawline tightened, "Grow up, my friend. She's going to wake up, feel terrible. She won't be concerned for you or anyone. She probably won't even notice you've gone. She'll have one thing on her mind. A fix. She'll grab the first cab in sight and scrabble back to her pad for a quick shot. We both know it. So cut out the guilt complex. You ready?"

Bustillo nodded, unsure of anything at the moment. "Where're we heading?"

"My place. But not for long. Kenji will soon pick up that trail."

Bustillo grinned awkwardly. "It figures. I couldn't see you sticking your neck out for my sake."

He had finally got under Tadashi's tough skin. The brown eyes were bleak, the voice harsh. "Just *what do you think* I'm doing this for?"

"For yourself, sweetheart. Let's go and talk over your angle."

Tadashi opened the door angrily but Bustillo turned back to Nikki. He took a blanket from his own mattress and covered her carefully. She didn't stir as he tucked her in. At the foot of the bed he held the exposed foot in one hand. It was a small foot, soft and

33

cold. He gazed down at it aware of its communication, its tender age, noting the heavily embossed veins of a much older person, carrying the poison that riddled her system. He crouched there for a while, sorry beyond belief and disillusioned at his own inadequacy to help. He was hoping that Tadashi would comment so that he could strike out at him but Tadashi had more sense. Bustillo lifted the foot, kissed it, then gently tucked it in. Poor Nikki. Poor girl.

They went downstairs where Tadashi insisted on the night clerk taking payment for the room and liquor and demanding a receipt with a warning not to worry the girl in the morning. He had the grace to give the change to the clerk and in return expected him to raise a cab.

It was after two o'clock when they finally reached Tadashi's place on the outskirts of town. It was a small studio apartment in an old building overlooking spare shrubland on the fringe of which operated a row of market stalls separated in the middle by a square. In the centre of the square was a huge iron cauldron full of ashes into which incense sticks were inserted to burn slowly while the providers prayed, wafting the smoke into their faces as a touch from the Gods. Tadashi had become too international to become intimidated, though one day Bustillo had caught him watching his countrymen and women, invariably in national dress, praying in this way. It was the only time he had seen Tadashi look guilty about anything.

Now the market and the square were in total darkness. The stalls were dead until daybreak.

Tadashi said pointedly, "You'd better have some coffee." And then, "I suppose you've had nothing to eat."

"All I want is to straighten things out."

"We can talk and eat too. Because of you I missed my dinner."

"To hell with your dinner. I should be wringing your neck."

"It would be untypical of you to do that before you'd heard me out. In the ice box I have shiba-ebi, kuruma-ebi or kani. I might stretch to some ika. It wouldn't take me long to prepare a tempura." Tadashi stood impassively in the doorway to his small kitchen.

Bustillo wanted to retch. After the amount he'd been drinking the sound of fried shrimps, prawns, crab and then as a last malicious dig, squid, reached right inside him. He was sure that Tadashi had done it deliberately. "Just bring me a hunk of bread. And don't procrastinate, Tadashi. You've got a lot to answer for."

34

The uncompromising journalist cooked his meal and an aroma reached Bustillo that he would have relished at any other time. Tadashi was a superb cook, but Bustillo, still thinking below top speed, reasoned that it was all done to gain time, to give Tadashi opportunity to preface his answers. It wasn't until Tadashi had packed his chop sticks away and had served coffee that he asked, "Okay. So why did you walk out on your job?"

"For the reason you engineered it for me in the first place."

"I don't understand." The small impassive face stared blankly at Bustillo. "Nikki got you the job."

"And Nikki was introduced to me by you."

"So? You imagine I knew she would persuade her father to give you a job?"

"That would be underrating you. No, you persuaded her to persuade her father. Maybe you guessed that the old man has a soft spot for her."

"You think I'm so calculating?"

"That's only the half of it. You are pretty certain, without proof, that the Miyotos are deep in corruption of some kind. Perhaps a disgruntled shareholder, a disgruntled member of the staff. I dunno. It doesn't matter. It could even be your nose. You hadn't a hope in hell of finding out without someone on the inside. You probably know more about me than I realise. I was God-sent. I bet you bunged in your little prayer sticks the night you ran into me. I had everything you needed. And if it came down to it, I was very, but very, expendable."

Tadashi showed neither denial nor confirmation. He sat in a huge armchair, almost lost in it, head barely reaching the top. His legs were neatly crossed, hands on the arms of the chair. He appeared completely relaxed, head slightly angled, like a jockey listening to advice from an owner in a completely non-committal way the night before an important race. Reasonably he said, "But Jimmy, I asked nothing of you. Not ever."

Bustillo grinned wolfishly. "That's true. Maybe I've done you an injustice. Let's drop the whole thing."

"But you walked out on the job. What made you do it?"

"Don't worry about it. I shouldn't have voiced such evil thoughts of you. Just drop it and give me a brandy."

Tadashi rose, leaving shallow indentations in the leather chair. He poured two brandies, handing one to Bustillo.

"I hope it mixes with the bourbon." He sat down again, raised his glass. "I can't let it drop. I've become involved. I discovered

Kenji's after your blood and now you're in my apartment. I've stuck my neck out for you. I'd like to know what for."

"You're smooth, Tadashi. Why should you think Kenji wants me ? Only because you know a reason. You planted me in Miyoto's and at a given time you were going to persuade me that something fishy was going on. What a lucky thing that I was there. Just the guy to winkle out a few truths and to understand what he saw. If I searched that is." Bustillo smiled ruefully, as he failed to ruffle Tadashi. "It was strange that I was alerted before you might have prodded me. Something I noticed that I simply couldn't let pass." Bustillo sipped his drink. "I really persevered for Nikki's sake. She's in enough trouble without family problems. But you want in on a Japanese Watergate."

"Okay. Let's stop there. I'm a newspaper man. What do you expect ? I got you a job via Nikki. You needed one. Right ? Is it so bad to expect a favour in return ?"

"Not if you level about it."

"I'm levelling now. I was going to bring it up. I wanted you to feel your way first. You were under no obligation."

"You're holding back, Tadashi. What do you know about me ?"

Tadashi spun his glass and watched the brandy swirl. "I know that the C.I.A. are looking for you."

"So you know who I am."

"I've always known."

"You reckoned you could apply the pressure when you needed me ?"

Tadashi glanced up. "I wouldn't have used my knowledge against you."

"But you'd have tried a little blackmail just the same."

"I would have. But I wouldn't have betrayed you."

Bustillo put down his glass and went to the windows, looking out at the frosty night. "It's easy to say now. Do you want to know my story ?"

"No."

Bustillo turned his head but Tadashi was still giving nothing away.

"Meaning that you couldn't be sure it was true."

Tadashi didn't move. Then with quiet anger he said, "Just what sort of a bastard do you really think I am ? You'll tell me when you want, not when I want to hear. The time you do that I shall hear the truth."

"Have you ever had to do a job that stinks, Tashi ?"

"In my game? All the time."

"Don't you ever feel like quitting?"

"Sometimes. I don't know what else I'd do."

"Well, I quit. In the middle of a job that choked me. That's the extent of my guilt."

"You worked for no one else after?"

Bustillo looked across suspiciously. "I was bailed out by a friendly hand. That leaves me with an obligation. But there was no treachery. I'm no traitor. I just want out from a lousy game I should never have joined."

"So you're floundering?"

"You could call it that. It would be easier if they'd let me go, if the lies would stop."

Tadashi nodded. "I won't press you for details. Not now. Maybe later I can help you."

Bustillo raised a brow in surprise. Tadashi was ruthless but he'd just exposed a strange loyalty that briefly touched the American. The good impression was immediately destroyed as Tadashi went on:

"You *must* tell me what you found out at the Miyotos'."

Bustillo smiled in relief. "You almost fooled me for a moment. You almost had me going. I shan't tell you, nor anyone."

"Kenji will kill you. He thinks you know something."

"That's going a bit far. He's safe."

"Kenji doesn't go searching for fun. He wouldn't be seen dead in Nikki's apartment. He wasn't looking for her, he was looking for you. So why do you imagine a man in his position should search for a minion, a lowly placed employee? You found something out and Kenji knows it. He's headstrong, stupid at times. He'll take the quickest course. That means you're dead."

Bustillo went back to his drink, raised it thoughtfully. He was calm under pressure. "It makes no difference. You must all assume what you like. I'm not getting involved."

Tadashi jumped from his chair his face contorting. "By the gods, you fool. *You are involved whether you like it or not.* You cannot keep burying your head, running away. *You have got to take sides.* Jimmy, if you don't you're committing suicide."

"I am, whatever I do."

*   *   *

Susumu Takama was awake at dawn. He left his sleeping wife's side, slipped on a dressing gown and went down the stairs of his sumptuous villa which faced the North Pacific some twenty miles south-west of Tokyo. Once downstairs he put on his half-rimmed spectacles and poured himself a full glass of tomato juice. The dawn light was creeping through the foliage of the delightfully planned garden, fronds moving on a cold wind. In the open spaces of several lawns he noticed the white frost and shivered in spite of the warmth of the villa. Through a cluster of huge cacti he caught segments of the dazzling morning blue of the kidney-shaped swimming pool. As the wind plucked at plants, the roughcast stone bridge over the pool shone coral pink in the early morning light. His surrounds were idyllic and sufficiently far from traffic and the airport to enjoy rural silence. The birds were already winging hide-and-seek flights among the subtropical vegetation.

Yet much of this was lost on Susumu. Unlike most of his countrymen, he failed to see the beauty of his heritage. He knew the garden was lovely for he had paid vast sums of money to make it so. He had played no part in its creation except as the provider of funds. The villa was the same. He appreciated its conveniences, again carefully planned by someone else. If the garden was Japanese, only the exterior of the villa was. Susumu dealt a good deal with Americans and had largely gone their way, losing, en route, the delicate art touch of his race.

He would see beauty in a gold brick, a perverse satisfaction in a junkie. The sweetest sound was the rustle of full bank balance sheets. An extension of this need of affluence was carried on to his wife who he made wear the most expensive clothes whether oriental or western and, of course, the finest jewellery. Her embarrassment was not important, she was an advertising sign of his power which was not only the power of wealth. Susumu had something in common with the Miyotos but only in outlook. They were kindergarten in his eyes. Keen amateurs who would never be professionals. Wealth was relative. Theirs was petty cash and, from the signs, in some danger.

As he sipped his drink he walked into a huge glass-walled lounge with so much space between the many silk rugs and easy chairs that it appeared misleadingly empty. His only concession to Japanese decor was a bank of Hiroshige prints on one wall. He never looked at them. He finished his drink, shaved, showered and dressed. His wife was still asleep.

Even the best tailoring couldn't quite hide the badly rounded shoulders and the paunch. Above middle height, the bleakness of his hard eyes was trapped by the glasses and not helped by a balding head. He appeared awkward in a suit as if he was afraid to move in case he spoiled the creases in trousers and sleeves. But the clumsy image was misleading. His mind was as sharp and as crisp as the external frost and as devious as the intricate beauty of his garden. His chauffeur called to collect him ten minutes later, just after the sun had slipped over the Pacific horizon. He sat back behind the armour-plated glass of the car and studied some reports on the way to town.

He was going to his office like any other business man. There was one stop on route, at the Chinese Theatre in mid-town where a shivering Hitomi stood on the sidewalk in a thick fur-coat. Susumu opened the door for her to get in, a vestige of gallantry not quite extinct. She huddled on the seat as far away from him as possible.

"You're cold? Not used to rising with the sun? It's a glorious day."

"You've forgotten you made me a night worker. This is the only time I can sleep." It was daring repartee to offer Susumu.

He took it with a thin smile, not yet confronted by the pressures of the day. "Miyoto left before you?"

"I wouldn't be here otherwise."

"Don't take too many liberties, Hitomi. You've turned out to be of little value. Perhaps you've grown fond of the old man?"

He had a way of subtly changing tone that sent shivers through her. She avoided his eyes. "I've done my best."

"It hasn't been good enough. Even this last piece of information is of little use. You should have got a name."

"He would have suspected me."

He didn't reply. For some seconds he gazed through his glasses at the plated partition between them and the chauffeur. Still without looking at her he said, "I'm giving you one last chance. If Miyoto continues to show strain, I want to know. If at any time he appears to be floundering, in need of help, choose an opportunity to mention my name. I want him pushed in my direction."

Hitomi stared at him, astounded. "He wouldn't accept your help." It was spontaneous, out before she could stop herself.

He turned towards her then, cold, impassive. She expected a blow but instead he put a podgy hand on her thigh pressing his fingers into her flesh. She dare not resist, well knew the dreadful coldness of his sudden rages. "Do as you're told," he countered with surprising softness. "That's your job. My job is to read the signs correctly and I've had vast experience of that. But you know that already." She cringed before he contined. "There are certain circumstances in which he will almost certainly turn to me. But he needs to be pointed in my direction. It's important that he knows I'm there. Do you understand?"

She nodded, wanted to remove his now caressing hand.

"Don't make a mistake, my love. I treasure old memories, and would hate for one to turn sour. Do this properly and you vindicate yourself."

She had seen Susumu's ostensible reasonableness before. And she had known of people dying soon after it. Susumu was giving her a last chance and if she made a mistake she would not be dismissed with a golden handshake. She suffered a few seconds of terror. The fingers relaxed on her legs and reached up to her face. "Then kiss me, my little one. Like old times." She suffered the fat lips on hers barely concealing a shudder. Susumu tapped on the partition window and the car drew in.

Hitomi was left to open the door herself, which she managed after fumbling nervously. Susumu leaned towards the open doorway. "You can find your own way back?" He was laughing at her from a face that didn't move. "Time to earn your keep, little one. Close the door."

After the car had gone she stood for some time watching its direction. Long after it had disappeared she still stood there, coat collar pulled up and held tight. It was cold but she knew it wasn't cold enough to account for the tremors in her limbs.

*   *   *

Nikki Miyoto awoke while it was still dark. She came out of a drunken stupor with a terrible fit of trembling as if she had spent the night in a cold room. She pulled the blanket around her and huddled into a ball, trying to stop her teeth from chattering. She finally emerged from the blanket still shaking violently but motivated by the insatiable need of water after the session on the dehydrating bourbon. Her mouth and lips were completely dry. Even a probing tongue produced no saliva. She staggered to the bathroom and splashed water into her mouth and over her face. While she crouched over the wash basin she clung on to it with one hand, her legs barely capable of holding her. For a while she retched on an empty stomach then staggered back to the bedroom.

Her first coherent thought was not who had occupied the empty mattress beside her but the fact that she desperately needed a fix before her body fell apart. Tadashi had been right. She gazed

40

round, red hollow eyes slowly picking up the visible signs of what might have happened. The dressing mirror showed a swaying, crone-like image and she turned away from it unable to face herself. She had to get back, had been mad not to bring some stuff with her.

She stood swaying in a torpor in the centre of the room slowly grasping the need to dress. It took so long that at one stage she almost left the room half naked. She was saved by the cunning of the addicted in not wanting to draw attention to herself. Too unsteady to make her face presentable, she finger combed her hair without use of a mirror and perhaps, by so doing, made a minor improvement. She staggered to the elevator, head partially hidden in the deep collar of her coat. No matter how she tried she could not stop shivering and her hands were pushed deep into the pockets.

The night clerk was still on duty at reception. When she pulled out her purse, against all natural instinct he told her her bill had already been paid. She handed him some yen and told him to get a cab. When he explained the difficulty at this time of morning she gave him a gaze that reflected her every feeling and threatened to scream the hotel down. Nor did he disbelieve her, with the secondary possibility of having a corpse on his hands if he didn't move fast. He'd have sworn that he could hear her bones rattling as she tried to stand upright before him.

It was light by the time the cab reached her apartment block. Unable to separate the notes she handed the driver her purse uncaring of the temptation she was putting his way. She staggered into the hall and the porter, with only half an hour gone of his new shift, immediately picked up the telephone.

Kenji Miyoto knew of her home-coming just as Nikki finally managed to get the key in her lock. He climbed out of bed, shaved and showered without hurry. From what the porter had told him Nikki was in no condition to leave her apartment, barely fit enough to reach it.

Once inside, Nikki went straight to the drawer containing the heroin, the syringe and the spoon. She took them to the kitchen hardly able to hold them. She cursed the amount of drinks she'd had. She always did. And she'd gone too long between fixes. Craving and necessity briefly fought her tremors long enough for the injection, then she sat back waiting for the heroin to bring relief. When Kenji arrived she was combing her hair, able to face her image in the mirror.

Kenji entered with a key from the porter. He did so silently, closing the door behind him. At the open bedroom door he stopped, watching her studying herself in the mirror, trying to salvage something of the wreckage with make-up.

"Where's Bustillo?"

She rose from the chair with shock, her face losing the colour that had crept back to it. A hand flew to her heart then she saw him in the mirror. "You bastard. You nearly frightened me to death."

"It wouldn't take much to do that." He shrugged indifferently. "Where is he?"

Suddenly it all came back to her. For once she could afford the truth. "He'd gone before I woke up. What's he done to get you up this early?"

He sauntered into the room, hands in pockets, making no effort to cover his disgust. She was calm about it.

"Did you know he walked out on his job?"

"No. It wouldn't worry me either way."

"You met him in the afternoon when he should be working, and you didn't wonder about it?"

She picked up a lipstick fervently thankful that she was steadier. "We didn't meet in the afternoon and had we done it would not have occurred to me. I'm your sister, not one of your employees. You're not welcome here, so go."

He cast his critical eye over the bed. "Where did you go?"

"Go to hell and get out."

He whipped round and back-handed her across the side of the face. She went sprawling from the stool, the lipstick making a red gash on the light carpet. Propping herself up on her elbows she blazed hatred at him. "I'll tell Father about that."

"Whose father? Yours or mine?"

She stared up at him, a pain suddenly shooting through her heart.

"What do you mean? Is this some more of your evil?"

He smiled crookedly. "You never considered why the old man tolerates you? You should think about it."

Nikki made no effort to rise. He wasn't beyond hitting her again. "I have thought about it. In my clearer moments I've thought quite a lot about it. And do you know what I've thought, brother Kenji?"

His smile stiffened at her challenge. Too late he tried to be nonchalant.

"I thought that he wouldn't care for me unless he *was* my

father. On the other hand I haven't noticed him doting too much on you. Maybe we had the same mother but it would still make you a bastard, half-brother."

"Shut up, you bitch."

She laughed scathingly. "Why? Are you going to kick me while I lie here? That's something Father could never do and Mother was certainly too soft. So where do you get it from, all your brutality?"

He did kick out at her but she rolled in time knowing that she had driven him to the limit. She scrambled to her feet then and grabbed a hairbrush. Her action sobered him. Viciousness showed in his tight mouth and eyes now barely slits. Belatedly he realised that he didn't want a scene here or anywhere. She had got under his skin. Not for the first time. He had only to be here to feel revulsion.

"Where did you stay?"

There was no harm in telling him that. He could chase his tail following that one up. She had made light of the danger to Jimmy Bustillo but now she realised she'd been covering her own feelings. Bustillo *was* in grave danger. She said, still gripping the hairbrush, "Why should you want him? He's not a man who could ever cause you trouble."

"Why should you say that?" He eyed her suspiciously.

She shrugged helplessly. "You don't come chasing up here at this time of day, knocking me about and demanding to see Bustillo in order to give him protection." With a feeling of utter hopelessness she suddenly realised that Bustillo meant something to her.

"So you've no idea where he is?"

"I told you. I was out cold. I don't know what time he left."

"But you're sure it was him you were with?"

She let it ride. There had been a time when she wasn't sure. When she thought back to her shudders she closed her mind quickly.

He went through the flat again. Just in case. In the kitchen he saw the syringe, the few grains of powder left on the small square of white paper. That she should do this. And leave it lying there as if discovery was unimportant. He was certain that the only reason she hadn't been picked up by the police was due to family influence and the fact that they had at least tried a cure on her. He took the syringe into her. "How much does it cost you for cocaine?"

She ignored him, sat on the stool again and started to brush her hair.

"How much, you bitch, before I break you?"

"I pay in dollars. About a hundred a day."

"A hundred dollars. Daily. Down the drain. The old man is crazy. I'd let you scream your head off for the stuff. You're paying that much to torture yourself to death." He was breathing heavily, almost beyond words. "The sooner the better."

She didn't flinch. She was too intelligent to delude herself and life had long since been a drudgery, which was why she crammed as much as she could into what was left of it.

"Who are Bustillo's friends?"

She had to think about that and whether it would do Jimmy any harm. She wasn't sure.

"I'll ransack this place and tip every grain of heroin I find down the drain if you don't tell me."

"I can get more."

"And then I'll buy off your pusher."

That could create problems. "The only one I know is Tadashi Fujuda. A journalist." She didn't think it mattered.

A journalist. The revelation was like an exploding bomb in his head.

When she looked round to see why he was so silent he had gone leaving the front door open.

4

CHIEKO LEACH LAY ON her side watching the restlessness of her husband in bed. A freezing dawn was peppering the long stretch of window like giant pink confetti as the light pierced the trees. She'd had little sleep, her mind anchored on what she had heard her husband say as he'd raised his glass to his own reflection. Kill a man? Why? Who? With oriental perception she had always known that a part of her husband was hidden from her. She had even found it contributed to his attraction for she could not believe that there was anything about him that was really bad. He was so gentle, so considerate. Her father thought he was also very clever.

He was lying on his back in bed, trying to speak at times but nothing was intelligible. He mumbled and stirred as if suffering nightmares. And she imagined he was. She put out a hand and stopped before it reached him. She felt wretched and numb from worry and lack of sleep. Something had happened yesterday. Something terrible. Apart from the one compartment in himself which she accepted and never probed, he had always been completely open with her. They had been happy. Now he was holding something back which he did not want to tell her, and, having overheard his promise to himself, she understood why. And she was terrified.

Chieko wondered how she would keep her secret. Now they both had something to hide from each other. It would be better out in the open. But how could he raise something so dreadful with her? Then should she raise it? When she considered that, a deep inner caution warned her not to and the resulting sensation was one of dread. She gazed at his form as she had been doing for most of the night but now she could see his profile clearly. It told her nothing except that he was disturbed. Slowly she withdrew her hand, her beautiful eyes moist. How little she really knew about him. Before it hadn't mattered. He had not sought her money for he had plenty of his own. He was a rich man. There was an age gap, she in her late twenties and he in his mid-forties. Yet that wasn't an impossible one and had never mattered. It didn't now. It was something else that had crept in that frightened her badly.

They had met at a party thrown by her widowered father. It had been dull, comprised mainly of businessmen and their wives but Chieko had grown used to hostessing after her mother's death. Leach, she discovered, had a good knowledge of computers. An Englishman, he had lived in London, New York and Sydney from where he had last come. He spoke Japanese and intended to stay in the Orient. His quick charm had gradually captivated her, his politeness matching hers. At the first sign of a courtship between them her father had been disturbed. Then the commercial interests of the two men had drawn them even closer and her father's objections had waned to silent acquiescence. Some time later she had wondered about Leach's background which he had revealed on occasion. It had not disturbed her. Men often exaggerated or played down matters as they saw fit. Only now did she admit that some of it had sometimes sounded rehearsed, with too much consistency.

She remained staring at the enigmatic figure of her husband, forced at last to face her own subjugated doubts. Inwardly she cried.

*   *   *

The open door worried Nikki Miyoto much more than the actual departure of her brother Kenji. It illustrated the panic of a usually logical mind and the importance to him of finding Jimmy Bustillo. She was thinking clearly but more slowly than she realised. Time was something she had ceased to estimate with accuracy. She didn't want to know about the passing of time so there were no clocks in the apartment. Time was protracted or condensed, depending on her state.

She closed the door aware of the urgency that must have seized Kenji for him to leave her apartment on view with readily available drugs. She picked up the telephone and rang Tadashi.

"Tashi, do you know where Jimmy is?"

Tadashi was immediately careful. "No. Why?"

"Kenji's after him. He's been here. He hit me and he needs to find Jimmy badly."

"I'll tell Jimmy if I see him. You all right now?"

"Meaning I wasn't too good before? That means you saw me. And Jimmy. Don't you play games with Kenji, Tashi, he's no good." She hung up because there was nothing more that she could do. She couldn't stay here. She couldn't face life alone. All that did was to give her time to think and that was the last thing she wanted. She tidied herself up, went downstairs to the garage and drove her car uptown. A few minutes later she saw her quarry walking towards her, a girl in a high necked silk trouser suit, with a severely tailored topcoat against the morning chill. Nikki pulled in, opened the passenger door and called out.

The girl came running forward with a wide smile. "Oh, Nikki, darling. I was ringing you all yesterday. Where have you been?" They embraced and caressed on the front seat of the car to the surprise of startled passers-by. Nikki had found her morning companion.

*   *   *

Tadashi put down the phone and said crisply, "Kenji's on his way. You'll have to go. I'll give you an address."

Bustillo, who had just managed his first breakfast for two days, said, "I don't mind facing Kenji Miyoto."

"Don't be naïve." Tadashi was looking through his front window. Across the scrubland, the market was preparing its stalls, some already in operation. Gay lights and paper buddhas linked the two sides of the main market street. The whole place was alive. A car drew up below. He couldn't see it and it hadn't come from the market direction. He assumed the worst. The brakes had squeaked, the car door slamming almost instantly.

"We're too late. Get up the stairs and sit on them out of sight. I'll call you if it's a false alarm."

"No. I'll stay. To hell with the Miyotos."

"If you can't think of yourself then think of me. Besides, an unshaven man is never at his best."

It was astute comment. The fair-haired American ran a hand over his stubble, an indication that appearance had once mattered. "For you," he said.

"*Hurry.*"

Bustillo left the flat and mounted the stairs hearing hurrying footsteps below him. One thing he had learned to do was to move silently. He did so now at a belated sense of danger. At times he considered his regard for himself was no better than Nikki's. Once he had been sure of purpose but that was now blurred out of recognition. He went no further than necessary, squatting on a half landing out of sight from above and below unless someone approached him. The knock on Tadashi's door was authoritative.

In the apartment Tadashi had quickly removed all signs of a guest. He opened the front door breezily, saw the barely contained fire in Kenji Miyoto's eyes. "Yes?"

"Is Bustillo here?"

Tadashi was too experienced. "Bustillo? You've got the wrong address."

"I understand he called."

"Did you? You're not very well informed. Do you realise the time? I'm just off to my office."

"I can give you a lift. May I come in?" Kenji was already trying to edge in, peering urgently through the space in the door.

"No, you damn well can't. And I have my own car. Who are you?"

"Kenji Miyoto. It won't take a moment."

"The Miyoto Consortium? You're way off your beat. All right, come in." There was nobody more adept at just getting it right than Tadashi. He held the door open and Kenji went in, hat in hand, hard eyes probing the place for tell-tale signs.

"Now, what's this about Bustillo? Doesn't he work at your place?"

"I discover so. Our paths aren't normally likely to cross." From anxiety Kenji was filled with a belated sense of danger. He should have thought first. His father's warning came to him. Here he was with an astute journalist, one with a reputation, and what was he going to tell him? Already the little fellow had his nose out for a story.

"May I speak to you in confidence?"

"I'm a newspaper man."

"Yes, of course. But you also know my sister. This largely concerns her."

"Yes, I know Nikki. I feel desperately sorry for her."

"We all do. We've tried to help so much. Were you not a good friend of hers I wouldn't have called like this."

"She told you we are friends?"

"She treasures your friendship. It is clear, too, that so do you. A man of honour. Otherwise some of her worst escapades would surely have appeared in your columns."

48

Tadashi conceded the neat turn with a nod of his head. "I protect her if I can."

"I believe Bustillo has behaved badly to her. I wanted to speak to him."

"Oh? Jimmy Bustillo? She hasn't said anything to me."

"When did you last speak to her?"

Careful. "Not for a couple of days, I confess."

"It's happened during that time. I want to stop it quickly. You understand. We are worried about it and about her all the time."

"Yes, I understand. But I still can't help you. I tried to contact Bustillo yesterday. There was no reply."

"I see." Kenji Miyoto gazed about him while Tadashi wondered whether the industrialist believed him any more than *he* believed Kenji.

"Will you be seeing him?"

"Certainly. If he surfaces."

"Will you then tell him that I would like to speak to him? If it's money he needs it can be arranged. I merely want him to leave poor Nikki alone."

"I'll certainly tell him that. When I see him."

"And, Mr. Fujuda, I do hope you'll keep this off the record for Nikki's sake. It is a family matter. And we haven't been ungenerous with our advertising in your paper."

"You have my word, Mr. Miyoto."

They bowed at each other, Kenji quick to catch the cue from the silently mocking Tadashi who then showed him out politely.

Kenji went down the stairs, got into his car, started it, moved off. He drove round a couple of blocks, the streets narrower, shabbier in this district. The buildings were old, some worn at the edges. Endorsing the age were more people in local dress, both men and women. Loose smocks and baggy trousers, kimonos, counteracting the drabness. The market atmosphere was cheerful.

Kenji came round behind Tadashi's building a short block away. He parked so that the car was hidden from the main entrance, then climbed out and waited, self-conscious in his expensive, western clothes, aware too that his features were more western than eastern. He rarely considered it; now he did. He stood, hands in pockets, feeling a stranger in his own country. His industrial world was not like this.

*   *   *

49

"He's probably waiting for me outside."

"He might be."

"Did you give anything away?"

"Do I ever?" Tadashi shrugged. "Kenji Miyoto trusts nobody. Not even his own father."

"He's not going to shoot me in broad daylight."

"He's not going to shoot you at all. He'll have it done."

Tadashi's cold assessment got through to Bustillo. "Can I have a drink?"

"It won't solve your problems and I don't want you stoned here."

"You're a cold bastard."

"Because I speak the truth?"

"What should I do?"

"If you were to help me expose him I could get him off your back. All you can now do is to go to the address I gave you and make up your mind."

"Okay, Tashi." Bustillo fingered the key Tadashi had given him. "I don't know whether to thank you or curse you. I wouldn't be here but for your conniving."

Tadashi smiled as he opened the door. "You're here because you won't stop running. One day you'll have to make up your mind to stay your ground."

Bustillo tossed the key, caught it. He smiled crookedly. "I did that once before. It was misunderstood." He left the apartment, going down the wooden stairs slowly. Halfway down he had to sit, a tremor starting in his legs. God, he needed a drink. Away from Tadashi, old uncertainties returned. There was something so realistically matter of fact about the journalist that in his company it was almost impossible to let the mind wander. Now alone, Bustillo was confused by the need for integrity, honestly to state his case, and the realisation that other people had other fears, that truth wasn't enough for them. They had to be *convinced* and the deviousness of their own lives permitted only one stable conviction in their own instability. Remove the doubt.

As he sat there Bustillo shuddered. He needed Nikki, then. He could lose himself with her, join her in the oblivion of depravity. He briefly wondered what she was doing, then quickly closed his mind to the possibilities. That left the bottle and the bottle was out of reach.

Shakily he climbed to his feet, leaning against the wall, then he descended the remaining stairs slowly. Beyond the door he was really on his own and he didn't want to take the step. He glanced back up the stairs, got a grip on himself then went out into the street.

The cold air took him at once. In spite of the brilliant sunshine he turned up his shirt collar. He'd better get a cab but it wouldn't be too easy at this time of day around here. Beyond the market it might be easier. He stepped across the street, to a footpath that cut through the wasteground to the market. Gossamers of frost still clung to the lower blades of grass, the upper stems wet with dew. The earth path was hard, but would soften as the day wore on.

Bustillo had only seen Kenji Miyoto twice, once from the rear, and once profile; both times only briefly and long distance. Their paths had been unlikely to cross in the hierarchy-conscious Miyoto empire. Yet without a second look he knew who it was who detached himself from the wall a block away. Habit dies hard. Bustillo swept up the image with barely a glance. Old instincts took over. He didn't change pace, hands were in his trouser pockets for warmth, shoulders hunched in the cardigan, hair barely combed, lifting on a slight breeze.

Training had induced him into the right action, yet he was near panic. On the open ground he was very exposed. *"He'll have it done."* Tadashi's assurance bore little comfort. He heard Kenji quicken pace, skipping across the street, then the small feet pounding the path. The market was still some distance.

"Bustillo." The breathless call was not far behind him.

Bustillo lengthened his pace subconsciously. His earlier willingness to face Miyoto had faded under Tadashi's logic and his own indecisiveness. Over the past two years his life had comprised of dilemmas without solutions.

"Bustillo. Wait." Much nearer. Kenji was running fast. *Kenji Miyoto running after him in a public place like this? He wouldn't normally be seen dead here. For Chrissake, doesn't that mean something?* Doesn't it put it on the line? Bustillo, his need for liquor never stronger, finally made his own decision and he ran, the crisp air biting into lungs that hadn't been properly exercised for some time.

As he neared the market his pounding feet attracted attention, his tall frame and fair looks, further interest. Behind him Miyoto was sprinting with surprising speed. Both men had discarded dignity and their motives for running were confused. Bustillo ran straight into the now crowded market, scattering people he couldn't avoid, drawing shouts and oaths of annoyance. His height was against him, his fair hair and complexion like a beacon above the others. Miyoto followed in his wake, fitter, smaller, deft and light-footed. He was intent on not losing contact. If he couldn't stop Bustillo it was imperative that he found out where he was going. While he raced he seethed.

The crowd favoured Miyoto not because he was almost one of them but because Bustillo's size was against him in trying to get through. When Bustillo sent a wizened old lady with a bundle tied to her back spinning the crowd took more positive action. They didn't like that and voices shouted behind him to those in front. Legs were stuck out and he went hurtling forward on his knees, the pain excruciating on the concrete. But he was up at once, becoming more ruthless, using his weight desperately until they got out of his way. The crowd split in two in front of him and as it converged again to form his wake, Miyoto was impeded instead.

Bustillo reached the open square. A couple of young girls and an elderly man were praying at the cauldron, the ashes already spattered with joss sticks, smoke being wafted into impassive faces. He rounded the huge cauldron, raced up the second main lane of stalls then turned right at the top. He guessed that Miyoto had fallen slightly behind, but people would still point out the way to him. Bustillo kept going. When he reached the end of the market there was more open space in the form of a huge patio filling with people even as he raced through it. Beyond it was the town proper, buildings, shops, streets, alleys. And a more thinned-out population.

Bustillo grabbed a cab as Miyoto left the market, twisted round to see through the rear window but the movement was too erratic, the angle wrong. When next he looked he had lost sight of Miyoto.

Kenji Miyoto, chest heaving, had seen the cab. He stood on the sidewalk aware that he had aroused curiosity and now furious that he had given way to impulse. There was no other cab, but he hastily made a note of the one that drew away. Instead of seeing the wisdom of his father's careful thinking he was annoyed that he had been told to contact Bustillo in the first place. He would have denied the thread of oriental behaviour that had made him reluctantly obey his father. It was not going to happen again.

He started to walk in a general up-town direction very conscious of the attraction he'd caused and now trying to restore some poise. His mood was one of white anger. At Bustillo, his father, and, though he'd find an excuse for it, himself. When he finally caught a cab he went straight to the Miyoto Building grateful that it was so far away from the scene of the chase. At his desk he used his private line and asked for a check-out on the cab number and the journey of the American. In the circumstances he considered it better not to go in to his father. Then he instructed his chauffeur to pick up his car.

*   *   *

Graham Leach was quick to realise the almost unobtrusive withdrawal of his beautiful wife Chieko. But for his need of ultra caution he might have missed it. Over breakfast she was just slightly over-anxious to please as if to persuade him that all was well when she felt that it was not. Her deep eyes lacked their usual soft lustre as she sat speculatively opposite him with an orange juice, her shapely fingers and long pink nails curved protectively round the glass.

He had to make a decision. All night long through restless bouts of sleep he had looked for one, unaware that for much of the time she had been watching him. Even so he could see the pale bruises under her eyes and he guessed that she, too, had suffered. There was a limit to the time factor in keeping up a pretence. Too much was involved, including his own safety. And his future. Chieko's too. It was important that the deal went through with her father. It would give him, Leach, new roots in sound soil. He liked it here. So once there were doubts he was in danger. He did not underrate Chieko, not in any way. She was intelligent, highly sensitive to his needs and easily hurt. He had quickly learned to be gentle with her, to over-explain rather than take her grasp of matters for granted.

Now she was unsure of him for the first time. His judgment was right, his plan politically sound. Most of his life he had been adept at living a lie. Now he prepared to launch a new one.

He finished his coffee and she quickly poured him another, eyes searching for explanation and detecting a change in him. As she lowered the pot she knew that he was about to tell her something. She still kept her grip on the handle as he smiled sadly at her.

"Chieko, I need a gun." Rivet her from the outset. He felt little emotion as he saw her pale almost to the colour of the slender coffee pot. He didn't expect her to answer. He leaned forward to pat her hand. "It's all right," he murmured. "I'll explain." She had been shocked but not visibly surprised and he wondered

53

whether she had overheard his threat the previous night. He decided to take the view that she had.

"There's a man in Tokyo who wants to kill me. I am sure that he's followed me here. That's why I was so worried when I came home last night."

Some of the tension left her and her hand released the coffee pot to reach for his. "*Why?* Why should someone want to kill you?" Expression was back in her face, her concern so clear. He knew that he was going to have no trouble.

Shrewdly, he said, "You may have guessed there's something in my life that I've held back. Until now it was something that had no bearing on our relationship and a matter I wanted to put right behind me. Before I tell you I must have your promise that it's our secret."

"I am your wife, Graham. If I must promise, then I promise."

"I don't want a blind promise, my darling. It's important that you believe me." Leach pushed back his chair and crossed his legs, holding an ankle with one hand. It had always been a favourite position of his when sitting at NATO meetings in Brussels. It was a habit he had tried to lose. With his free hand he removed a cigarette from an ivory Shibyama casket, and lit it with a gold lighter. He would have given up smoking if he couldn't have afforded the finest tobacco and addendum. He straightened his story and started to speak with a quiet, cultured persuasiveness that had convinced intelligent people for so long. Chieko, who wanted to believe, hung on every word.

"For much of my life I've been a British Intelligence Agent. Even now I've retired from the game I'm still bound by the Official Secrets Act. It's second nature to me, my sweetheart, not to discuss it. Even with you. The reason I tell you now is because there is an American in town, a defector, who would recognise me. That wouldn't matter so much except that the Russian K.G.B. have good reason to want me dead."

Leach smiled bitterly. "You will probably wonder why should they want to do that if I'm out of the game. Well, you know, other intelligence sources would never believe it. The Russians in particular are suspicious of their own shadows. In this game one cannot hang up a declaration of retirement and even if it were possible it would be considered a forgery as a matter of course." He drew on his cigarette, giving Chieko time to ask a question and himself time to tidy the next phase. Questions never worried him.

Chieko took what he said with combined misgivings and relief. She knew that he tinted his hair, had suspected a little vanity, but now there might be another reason.

"Why should *this* man be a danger to you? Will there be others?"

Leach shook his head. "He's the only man on the other side who knows what I look like."

"But you say he's American."

"A defector from the Central Intelligence Agency. He went over to the Russians." He paused the right amount. "We met in Cuba. By accident. I was there as a British business man. He was there 'singing' to the Russians. Chieko——" He held out a hand. "I shouldn't be telling you any of this. There will be gaps, parts you won't understand. Please take my word for what I'm saying. This man alone represents my only danger. I had to inform the C.I.A. of my discovery after I left Cuba. They want him. And he wants me."

"Enough to *kill you*?"

"We represent a danger to each other."

"But . . ." The hand wave was a delicate flourish. Chieko was groping with something beyond her scope. Spies. Killing. It was something transitory she read about in the newspapers. Her mind was reeling but she wanted to understand, to help. "Couldn't you tell these C.I.A. people that he is here? Couldn't they help?"

"There is a C.I.A. office, of course. In the U.S. Embassy. But to do that is to reveal myself. In no time at all official Japanese sources will know who I am and will then wonder why I'm here. The circle of suspicion is never-ending, my dear. My past is buried. I'm here. I want to live here, not to suddenly find myself deported because they can never be sure of me. And what would your father think?"

"Oh, Graham! What do we do?" She came round the back of him, her slender fingers splayed up his face with an expressiveness her features tried to hide. She held his head to her, stroking him, worried for him beyond measure. Her loyalty was simple. It was to him. Her innocence had trapped her into believing, but greatly experienced experts had been misled by him before.

He took one of her hands, gently kissing her fingers. "The first thing is to find a means of protecting myself. I must get a gun." He felt her stiffen. "It has to be faced, little Chieko. Until this is resolved life might be ugly. Better to look this ghastly business straight in the eye." Stoic. British.

"And then what?" He hardly heard her, she spoke so softly. He was glad she was standing behind him, it made it that much easier.

"I must find out where this man is. That will help a great deal. Perhaps you can help me there."

"All aliens must register. Father knows the Police Chief. He could soon track him down."

Leach resisted a shudder.

"We can't use the police. They will wonder why your father wants to find him."

"Perhaps a detective agency?"

There were snags with that too, when the American was traced after being killed. But what surprised him most was the unexpectedly quick adjustment Chieko was making. She had produced two relevant and positive suggestions.

He hesitated, knowing that he was taking a risk. "I was thinking of more underworld channels."

"Underworld?"

He stood up and held her to him, his fingers exploring the rich black hair of her head as he held it against his chest.

"Someone who will keep it to himself."

She tried to break away, to search his face but he held her tightly. "Don't be frightened, Chieko. It will be all right. Once I know where he is I shall know what to do."

"Kill him?" She broke away at last, panting heavily, her hair falling down over one shoulder. "Kill him?"

"I think there's another way. But I must find him, speak to him."

She stared at him in silence, breathing erratically through her mouth, the white tips of teeth visible. Not convinced, she didn't know what to say. If it came to a question of her husband's life or the other man's she was left in no doubt. The very prospect was nightmarish.

"There really might be a way," he insisted. "But I must be prepared for the worst. Do you know someone who can get me a gun for my own protection?"

Her hesitation was a giveaway. There had been no denial.

"Chieko. Please, darling. It's my life that's at stake. Our future."

She leaned against the table, fingertips on it to steady herself. "I have a girl friend who went out with an employee of a dreadful man. A gangster. I used to warn her."

"Does she still see him?"

"I don't know. I can find out. I don't know what job he had but he seemed to have money."

"Tell her that you've had a bet that you can obtain a gun illegally. She knows you're rich. Tell her that you'll pay more than the gun is worth. I'll cover the cost, of course."

"Wouldn't it be better to buy a gun openly from a gunsmith?"

He didn't want anything traceable. "It's almost impossible for a foreigner. I'd never get a licence for it. I could never state the reason I wanted it. Please ask her, Chieko. It's imperative."

In the space of half an hour her world had stood on its head. From infancy she had been nurtured, protected, probably too much. Now she was being asked to do the sort of thing she had been taught to abhor. She wanted to run from the room. Suddenly she was directly involved, unaware that perverting innocent people was nothing new to Leach. It did not matter that she was his wife nor that enquiry could lead back to her if things went wrong. And that he would let her take the consequences if that proved the right course for him.

She looked at him and saw none of this, only his helplessness, his open looks, and his reliance on her while he was in peril. "Now?"

"Absolutely now. I want it by tomorrow whatever the cost."

Chieko picked up the telephone, not sure of anything any more.

*   *   *

Kenji Miyoto did not receive the information about Bustillo until the following day. Bustillo had paid off the cabman at the next set of traffic lights from the point he had picked up the cab. Kenji rammed down the telephone angrily. Well, that was that. He went into his father's office.

Fujio was standing at the window looking at the blue sky speared by the radio mast of Tokyo Tower. He glanced over his shoulder, saw his son. "Were you ever told that Tokyo Tower is six feet higher than the Eiffel Tower in Paris, France?"

"Is that all you have on your mind, Father?" Kenji spoke in English, deliberately to annoy his father.

Fujio turned from the window, the backdrop of light seeping into the lines under his cheekbones that had deepened over the last few days. He was beginning to look his age. Kenji gave him a much watered down version of what had happened the previous day, emphasising Bustillo's obvious unwillingness to talk. "I tried

to do what you wanted. It didn't work. I don't know where he is."
And then sharply, "Do you know a journalist named Tadashi
Fujuda? Works on the *Nippon Sun*?"

"I've met him, perhaps twice. I understand he's good at his
job."

"Maybe too good. He's tied in with Bustillo. You realise what
that means?"

Fujio looked uneasy. He didn't reply.

"It means that it's far worse than we thought. The whole
business will collapse around us if we don't move fast. We stop
procrastinating, Father. As from this moment. I'm going to find
someone to do the job."

Fujio sat on the edge of his desk, thoughtful and surprisingly
unargumentative. He shrugged almost imperceptibly. "Who will
you contact?"

Kenji accepted his father's surrender, pleased that there was no
further barrier. "I don't know yet. It's got to be a professional job.
No comebacks. We pay and the job is done. We won't even know
by whom."

"Oh, we'll know who. It will be us. But we won't fire the gun."
It was Fujio's last concession to reluctance. He well knew the
grave urgency and that he'd delayed matters. It was bad news
about Tadashi Fujuda's involvement. That meant a deliberate
conspiracy. Perhaps Tadashi would have to go, too. He studied
his son. "Try a man called Susumu Takama. He won't press the
trigger either. But he will arrange it. At a price."

Kenji was shaken. "You could have told me before."

"I didn't know before."

"Who told you?"

"Don't be childish. You don't imagine I've discussed murder
with an outsider. I leave that for you to do." He still felt the
humiliation of Hitomi being unable to rouse him. She had
straddled him, tried everything to illustrate her experience, things
even he hadn't known. Yet he was so deep rooted in worry she
had failed, taking the blame herself. Yet the failure was his and it
was nothing to do with age.

"You are worried about something. Worried sick." Her hair
was hanging round her face, sweat beads moistening her forehead
after her fruitless efforts to excite him. He couldn't deny it. It was
so obvious, what was the point?

"Is there something I can do, Fujio?"

He'd smiled grimly. "Don't you think you've tried enough?"

"Not that. I don't mean that. You're in trouble. You wouldn't be like this otherwise."

"Perhaps, Hitomi. You can't help me."

"It depends on the sort of trouble."

He gazed up, pleased by her young body, still unable to take advantage of it. "This trouble I can't share. Not with anyone."

"I once knew a man who was very good at fixing troubles. He helped me. He dealt with the sort of troubles that the police and lawyers couldn't touch. There are such troubles. I believe his prices are high though."

It had gone on from there but he had no intention of telling Kenji. It might prove to be an abortive contact but one had to start somewhere. Quickly.

"Okay, I'll contact him. I'm sure I've heard of him."

"Tread carefully. There are many forms of danger."

"I know. Don't worry."

The intercom rang and Fujio flicked it down.

"Mr. Bustillo to see Mr. Kenji, sir." There was doubt in the tone.

The two men locked gazes. "Send him into my office," said Kenji. "And I want no interruptions while he's with me."

5

KENJI WAS SEATED AT his desk when Bustillo came in. Old rancours stirred but this was no time to lose his temper. The American came into the room uncertainly. Everything about him was ambiguous. His clothes were shabby. No tie. His eyes looked as if they were healing after being punched. The hair had been combed and he had now shaved, some kind of conflicting concession, reflected Kenji, as he studied the man for the first time full face. There was nothing there to frighten him that he could see. Bustillo would never have crossed the threshold of this office as an employee, but his role had changed.

"Sit down." Kenji just fell short of being curt; he didn't want the American scared into running again.

Bustillo sat, crossed his legs, fingered his cardigan, aware of his comparative shabbiness. From the shadows of his eyes he took stock of the forceful Kenji and of the suspicion on the sullen face. The son was not so capable of oriental impassiveness as his father.

"What made you change your mind?"

Bustillo grimaced. "It seemed kind of ridiculous. Running like that. It's best we clear the air."

"About what?"

"If you don't know, I'm wasting my time here. You came looking for me."

There was a quiet authoritativeness about the American that warned Kenji to be cautious. This was no book-keeper confronting him. Bustillo was nervous, doubtful, but he wasn't in awe. Not in any way. Kenji reminded himself too, that this quiet man had been frequently with his sister. An all-round enigma.

"Okay. Let's start with your reason for walking out on us?"

"What difference can it make to you? I had a bit part here."

"You tampered with a safe. Why?"

Bustillo shrugged. "This may sound sort of corny but it's true. Either your chief accountant got careless or I'm quick sighted but I spotted something that made me curious. I'm an inquisitive sort of guy. I guessed he wouldn't tell me, so I tried to find out for myself. I just wanted to check a discrepancy, that's all. To satisfy myself. No more than that."

"And did you?"

"Check? No."

"I don't believe you. The lock was jammed after you tried to re-lock it."

"No. It was jammed as I was trying to open it. I never got anywhere."

"Would the kind of discrepancy you say you saw be understood by a book-keeper?"

"No. Only by a trained accountant. I am one. But I don't know whether my qualifications hold up here. I was grateful for any job. I'm not complaining."

"Then why are you here in Japan? Why not work in your own country?"

"I wanted out. For all sorts of reasons. None are connected with you or this business. I just wanted to get away."

"Are the American police after you?" Kenji knew that his father had checked on Bustillo but he preferred to test reaction himself.

"No." Well, that was true. Not the police.

Kenji swivelled in his chair. He picked up a gold inlay rule, running his fingers up and down it. "You've given me a strange story. An American, for some reason quits his own country, comes to Japan, strikes up a friendship with my sick sister through whom he gets a menial job then promptly starts breaking open a safe. He isn't paid much, he speaks fluent Japanese, walks out of his job without notice, then runs from me when I approach him. What would you think of that if you were sitting here, Bustillo?"

"I'd think it stinks. I'd equally think it suspect that a man in your position should chase a guy like me through a section of old Tokyo. And that you haven't asked me about the discrepancy."

There was silence between them. Kenji was now gripping the rule fiercely, the edges cutting into his palm.

"All right, Bustillo. How much?"

"That's why I came here at last. I've nothing to offer."

"Thirty thousand American dollars?"

"I can't sell what I don't know. That's what I wanted to tell you."

"We wouldn't be talking like this if you had nothing to sell. *You express no surprise that I'm offering.*"

"That's because I can guess. But it's only guessing. I couldn't show a thing against you."

"How much is the *Nippon Sun* offering you? I'll double it."

"Tadashi is merely a friend. He knows absolutely nothing. He doesn't know why I quit. I wouldn't tell him."

"That's what's so suspect. That you walked out yet claim you know nothing."

"For Chrissake, I didn't want to be involved, don't you see? Once I realised what I might get caught up in I didn't *want* to know. I've escaped from one situation, I didn't want to land in another. *That's why I tried the safe.* I wanted confirmation that I'd landed in the shit. I needed to know to decide what to do. For myself. Stay or leave. When I couldn't open the safe, I decided to take no chances. I split. That's all there is to it."

Kenji waited for Bustillo to cool down. He was watching the American closely, thinking that there was too much unknown about him. The need to assess the position made him think without a hot-headed response. "I accept some of what you say. This is what I propose. We'll accept liability for you losing your job. Wrongful dismissal. We prefer our staff to be Japanese. A mistake was made. In view of this we will give you a sum of fifty thousand American dollars compensation for loss of office. You will have to sign a receipt for it. You then leave the country."

Bustillo rose. "I can't get it through to you. I don't want your money. You have nothing to fear from me. I don't want to be on the run from you or anybody. And I want to stay in Japan."

"I'd be happier if you took the money."

"Sure you would. And the hold you'd have over me. Forget it, Miyoto. I was hoping you'd believe; that my calling here was indicative of some sort of integrity. Can't you imagine anyone being straight?"

"Think it over at least. See it from my end."

"The hot seat you're in isn't one I made. Okay, I'll think it over."

"Where can I contact you?"

Bustillo smiled wearily. "I'll let you know." He sauntered half-way to the door, looked back over his shoulder, then turned a little. His shoulders were hunched in resignation. "I'd guessed I'd be wasting my time. I just thought I'd give it a twirl. I must repeat that you can safely forget about me. Don't try anything stupid, for that really would place you in danger. Stick to what you know."

Kenji didn't answer. After Bustillo had left he gazed blankly at the closed door, not reaching for a telephone, nor changing position. It was pointless having Bustillo followed for who could do it? After some time of unblinking silence he went in to his father who was restlessly waiting.

"He knows something. He tried to whitewash himself and he may even have meant that we have nothing to worry about from him. The thing is he *knows*. And if he knows someone is going to try to winkle it out of him and they won't be fussy how. I'm going over to the Tokyo Prince to make a phone call I don't want to make from here."

Fujio understood. He nodded without comment.

The Tokyo Prince is a superb hotel near the Tower in the green folds of Shiba Park. Kenji entered the white-furnitured lobby and made his call from a booth after looking up the number. He was talking to Susumu Takama within seconds. "I wondered if we could meet. I have something to say that might interest you."

"I shall be delighted to meet both you and your illustrious father, Mr. Miyoto. Is it a matter of some urgency?"

"Extreme urgency. And my father's not involved."

"I am old-fashioned, Mr. Miyoto. I believe in the correct courtesies. Your father must always ultimately be involved in the affairs of his only son. You see you are famous enough already to have drawn my attention. I suggest the three of us meet at my town apartment at six." He gave the address then the phone clicked in Kenji's ear.

*　　*　　*

It was luxurious but not big. A disharmonious mixture of east and west and not the best of either. But the apartment was central, and convenient. Susumu Takama had opened the door himself. He assured them at the outset that nobody was there but himself. They could speak freely. Then he beamed as he passed them drinks. "When people come to me it is usually for a specific service they themselves cannot perform. What can I do for you gentlemen?"

Shoulders rounded forward from the chair, belly pushing his

jacket out, carefully benign eyes studying them through the rimless glasses, with podgy hand stroking the exposed flesh of his scalp, Susumu appeared almost grotesque. Yet he had a presence both the Miyotos sensed at once. And something else. It was seldom that Fujio Miyoto felt uncomfortable in any company. Now he did and he wondered if Kenji was as sensitive to the man facing them with a smile. Certainly he was cautious in his approach.

"We want to find a man."

"Someone you can't ask the police to trace?"

The Miyotos stared at each other. Susumu said, "Come gentlemen. We are all business men. If you intend to be naïve we'll be here all night."

"We want you to find him."

"And what do you want done to him when he has been found?"

Again the Miyotos hedged through an uneasy silence. It was difficult to relate to a stranger whatever his notoriety.

"Do you want him beaten up? If so how much? Or do you want him killed?"

"We want him killed." Kenji blurted it as if the words had been choking him.

"Good. Now a description."

Kenji gave a detailed one and Susumu made a few notes on a pad. "The paper will be destroyed," he assured them. "You've no idea where he is?"

"No. Only that he's probably in Tokyo."

"Any friends that could lead us to him?"

Fujio Miyoto said reluctantly, "My daughter Nikki knows him. I don't want her harmed in any way."

"Naturally. My employees do not believe in giving free service. If there is payment for one then one it will be."

Susumu considered the problem. "The fact that this man is an American creates some little difficulty. It would be unwise for a Japanese to do it. Another American would draw attention away from Japanese involvement. It would be useful if the police discovered that it was done by a compatriot of the victim. It provides a false focus, something for them to occupy themselves with."

"Can't it be an accident?"

Susumu pushed his glasses up with a stubby finger. "In my experience there are so many accidents with accidents. They have to satisfy highly qualified forensic and medical experts if there's the slightest whisper of something wrong. And that can lead to exhaustive enquiry. A straight killing is better. Apparently motiveless, or a presumed motive beyond these shores. I am not open to argument on method, gentlemen. If it is placed in my hands I decide how. When do you want it done?"

"Now. Tonight, tomorrow."

"That's impossible. We have to locate him, find a contractor. The absolute earliest, with all the luck on our side, tomorrow night. Probably later."

Fujio Miyoto thought his head was splitting. They were sitting here talking, drinking, deep in easy chairs as if they were discussing the day's share index. Susumu made the whole thing sound so ordinary. Perhaps killing to him *was* his everyday work. Like going to the office.

"How much?" asked Kenji with the brashness he had used on Bustillo.

Susumu raised an almost hairless browline. "It's usual that I state the fee, Mr. Miyoto. Precisely; forty-five million yen."

The Miyotos were stunned. It was unbelievable. Kenji was doing rapid mental calculations. Where money was concerned he did so much business in the United States that he was inclined to think in dollars as an international currency.

"That's about a hundred and fifty thousand dollars."

"Really? I haven't converted it."

"But that's ridiculous."

Fujio Miyoto left it to his son. He had expected to pay a lot but on this he was inclined to agree with Kenji.

Susumu folded into his seat, his eyes suddenly veiled.

"I never haggle over a fee. I have to get a man over from the mainland of America. His expenses have to be met. There may be complications. His fee will be high. So is mine. It is a rush job. You take it or you leave it."

After a continued silence Susumu added, "I suggest you sort out your priorities. I can't decide for you the value of this man's death. I can only tell you what it will cost you. Meanwhile, gentlemen, you are wasting my time."

Kenji was glowering, disliking being on the receiving end of a bite. His father spoke calmly. "If that's your fee then we must accept it or go elsewhere. For that money we would expect a job that would be not only efficient in execution but would not remotely touch us in any way."

"Of course. Except for payment. Unless someone else is meeting the bill."

"We'll meet it. How exactly do you want it?"

Susumu lifted the decanter near his elbow, holding it out to each Miyoto in turn. When they shook their heads he charged his own glass and sipped thoughtfully. His action ejected a nuance that Fujio Miyoto caught and it made him stiffen. His face tightened as he tried to read the smooth features before him and to explain his feeling of sudden sickness. Kenji seemed unaware of any of this.

"I don't want it in cash. I want the equivalent amount of shares in the Miyoto Travel Bureau. One of your more neglected subsidiaries, I believe."

The Miytos, recovering from the first shock, were not prepared for the second. Fujio, with the hindsight of experience had sensed something bad coming, but not this bad. It was difficult to run over the many implications of the suggestion with so much on his mind. Kenji was looking across to his father for guidance, belatedly realising that his father still had a part to play.

"I'd rather pay you in cash: or, perhaps, gems."

"I'm not suggesting, Mr. Miyoto. I'm telling you how I want it. It's a fair instruction."

"No. A transfer of shares will link us on paper. That's the last thing I want."

"I would naturally use a nominee."

"There is no single block of shares to cover that amount. We can't go asking people to sell."

Susumu smiled, completely unruffled. "There are two blocks that more than adequately cover the fee. Yours and those of your son."

Fujio Miyoto rose with his empty glass. "I will have that drink after all." He held out the glass while Susumu willingly poured, eyes scarcely leaving the older man's face.

Fujio remained standing. Now that it was in the open a part of him was enjoying the kind of combat he had encountered in the early days of business; the ruthless manœuvring for position. But then he had always been in Susumu's present position, and the cards known. It was a matter of weighing one thing against another and there was really no choice. "I'd like to talk this over with my son. This is a totally unforeseen development."

"Very well." Susumu rose with difficulty, his breathing heavy. "There is only one question for you to ask yourselves. Do you want Bustillo dead or not? The remainder is not for discussion. I will give you five minutes. If you've decided before that time please tap on that door. Otherwise I will come in at the end of that time and assume a refusal."

As soon as Susumu had gone Kenji rose, releasing his feelings. "That fat bastard drives too hard a bargain."

Fujio smiled bitterly. "He's done his homework."

"Let's call his bluff." Kenji was venomous.

Fujio placed an arm on his son's shoulder. "There are times when I despair about you. You have your drive, your ambition, your ability. But when will you learn about people? That man is not bluffing. Not at any point."

"Then let's go elsewhere."

"Where?" Fujio Miyoto was looking round the room, inside lampshades, behind the central heating radiators.

"You think we're bugged?" Kenji had caught on.

"In his position I would have recorded."

Kenji was pale now. They were in a trap all ways. Then his natural defiance returned. "To hell with it. He's implicated too. Let's leave."

Fujio turned to him. "Do you intend to kill Bustillo yourself? You were seen running after him. Some will remember."

Kenji could barely contain his chagrin. He'd had his way for so long he couldn't bear the sensation of psychological imprisonment. In too short a time he had run up against too many unfamiliar barriers. It was a bitter pill to discover that he'd enjoyed the vast experience of his father for so long, that he'd been protected in ways unknown to him. Almost at that moment he took a big step forward in learning. Okay, so the old boy wasn't such an idiot but his methods of dealing with a problem were still archaic. Right now they were in a vice. They wanted Bustillo dead and by so doing placed themselves in another kind of danger. When he equated one with the other there was no problem. He finally faced and acknowledged it. But his resentment still burned. "You realise he'll have a big stake in the travel company?"

Fujio nodded. "But not control. What worries me is why he wants it."

They were speaking in whispers now as if it suddenly mattered. Fujio glanced at his son, crossed the room and knocked softly on the door.

Susumu came out calmly, no portrayal of triumph. He had never been in doubt. "I take it you will draw up a transfer first thing tomorrow."

"Yes. One from each of us. The price to be taken at current stock-exchange value."

"Of course. I shall want one half signed and witnessed before the execution and one half following."

Fujio nodded slowly. "Why do you want an interest in the travel agency?"

"I feel that it's a small stagnant part of your empire. I can provide business for it. Do you see the irony of it? Given a little time you could recover the cost of my fee." The eyes were twinkling behind the reflection of the glasses.

Fujio Miyoto drained his glass and put it down. He looked tired, beaten. With some dignity he said, "I hope you're worth the money."

Susumu laughed openly. "Come now, you have done the right thing. Nothing more? Then I must make a telephone call, if you'll excuse me."

Being shovelled out, Kenji called it afterwards. He'd done it so often to other people that he didn't like it happening to himself. The whole distasteful episode had been a complete reversal of everything he had known. Yet it endorsed the need for Bustillo's death. Too much was at stake. Viewed in this way he accepted Susumu's fee as petty cash. On the way back Fujio said uneasily, "We'd better get a complete list of shareholders and their holdings in Miyoto Travel. Get Kasaka on to it first thing."

Susumu, meanwhile, glanced at his watch and booked a person-to-person call to San Francisco. When it came through he spoke in a clear, clipped English with a slight American accent. "Enrico? Susumu. I think I've solved our distribution problem. I've gone into the travel business. Freights and passenger. There is a branch in San Francisco. Give me, say, a month, then I'll come over and discuss the detail with you." He chuckled. "It's a *very* respectable group."

The two men laughed down the wire before Susumu continued: "Part of the price requires a contract over here. It must be finalised at once. Will you send one of your best lawyers? Now. It's *very* urgent. Say twenty thousand dollars plus expenses. *Fifty thousand?* But that's . . . all right, Enrico, so we're all in the grip of inflation. It's a dreadful world we live in. A really top man for that." Susumu wiped his brow, thinking that he had fared well. "I'll leave half his fee in the deposit box we used before. He will be met on arrival. I'll leave the contract and the pen there. All he need do is collect them. A hotel reservation will be included together with a day or night telephone number. When the contract is complete he should return to the box to collect the remainder."

When he hung up Susumu considered how nice it was to deal with Enrico. When things were going right. He had no illusion about getting a top hit man at such notice. The distribution had been the carrot, not the fee which would go wholly to the contractor.

He dialled a local number, his voice changed, all bonhomie gone.

"I want an American found. Tall, fair, grey eyes, dress irregular western style. Last seen wearing light brown ruckled trousers, brothel creepers, open shirt, fawn cardigan. Name James Bustillo but might be using any name. Probably has limited funds on him. Try small hotels, doss houses. Check any addresses belonging to *Sun* journalist Tadashi Fujuda. He may have provided a room somewhere. Get it out of him in any way you can but don't overdo it. If you can find Bustillo without Fujuda do so. Fujuda is the last resort. Also watch the apartment of Nikki Miyoto. Bustillo has contact there. Do not touch her in any circumstances. She's protected property. Use all the men you want. I'll underwrite expenses and justified bribes. A bonus for whoever runs him down. And I want him found before dawn. When found try to get a photograph. Now report back."

He hung up again, satisfied. A whole stream of enquiry was set in motion through receptionists, landladies, cabdrivers, shopkeepers, waiters, newspaper vendors, covering right across the board. The only stronger incentive than money was fear. He exercised both with the right amount of adjustment as necessary.

Satisfied with a short evening's work, Susumu showered his ample body, pondering which of his many clubs he would delight for dinner. He began mentally to run over the hostesses. It was a night for celebration.

*   *   *

Jimmy Bustillo sat on the edge of the bed, a bottle in one hand. It was a woman's room, pastel shades and delicate arrangements. It belonged to one of Tadashi's girl friends at the moment covering an assignment in Hong Kong. It could have been far worse. He stared at a wall, the palest blue with a subdued cherry tree motif, and took a swig from the bottle. His eyes were distant but not glazed. He got off the bed, went to a small bureau and found notepaper and pen. He sat down, still holding the bottle then used it as a weight to anchor down the notepaper.

He started to write, wrinkling his brow with the effort of concentration. Occasionally he would drink from the bottle to relieve the monotony. At one time his head fell forward on to the paper and he slept for some minutes, coming to in a confused state, not quite knowing where he was. Then he recalled the mess his life was in and started to write again. For a spell, as fear bit into him, he didn't touch the bottle at all but examined closely what he'd written, checking out on a well-trained, but ill-used, memory pattern. What he'd written was enough to open the floodgates if they killed him, but it couldn't save him.

The bottle was almost empty. So used to quantities of liquor by now, he could remain in this state of dulled consciousness, reflexes slowed, but completely aware of what was happening. Right now a big boredom was happening. For his own protection he was being reduced to doing what he'd been trying to avoid all along. What he had told Kenji had been partly true. He had wanted to help Nikki but also to check the direction of the bus before staying on or getting off. And the only reason he'd wanted to do that was because he had sufficient complications without adding to them.

He'd bungled it. Left a trade mark like an amateur. And then he'd stepped off the bus while it was still in motion, which left the third alternative. Stupidly, he had placed himself in a position of being run down by it. It seemed that he could do nothing right any more. His judgment had wavered ever since Chile. The downhill rush had terminated with the bottle, not been caused by it. His own momentum of confused loyalties had carried him there. Nothing had been solved and his problems had multiplied. Now his life was at stake.

He read through his notes once more, folded them and sealed them in an envelope, placed it in his trouser pocket. He held the bottle up, reluctant to finish the little left to leave himself without but needing what was there. Finally he lifted the bottle to his lips, keeping it there until it was drained. He put it down, careful to wipe its base so that it would leave no ring on the bureau. It was a throwback of consideration for which he had once been known. He'd always had respect for other people's feelings and property. Too much for his own good.

Taking out his wallet he produced a crumpled photograph of a wide-eyed girl. Jenny. She had once sustained him the few times they'd spent together. Even looking at the photograph had once helped. Now the magic had gone. He'd burned his bridges and she must have long since forgotten him. Yet he'd clung on to the well thumbed print in the forlorn hope of putting the clock back. He took a brief step towards reality and with a feeling of great sadness burned the photo in an ashtray. The sweet face curled away as he held it.

He rang Nikki. As soon as he spoke she cut across him. Like him she had been drinking. She was verging on hysteria. "Kenji's out looking for you. That lousy swine hit me."

"Take it easy. Can I come over?"

"Oh, please, Jimmy. I've missed you." And plaintively, "You walked out on me."

"I know, honey. I'll explain. Is there a back way in?"

"Only the fire escape. Where're you hiding, Jimbo?"

"I can't tell you. They are sure to have your main entrance staked out and the entrance to the courtyard that leads to the fire escape. Isn't there another way?"

She thought for a moment. "Each wing has its own entrance and they are not interconnected. I have a friend on the second floor of the west wing. I'll call her. She can let you through to the back and then you can climb up. I'll call you back."

"No. I'll call *you* in five minutes." He hung up, annoyed now that he'd finished the bottle. This was how it was going to be from now on. Minute by minute. It was risky going to Nikki but he couldn't meet her elsewhere, she wouldn't know if she had a tail or not. And, in a strange way, she was the only one he could rely on for what he had in mind. When he rang back she gave him the apartment number and told him it was okay.

Outside, he fought off the impulse to call a cab because of the obvious dangers and, anyway, his funds were low. By a mixture of walking and public transport he reached the apartment block almost an hour later. By this time he was cold and hungry.

Avoiding the main wing completely he approached the west wing by a circuitous route and waited in a side street opposite to watch the brightly lit portico. As he stood in shadow he cursed the fact that he'd left his topcoat in his own rented room to which he dare not go back. Had his head been clearer at the time he would have organised himself better but self-recrimination was too late. He didn't care that much anyway. To prove it to himself he crossed the road and entered the west wing. The porter saw him but made no comment as Bustillo went to the elevators. There were times when he could carry himself impressively no matter how he looked.

At the second floor he found the apartment and rang the bell.

The petite beauty who opened the door wore a Japanese Airline stewardess's uniform and bade him enter with a smile. "Do you speak Japanese?"

"All the time."

"Good. If you want to come back this way will you make sure the front door is closed."

They walked through to the kitchen. "It will mean leaving this door unlocked. You look as if you're going on duty."

"I don't mind. I have nothing worth stealing."

"Except your smile. This is very kind of you. And no questions."

She shrugged. "I feel sorry for Nikki. She hasn't much to look forward to. I hope you're not adding to her problems."

"I hope not too. Do you mind putting the light out until I'm clear of the escape?"

She switched it off. "Thank you," he said again. "One day I might explain."

Bustillo slipped past the door on to a small iron balcony on which were pot plants he was careful to avoid. Below him was the rectangle of lawn and surrounding paths shared by the tenants. The block almost completed a square but at right angles to him was a wide gap in the buildings closed off at ground level by huge, wooden gates kept open during daylight. It was the entrance the garbage collectors used and a fire exit for those using the rear escapes. He had no doubt that it was being watched at this moment. Crouching first, he began to descend the two floors treading lightly all the way.

When he reached the ground he stood still, peering across the rectangle which was hazily lit by the glow of apartment windows. It was a tricky, insufficient light that left far too much in shadow. He saw the gates. Closed. But in one of them was a small door giving access to those on the lower floors who might want to short cut in or out that way. It was open. Bustillo could just make out the pale frame of it. When it partially blacked out he realised someone was standing by it. As he concentrated more it seemed that someone was peering in. He stayed exactly where he was, not moving, back against the wall.

6

WITH THE ADVENT OF real danger his head cleared rapidly. He could see his own frosted breath change colour as it crossed the lighted window at his side. The shadow moved, stepped through the gate and it was clear that he was looking around trying to penetrate the uncertain darkness as Bustillo was. By movement and outline Bustillo could see that it was a man who stepped outside again. The doorway became clear but Bustillo waited a little longer before moving. When he did he crouched below the window levels, at times crawling on the concrete.

Reaching the escape leading to Nikki's apartment he pierced the gate area before reaching up and starting his climb. After the first floor he was already panting and he had eleven more to go. Jesus, it's going to kill me, he thought. At the fourth platform the sweat was soaking him and as the cold air cooled it he was fluctuating between hot and cold as if he had a fever. He rested at each landing, his breath so rasping that he had to cup his hands over his mouth to keep down the noise.

By the time he reached Nikki's his legs were rubber and he had to tone down before tapping lightly on her back door. When Nikki didn't reply, and as he dare not tap louder, he sank down and opened the door slowly, dismayed that she'd left the kitchen light on. He went in on all fours reaching up to close the door behind him. Nikki wasn't in sight so he crawled to the dining room door, switched off the kitchen light, then rose, leaning for a while against the door. At that stage Nikki heard him, came rushing from the lounge and fell into his arms. She helped him back into the lounge, her hand rubbing his chest sensuously.

"You made it."

He flopped into a chair, waving her entreaties away. "Only just. Give me time, for Chrissake. Get me a drink."

She returned with a tumbler full of bourbon, realising at last what it had cost him to climb twelve floors. He sipped and spluttered and then coughed. "I didn't know I was so out of condition," he confessed.

"You ready for bed?" Nikki was already in a negligée, her insatiable demands still unsatisfied.

He looked around at the disorder and saw a self-reflection which urged him back to the drink. "I've got to talk to you," he said. He groped in his pocket and produced the now crumpled envelope. "I've got to rely on you, Nikki. Are you capable of listening?"

She blinked at him, pushing her belly forward. "Can't we talk later?"

Oh Christ, was this just one more mistake. "Sit down and listen or I'll leave you now."

She sat, cross-legged in front of him in a careless posture. "I mean it, Nikki." He rose.

"Damn you. All right, I'm listening."

He waved the envelope at her. "I'm leaving this here. If anything happens to me I want you to sober up long enough to deliver this to the British Embassy."

It caught her attention. "The *British* Embassy?"

"That's right."

It silenced her for a while. "Why them, Jimbo?"

He didn't answer, sitting down again wearily.

She came forward, took the envelope, tapping it against her other hand. She looked down at him, more serious than he had seen her. Like this it was easy to detect her finer points, not only of feature but of unconscious poise, pride even as she held her head back. He wanted to weep for her. "Why me, Jimbo?"

"I've no one else. They wouldn't expect something like that to be here. They don't understand you."

"And you do?"

"A little. Just a little."

"Don't let anything happen to you, Jimbo." Her emotion was welling visibly. "I'll probably fail you. Forget."

"It'll be too bad. I won't be in a position to criticise. It doesn't matter that much."

She knelt in front of him, all promiscuity gone as she held up the envelope. "Why not give it to them now?"

"I don't want to stir it up." He leaned forward, stroking her hair with a smile. "There are other reasons I can't explain."

She understood his underlying attitude of resignation; she'd had it so long herself. But for him there was some hope. Not realising she was reversing her earlier desire to take him with her, to have someone's hand at the end, she asked, "Could this thing save your life?"

He shook his head. "No. Stop worrying about me, Nikki. It's not all you think it is."

"I could open it."

He smiled wearily. "It wouldn't help. It's in code."

"Are you asking me to sacrifice my own family?"

"That's part of it. But only if they kill me."

When she sank on her heels he said softly, "Forget it, honey. I shouldn't have asked. Here, give it back." He held out a hand.

Nikki tucked the envelope behind her back with a child's truculence. Her expression was pleading as she gazed up at him.

"It's not them that worries me. Kenji's a louse. And my father's made no effort through his life. He destroyed my mother and he's largely responsible for destroying me. Does that sound like self-pity?"

"Not if it's true, Nikki."

"It's true. I finally got through to him when I got hooked. His belated sense of duty to me came as a kind of conscience that ensured my supply. He's helping to kill me by pandering to my needs because he has no example to set, no character to follow. Jimbo, I'm scared."

He slid off the chair and held her to him, her hands still behind her back, holding the envelope. "Can't you really make a try, Nikki? It *can* be done with guts. I'll help all I can."

Her face was next to his and he felt her tears. Her arms crept round him with surprising strength. "Will you be able to take the pain from me? The craving? Can you give me a different life?"

He stopped the false promises springing to his lips. She would know. She knew now. She pulled her head back.

"I'll let you down, Jimbo. You're asking me to cut off my own supply."

"Then don't do it. It's not important."

"If they kill you I'll try. I really will. But I'm only as strong as the hope for the next shot."

"I know. It doesn't matter."

Still looking at him she wiped her eyes with the back of her hand. "You've no one else to ask. You really are a loner."

"I can't trust Tashi with it. Nikki, can you get me a gun?"

She pulled back from him.

"As things are I feel kinda naked." He didn't know that he was almost echoing Graham Leach's words to his wife Chieko.

"I can try."

"Your pusher must know someone. I need it quick. And ammunition."

"I'll see what I can do."

"I can't pay for it, Nikki."

She kissed him lightly on the lips, then smiled wickedly.

"Father can pay for it. How's that for poetic justice?"

He gave her a squeeze then stood up, helping her rise with him.

"I can't stay, honey. I dare not leave in daylight and I must get back before the public transport stops operating. Try to understand."

The prospect of a long, lonely night loomed before her and Nikki shuddered. Yet she well understood his danger. "Are you going to stay on the run, Jimbo? How long can you keep it up?"

"If I can stay low for a few days and nothing happens either way, Kenji may get it through his thick head that he has nothing to fear. He may even come round to believing that I know nothing."

"Sure. And I might sign the pledge."

He shrugged. "I don't want to leave Japan. I'll do that only as a last resort."

She slunk up to him making a last effort to get him to stay, putting her own fears first, but he held her off.

"I'm sorry, Nikki. I don't want to leave you." He was holding her at arm's length very firmly. When she eased he picked up his drink and finished it. "At least it's downhill this time. Thank your friend for me when you see her."

She didn't try to detain him again, her face crumbling back into lines of defeat. "You're used to this, aren't you? Being chased, I mean."

"Does it show that much?" He went to the rear door where she was now leaning, her head against the wall. "I'll tell you this, Nikki. You never get used to it nor to like it. It's my own fault. I should come to terms. I'll ring you tomorrow about the gun. So long, hon. And thanks."

Stepping out on to the fire escape was like walking into a refrigerator. After the excessive heat of Nikki's rooms he huddled on the platform rubbing his arms and crouched low. He went down carefully, halting at each stage, to listen and to try to spear the gloom. He reached the ground. The gate was clear so he moved along the pale strip of perimeter path until he reached the other escape. The climb of two floors returned the heat to his body. He entered the stewardess's rear kitchen door on hands and knees. Once inside he locked the door and felt his way forward without using the lights.

Another man joined him at the elevators, eyeing him curiously while Bustillo was only too aware that he was not only a westerner but a badly dressed one. They went down together without exchanging a word, Bustillo holding back when they reached the bottom. He refused the porter's offer to get him a cab and tried to satisfy himself that there was no one lingering outside. Looking from light into darkness made it impossible to decide. He went outside, hugging the wall but aware that he'd been on view. He started to walk, listening as he went.

*   *   *

The frost crackled on the sidewalk, sparkling like diamanté under the dull glow of a solitary street lamp. Yet the three men trod softly, light of step with the practised silence of the furtive. They were small men, hunched in topcoats, hats on, surgical masks covering their faces to just below their eyes.

In Tokyo it is a common sight to see ordinary people wearing gauze to cover mouth and nostrils, particularly in winter. Hygienically minded, they've no wish to pass colds on to their neighbours. They are also a protection against pollution. Either way it is unlikely, even in daytime, that one can travel in Tokyo without seeing them worn at times. Certainly they provoke no curiosity.

It would have been difficult to decide therefore for which reason these three swiftly moving figures wore their masks until they stopped outside the near-dilapidated building in which Tadashi Fujuda lived. As they manipulated the main door lock it became clear that their masks were worn for neither of the accepted reasons. The lock was no problem to them and it clicked as the tumblers spun. They went up the darkened stairs without a sound.

At Tadashi's door they used a torch while one of them picked the lock. Because of the relative noise in the confined space they waited a minute or two after the lock had sprung, one of them

77

with his ear to the door. At a nod from this man, another slowly turned the handle. They went in completely noiselessly. Even when they closed the door they made no sound. One of them used a small torch, pointing downward to obtain location, then all three moved towards the bedroom door.

Their understanding in the darkness was uncanny as if they were well rehearsed. The bedroom door was opened and Tadashi's soft breathing was barely audible. One man closed the door and stood by the light switch. Another drew a gun, made certain that the curtains were drawn across, used his torch carefully and went to the far side of the bed. The third drew out a gag and approached the nearer side of the bed. The one with the gun said quite clearly, "Right."

The light was switched on, the gag was brought down over Tadashi's mouth and a gun with a silencer was rammed against his temple. The shock might well have killed a lesser person but even the hardened Tadashi believed he was having a terrifying nightmare and his heart thumped agonisingly. Straight from sleep to this frightening tableau was almost too much and he couldn't breathe. He struggled to get the gag away and it was then that he saw and felt the gun. His brain was near bursting before the truth struck and when it did he began to sober quickly, his heart still banging, his lungs bursting for air.

With the coolness of expertise the three men waited patiently for him to come out of shock and once they saw the terror fade from his eyes to change to recognisable fear, the one with the gun said softly, "If you shout I'll blow your head off. We're taking the gag away. Nod if you understand."

With staring eyes Tadashi nodded. The gag was taken away but when he tried to sit up he was pushed back on to the bed. If the gun and the three masked men were not enough he felt at a total disadvantage lying on his back staring up at three pairs of disquietingly impassive eyes.

The one with the gun was spokesman. He moved away slightly to halfway down the bed so that Tadashi might see the pointing gun better. The journalist's heartbeat was steadying, his thoughts collecting but he found no comfort. The calmer his reasoning the more imperilled he felt himself to be.

"I shall ask you one question and I want a simple answer. Then we will leave you. Unharmed."

The man had a slight lisp which might well be an affectation. Tadashi anticipated but kept quiet.

"Where is the American Bustillo ?"

Knowing what was coming made it no easier. He was staring at the gun. His thoughts were scattering in a subconscious protective pattern to avoid an answer. The question wasn't repeated and the deadly silence unnerved him into speaking.

"I don't know where he went. He left here this morning."

"Try again, before we make you impotent."

"Look, he was here. I've told you. But I've no idea where he went. I gave him a bed for the night. That's all."

With his eyes on the gun he didn't see the arm come down from the man the other side of the bed. The gag was rammed in his mouth while he was still speaking. Immediately he struggled, but both the gunman and the man by the door moved in. The three of them held his limbs. One of them produced a cord and with practised speed legs and arms were splayed and tied to the ends of the bed. They taped the gag to his mouth and let go of him. He struggled as he'd never struggled, his eyes whitening around the iris.

They opened his pyjama jacket and pulled down his trousers. Virtually naked he stared around at them in fear and closed his eyes as one of them produced a short bamboo cane. Sweat sprung to Tadashi's forehead. Two men held the bed each end to stop it banging on the floor as Tadashi strained in terror. The gunman gave a brief nod to the man with the cane.

Tadashi's scream filled his own head. His body arched and he tried to turn it in a crazed effort to cross his legs to protect himself. There was nothing he could do. He closed his eyes as the cane whipped down again and the gag began to choke him as he screamed, ankles and wrists tearing at the cords and drawing blood. The sheet under him was already stained with his own sweat. He couldn't take any more.

He tried to signal to them with his eyes but they seemed unaffected by his agony or his frantic effort to implore them to stop. But they did stop. For some time they stood looking down at him unmoving, seeking no direction from each other. Tadashi wanted to bring his hands down to cover the injured parts which were searing with pain. As the silence increased he became aware of only one sound: the tinge of whining through his dilated nostrils in his own strange breathing. He felt ashamed and humiliated and turned his face. At least they had stopped. Tension began to ease from him just before the cane came down again, harder than before.

He almost passed out. The excruciating agony was a terror ridden sensation wrapped in darkness. He was going mad in futile struggles he was barely aware of. When consciousness did creep through he didn't want it, he'd rather be unconscious. Hot coals had been poured between his legs and were burning through him. Tears of pain were scudding down his face, accelerating in the hollows under his cheekbones. Please end it. *Please.* He tried to shout through the gag but he refused to open his eyes. He just waited, tensed and terrified, for the next blow.

A voice from somewhere above him said, "One more like the last one and you'll never have another girl. We'll take the gag away and ask you one more time. Try screaming and you're dead."

Tadashi knew the gun was back against his head but he couldn't really feel it. When the gag was removed he gulped in air turning his head from side to side as if the sudden relief also brought agony. He opened his eyes; the three images were blurred through the film of water still welling up under his lids.

"Where's Bustillo?"

He told them in a painful, rasping breath. They cut the cords and by the time he had struggled up on one elbow they had gone. Tadashi stared down at his body in despair. It didn't look as bad as it felt but the pain was excruciating. He carefully dragged himself to the edge of the bed and reached for the telephone. It came as little surprise to find it dead. When he bent forward he saw they had torn the wire out before leaving. There was no other way of warning Jimmy Bustillo. Walking was out for some time.

Tadashi dragged himself to the bathroom where he was instantly sick. He ran the tap and splashed cold water in his face. Only then did he realise that the cords were still tied to his wrists and ankles. The blood grooves retold the story of his futile struggles. He freed himself after a time and with difficulty and bathed the blood away. He sat on the bed again with a blanket round him. Six o'clock. Still some time before light.

Apart from being unable to warn Bustillo, the useless telephone offered some advantages. It had prevented him from ringing his newspaper, which by now he would have done. To tell them what had happened meant involving Bustillo which he didn't want to do. Not yet. His journalistic mind began to tick over with possibilities. There was one hell of a story behind all this. But if they killed Bustillo he'd release what he had; to the police, to his paper.

He'd owe Jimmy that much. Practical as ever, he started to **work** out his lines of communication until he was mobile.

*　　*　　*

Jimmy Bustillo awoke parched and gasping. He drank some mineral water from the small ice box and the sharp taste brought him round quickly. He was hungry. There was no food in the apartment, which meant he must go out if he was to eat. The stores weren't yet open but there was a small restaurant down the street that opened early and closed late. It was eight a.m. With no shaving gear there was nothing he could do but bath.

He left the apartment, turning his shirt collar up and wearing dark glasses he had found in the bedroom which had fitted him after a little careful bending. Luckily, they weren't obviously feminine. The cold was biting into him now, a night of restless sleep having lowered his metabolism. Hands in pockets, he hurried along. Tokians were already on the move. He turned a corner and entered the restaurant already surprisingly full. He hooked himself on to a bar stool opposite the two white-capped chefs, watching their dexterity with the extra long chopsticks as they served. He ordered cinnamon toast, shirred eggs and ham with coffee, curbing himself when it was put in front of him and realising it wouldn't be enough after yesterday's virtual fast.

Outside the restaurant an early rising Japanese tourist, camera slung over shoulder, peered at the menu on the window. In sight of the restaurant he stood back and took a snapshot of the morning street scene. He was still there but not so obviously when a warmed and fed Bustillo emerged. From the cover of a deep doorway, the tourist took a shot of Bustillo as he came out and before he put the glasses back on, and another, side view, as he walked along the street. He then went slowly in the opposite direction to the American, rounded a corner, stopped at a parked car and gave the camera to the driver. The car pulled away immediately.

Bustillo went to the nearest supermarket and bought some tinned food and a half bottle of bourbon and took them back to the apartment. It was the back end of the morning rush hour. There were too many people on the streets to determine whether or not he was being followed. He didn't think so but he was too experienced to back his impression. Before reaching the apartment he used a few ploys and didn't turn into the apartment entrance until he was satisfied that he had no tail. And he was right. They

81

already knew where he was staying. Once satisfied that he was returning they had merely taken up stationary pre-planned positions.

In the apartment he put the goods away, checked the time and rang Tadashi. When he got the unobtainable tone he was uneasy. A telephone was a lifeline to a journalist. Their phones went out of order like everybody else's. But he didn't like the inconvenient timing. Later he would ring Tadashi's office. It was much too early to contact Nikki about the gun. There was nothing more for him to do but to stay out of sight.

Two things worried him. From time to time he would have to replenish food stocks and he was desperately low on money after his last purchases. And the bottle distracted him. It was all he could afford and he was loath to start on it so early. He put it away in a drawer but there was another reason why he was trying to keep away from it. Whatever his feeling about the lack of importance of life, his own in particular, the fact remained that as he sensed the increasing danger the need to keep his mind clear became obvious if he was to try to survive. He was pulled in two directions, feeling also the strong need to blanket his mind, forget his danger. Forget everything. For the moment he left the bottle alone.

Grappling elsewhere, anywhere to relieve the strain, he examined the toiletries in bathroom and bedroom and then searched through all the drawers, tidying as he went.

*   *   *

He had been born Piero Vezzozi on the beautiful little island of Ustica cradled in the Tyrrhenian Sea thirty miles north of Palermo. He had killed his first man at the age of eleven and had placed a bomb in the printing press of a Palermo newspaper at the age of fifteen when it had printed derogatory remarks about his father who, quite incidentally, was shot soon afterwards. He was now in his early forties and of limited ability which explained his lack of progress in an organisation to which he had been born.

Now called Peter Vence he was wealthy by all normal standards and was strong on loyalty mainly because he lacked the imagination to be devious. The only thing going for him was an ability to kill accurately, without fuss or clumsiness. He had done too much of it still to find it enjoyable but his detachment had merely made him more proficient. Average height and build, almost black eyes, neither ugly nor attractive, he aroused no interest unless, in the line of his business, one stared him in the eye for too long; a fraction of a second, say. A man empty of all feeling except the need for occasional self-preservation. A man with no aim in life other than to serve those he respected.

At roughly the time Tadashi was being tortured, Vence was at San Francisco International Airport with one suitcase, always ready packed, and a passport in quite a different name which proclaimed him to be a salesman. When he went through the security check no gun was discovered and the X-ray gave his suitcase the all clear. And rightly. He had no form of weapon with him.

He caught Pan American flight 001 which took off at 12.30 p.m. local time. He sat in the first-class compartment, ate, but refused all drink. The plane was a Boeing 747 Jumbo Jet that would fly the five and a half thousand miles to Tokyo non-stop, taking about ten and a half hours. Due to the fact that it crossed the International Date Line and that there was a time difference between west coast America and Japan, its calendar arrival would be the next day at 4.45 p.m.

Vence had no feelings about flying or any form of transportation. He relaxed in his seat, paid to see the movie and plugged in his ear phones. It was a gangster film. He'd enjoy that.

*　　*　　*

While Vence was high over the North Pacific Susumu and the two Miyotos met in the office of one of Susumu's lawyers. For reasons of secrecy the Miyotos hadn't brought a legal representative but they had already prepared the transfer of shares certificates which Fujio carried in a document case.

The men clustered round the lawyer's desk and Fujio pulled out the certificates. "They need signing and witnessing." When the lawyer reached out Fujio kept his hand on them while Kenji said, "What guarantees have we?"

Susumu looked pained. "Nothing in writing, gentlemen."

It sounded ludicrous. Yet as Fujio reflected he realised that in Susumu's place, honour in deals would be an essential part of survival.

"It's not good enough." Kenji was nervous of the whole business.

Susumu turned to him scathingly. "I thought you might have learned something last night. I'm afraid of you, young man. Afraid of your mouth."

Kenji went cold, then hardened. "Don't worry about my mouth, it's yours that concerns me."

Susumu hid his feelings, expanding with a smile. "You are not used to my ways or my word. Of what use to me are shares in an organisation that will collapse if I don't carry out my part of the bargain?"

It was unarguable. Kenji persisted. "You've got to find him first."

"He's been located and photographed and is ready for the oven. Since well before dawn. The plane arrives late afternoon." He spoke precisely and with contempt. "He will be burned as arranged, gentlemen."

Fujio took his hand away and the lawyer picked up the documents. When the necessary signatures had been made the lawyer took the documents to another office for witnessing. When he returned the deal was complete. The lawyer opened a small ice box and took out a bottle of champagne.

"A toast, gentlemen."

It was too much for Kenji. He didn't lose his temper but he didn't disguise his feelings either. "I'm not drinking to a loss of shares."

"Not losing. Buying a service." Susumu's expression changed, sinking behind bland folds like the sun going down and leaving a clear sky. With it his tone changed noticeably. "I want the present managing director of Miyoto Travel dismissed at once. Pay him what compensation is necessary but get him out within a week."

The atmosphere was almost physically painful. Fujio straightened slowly then turned towards the window displaying that deceptive pose of relaxation he maintained so well from the rear. Kenji was less controlled. He didn't speak at first but he made little attempt to hide his feelings as his rock hard gaze swept up to Susumu's. The lawyer maintained an indifferent pose behind the desk.

"Well, well." Kenji sensed the danger. "Do you imagine these share transfers give you control over our travel company?"

"I know that they do."

Fujio faced the room. "We checked the share holding. Who is your other nominee?"

Susumu nodded pleasantly to the elder Miyoto. "If only your son had your perception. I've had shares in the company for some time. I'd rather not name the nominee at this stage."

"Then our managing director stays."

84

"I have sufficient votes to call a shareholders' meeting. Mr. Isoga here, to whom your shares are transferred, will represent me. The meeting will confirm my control through the vote."

"It will also reveal your other nominee."

"Perhaps. Perhaps not. It's not quite so simple. Perhaps I have several nominees. That would confuse the issue would it not, Mr. Miyoto? Be sensible. Let's save ourselves time and effort."

Kenji took up the trend from his father. "If you have control you prove it the hard way."

Susumu spread his hands. "I thought you wanted secrecy. A public meeting will show my power *and* remove your man. It will also create widespread speculation. I presumed it better to arrange this quietly. Dismiss him. Compensate him. Give him a post in one of your other companies if you want to salve your consciences. But one way or another he is going. If you have trouble with him let me know."

With half the transfers made there was no road back for the Miyotos even if they now retracted their request for killing Bustillo. Yet when faced with it they both considered Bustillo their greatest danger. They had much more to lose through him than through Susumu.

Fujio signalled his son with a glance. "Call your meeting. The minimum notice is six weeks. I refuse to issue a dismissal notice."

Susumu didn't move. It was impossible to judge his reaction.

"I really don't want to wait that long. It's a pity. You've just condemned another man to death. But it won't take me anything like six weeks to arrange that." He looked at his watch then at the paled faces of the Miyotos. "You've nothing more to say?" He suddenly smiled and they both knew he had made his decision. "Perhaps you've already realised that you now have nobody else to turn to. The Police are definitely out, wouldn't you agree? Gentlemen, if your man is to enjoy a reprieve I must know by six this evening. Meanwhile I still have a contract to honour."

The Miyotos were left as bewildered as the previous evening. They returned to their own offices after Susumu had gone without saying another word to the lawyer. "His control must depend on the second share transfer," observed Kenji in the car. "And he doesn't get that until Bustillo is dead."

Fujio smiled sadly. He had a certain appreciation of Susumu's clever ruthlessness. "That's academic."

"We could keep them back even when he's done the job."

"There are better ways of committing suicide."

Kenji looked dejectedly at his father. "Papa, have you ever had the feeling that you've lost your way? Lost sight of what something's about?" It was a long time since he'd called his father, Papa. Then he spoiled it by adding, "Anyway, let Susumu do his worst. Let's call his bluff."

His father stared at Kenji, noting the unrelenting profile.

"You've just condemned a perfectly innocent man to death."

7

JIMMY BUSTILLO HAD SPENT some time at the small dressing table. With a hand mirror and scissors he had crudely shorn the long locks of his fair hair. It was difficult for him to remember his last hair cut. After he'd tidied up he rang Nikki.

"Any news?"

"I've been waiting for you to ring, Jimbo." She explained the arrangements.

"Have you told him my name?"

"I'm not that stupid."

"What about payment?"

"I've promised it. He knows I'm good for it."

"Thanks, Nikki." He felt wretched but he had to ask it. "Can you loan me some money? I'm nearly flat."

She laughed. "It's good to feel wanted, to know I'm of some use. How will you collect it?"

"I'll call like last night."

"My friend won't be back. She'll probably be in India or somewhere."

He thought quickly. "Can you get it to Tadashi? I'll be calling on him later."

"Okay. I tried to call him but his phone's out of order."

"Me, too. I'll see you, honey. And thanks."

He fought off the resurging need for a drink and had a light lunch instead. Time slowed, the urge more difficult to stave off. He dozed for a while half wondering whether he should simply go to the police and leave the rest to them. But there would be innumerable problems if he did that. He didn't want identification nor the risk of a false name or passport coming to light. Yet that was only part of it. At times it seemed that his life had become so complicated that he had difficulty coping day by day.

He got the bottle out and half emptied it before he left. It was warmer outside now, the sun well up. He had a long, loping stride, deceptively fast when in a hurry. It wasn't long before he knew he had a tail. There were at least two of them. He varied his pace to make absolutely sure. He decided to make no attempt to shake them. That they hadn't molested him, told him that they were merely keeping him in wraps. And he knew what that meant.

He travelled by bus part way and dropped off near the Tower, slowing his step through that section of the Shiba Park. At any other time it would have been a delightful walk, the winter sun and the splendid greenery of the park pulling in the sightseers. He stopped a little distance from the Tower, drawing his head back to view its full three hundred and thirty-three metres of height. And to make sure that his tail had closed in on him.

The highest iron tower in the world. The atrocious colouring had roots in his own country. The orange and white bands the accepted warning to air traffic in the U.S.A. to be seen even in bad weather. (There were three of them. He located the last man just ahead of him.) Nearer to the Tower, as he mixed with the loose crowd, they had to draw in even closer. He was well aware that he was head and shoulders above most of the people although here they were cosmopolitan; some Americans, Europeans among them. He went in the huge lobby, over to the elevator bank taking one to the fourth floor. None of the men rode up with him. It wouldn't matter to them where he went in the Tower provided they could pick him up when he came out.

He got out at the fourth floor, heading for the Tower television studios. With over half an hour to go for the Tower Variety transmission at two o'clock there was still a long public queue awaiting admittance. In this kind of assembly the dress difference of the Japanese was even more noticeable, only a colourful sprinkling of national costume among them. He considered it sadly while he kept well away from the queue which had started to move forward as the studio doors opened.

No one approached him although there were a few people lingering on the landing. He studied them one at a time aware that Nikki would have given a description of him. He made up his mind and approached a tallish Japanese with furtive eyes.

"You looking for an American?" Bustillo spoke very softly.

Immediately the dark eyes looked away. The man, afraid to

commit himself, didn't reply, nor did he move away, leaving Bustillo to convince him. "It's okay. Give me the package."

The furtive eyes were now roaming freely. The man wasn't sure.

Bustillo had the almost overpowering belief that this was Nikki's supplier. The impulse to strangle him there and then was almost overwhelming. Some of his feeling communicated, for the man stepped back but Bustillo grabbed him by the arm. It was a long time since he'd had a feeling so strong.

The queue had almost gone now. Bustillo eased off, expelling air slowly. "Nikki sent you. Give me the gun."

The man nodded sullenly. "Not here. Follow."

They went to the washroom and only when it was empty did the man take a cloth-wrapped package from his narrow waistband and hand it to Bustillo who pocketed it at once.

"Five hundred dollars," said the man, side mouth, holding out a hand.

"Get out of here, you peddling bastard. Before I kill you."

The man backed towards the door. Viciously he demanded, "Your name Bustillo?"

Bustillo didn't reply.

The man got nearer the door. "If it is, that won't help you." He pointed to Bustillo's pocket. "You'll be dead before tomorrow." He left without looking back.

Bustillo stood in the middle of the floor until two men came in. He had guessed a contract was out but receiving vindictive confirmation did nothing for his confidence. The two men eyed him curiously and he broke his spell and left, going down the stairs to the second floor.

The front main entrance to the Tower is on the ground floor. There is a rear exit which, due to the split level, is on the second floor. Bustillo knew that it would be covered. To slip them meant conveying that he knew they were there and there were reasons why he preferred not to do that.

The sun was already dipping low by the time he reached the journalist's home. He knocked on the door.

"Who is it? Tadashi's voice was strained, suspicious.

"Jimmy."

The door opened and Bustillo slipped through. He was shaken by the clear privation on Tadashi's face. The journalist was wearing a dressing gown, bare legs below it. His face was drawn.

"What's happened to you?" Bustillo didn't like the painful way Tadashi walked into the room.

Tadashi gave him the story without frills. He apologised for giving away the address, but Bustillo was touched by Tadashi having made any effort at all to protect him.

Bustillo made some tea, took it in to Tadashi. Observing the drawn, pale face he winced. "I'm sorry, Tashi. I didn't want to bring that on you."

Tadashi stirred his tea. "They only beat me. That's not what they will do to you."

"I know. They're outside."

Tadashi's bright eyes showed alarm and there was an involuntary jerking of his legs. Then he shrugged. "It's you they want." He inclined his head towards a small lacquer cabinet. "There's an envelope in the second drawer. Arrived by cab not long ago." He smiled ruefully. "I'm getting quite good at walking to the door like a jockey."

Bustillo ripped open the envelope and riffled through the notes thoughtfully. "She's a good kid. So good."

"I could have lent you money."

"I know." Bustillo sat down again. "But there would have been strings. From Nikki there are none."

"Except a sense of obligation that might make you go out on a limb for her."

Bustillo shrugged. "What do you *really* know about me?"

"Sufficient to see a good story. Do you mind taking my cup."

Bustillo reached across. "Tell me."

"Will you fill in the gaps?"

Bustillo smiled. "Some of them might be blackouts."

"You were presumably trained in Virginia. They should rename that State C.I.A. County. I know that you were dried out at the Farm near Warrington after you came back from Chile. It's a sad indictment that some agents have to be dried out at all."

"Anything else?"

Tadashi pretended sudden pain. "They've ruined my sex life." He stirred awkwardly on his chair.

"If you ever had any. You're too busy chasing ghosts. Anything else, Tashi?"

"The rest is rumour."

"You going soft. What's happened to the single-minded ruthless truth chaser?"

Tadashi grimaced. His eyes glazed over for a second. "You wouldn't have said that if you'd seen me last night. Screaming for mercy and choking on the gag. I was crying, Jimmy."

"It takes a man to admit it. You're being less of a man with your hedging, though."

"I heard you'd defected."

"It was a lie put out by a peeved administration. There was no chance of my defecting. Then or now."

"So why did they persecute you?"

"I told you before. I walked out on a job I couldn't stomach. They didn't like it."

"Would you expect them to?"

"No. But I would expect them to believe me. They didn't." Bustillo gazed at his cup, memories stirring.

"They certainly made sure you became unpopular."

"It didn't stop you using me."

"You were fair game." Tadashi looked down. "This is all that it brought me."

"But you still see a story in it?"

"I see a better story in *you* than in what you're supposed to have done. And in the Miyotos, which affects my own country. Anyway, I believe what you say."

Bustillo wasn't drawn. "If they kill me you'll have enough to force an enquiry on to the Miyotos. It'll make good copy."

"If they kill you it means they'll be well covered. The three who called on me didn't come from the Miyotos. They've contracted out. The Miyotos are scared silly of the specifics you plucked out *before* they put up the shutters. You still won't tell me?"

"Not anybody. It'll be okay if I can last out for a while."

"I'd hate to lose a new friend so soon."

Bustillo pushed his leg forward to get at the package in his pocket. He unwrapped the cloth and took out the gun. There was a bonus in a spare clip.

"It looks like a Luger." Bustillo removed the magazine and made sure there was no round in the breech.

"No." Tadashi leaned forward painfully. "It's a Japanese Nambu type 14. Eight millimetre, eight shot. They were standard equipment during World War II. The only ones around are souvenirs. They're pretty rare now."

Bustillo unloaded each magazine, counted the rounds then returned them. He slipped one magazine in the butt, pulled back the breech to insert a round in the chamber. He applied the safety-catch.

"You look familiar with one," observed Tadashi dryly.

Bustillo grinned. It transformed him, which set the journalist wondering yet again. "They didn't just dry us out in Virginia, Tashi."

"You've got to know who to hit. They already know."

Bustillo made no comment. He knew what he was up against and if he dwelled on it too long hopelessness crept over him. Tadashi allowed him to shave. None of the little Japanese's clothes would fit him so he was left with what he wore. He made sure that Tadashi could cope and learned that neighbours were keeping his office in touch without knowing what had actually happened. When he left he had the feeling that he might not see his friend again. His handshake was accordingly warm, a fact not lost on the shrewd Tadashi.

★   ★   ★

Graham Leach looked through the long window at the sweeping undulating green vista now being shadowed by the lowering sun. It was superb, lush scenery backwashed by the lightest of blue skies, the emerald sheen of trees enamelled by the deepening light. It was his favourite position, one of his favourite views. The artist in him kept him there, absorbed by the delights of nature as a cloud wisp flirted with the sun, creating moving fantasies in the hills and valleys.

He almost missed the sound of Chieko coming in. If it took a second to register the sound it was only a fraction of that time before his face snapped out of its pose and accepted the realities of life. By the time she entered the room he was completely down to earth.

"Chieko, my love. You look beautiful." This was no more than true but the appreciation of her wan beauty had sprung from the same artistic appraisal that had been admiring the view. Her sympathy was finely drawn. Had his heart been able to take in the gently cautious personality, the layers beneath, his cup would have overflowed. Leach always got first things first. "Did you get it?"

Her smile at his compliment was wiped away. She removed the shopping basket from her arm and handed it to him. It lay under a piece of silk like something picked up in a supermarket. Yet at the bottom of the basket the black significance of it removed any possibility of its being a toy. As he picked it up Leach was aware of its unfamiliarity. He was equally aware that he would have to use it. And soon, if he was to have peace of mind. That commodity was worth far more than one man's life.

With the strange-feeling weapon in his hand he was aware of Chieko watching him. She stood straight-backed, hands to her sides, kimono a fraction above the floor. He smiled at her awkwardly.

"I'm not used to these things."

"How, then, will it help you?" No admonishment, just fear for the safety of her husband.

"I'll sort it out. Thank you, Chieko." He paused, gaze on the silk rug before returning to her. "Do you think it possible for me to meet the man who supplied this? He can advise me."

"You want to meet a gangster?"

"I've no wish to! I've just realised my limitations with this thing."

"I'll arrange it through my friend." Chieko turned on her heel and left the room. Her suffering was lost on him.

"Tonight, if possible, darling. The sooner the better," he called after her.

*   *   *

It was like any other airport anywhere he'd been before. Peter Vence watched the two rows of runway lights come up to meet them like a pair of illuminated tweezers in the gloom. Headwinds had put the plane behind schedule but the Captain had assured them that there was enough gas on board to cope and he was the guy who ought to know. Vence had always felt comfort in the expertise of others. He was an expert himself.

The plane turned gently and the runway lights were lost to view. Vence took sight of those passengers he could see. The fat guy was near croaking with fear, holding on to the arm of his seat as if it was his last moment. Vence smiled. He enjoyed watching fear. He'd seen it, staring him straight in the eye more times than he could remember. He'd seen it expanding in the eyes, had heard the initial whimper of it, then the drying mouth as the tongue had flicked out. He'd heard the tearful pleading before the throat had seized up and all expression had then been conveyed through terror-stricken eyes, beseeching, imploring, silently pleading for life. Boy, they were the moments. Just before he squeezed the trigger and the surprise bit their faces and their lamps went out, like switching off. That's why he preferred the gun to the garotte; he could prolong the sweet feel of power.

They touched down and Vence thought the fat guy was going to pass out from relief; he was suddenly speaking garrulously to anyone, everyone. Vence chewed on his gum, watching, enjoying the suffering and thinking the guy had better change his pants at the first opportunity.

He collected his one large bag from the baggage hall, passed through customs and waited outside the building. He fingered one lapel, an agreed signal. There were cabs available. Some passengers had taken the normal monorail directly in to town. A cab drew forward, a head poked out of the window. "You have some baggage to collect, sir?"

"Yeah. Some."

The driver climbed out, heaved the case into the boot then held the door open for Vence. When Vence was seated in the back the driver handed him a sealed envelope.

"We can pick up your goods and then carry on to the hotel, sir."

"You know where I'm staying?"

"The Tokyo Hilton."

"Take me there and then blow."

"But, sir . . ." The driver looked into Vence's casually questing eyes and decided against arguing. "Yes, sir."

The matter had never been in doubt. Vence had no intention of anyone being testimony to him making a collection. He checked in at the Tokyo Hilton, and in the privacy of his room opened the envelope. There was a key with a tag and an address. Nothing else. He pocketed it, straightened his tie in front of a mirror and left the room. Tired after the long journey, sleep would have to come later. He didn't like rush jobs but the bread was good.

The concierge called a cab and Vence travelled the short journey across town to the Tokyo Railway Station. He paid in dollars unruffled by the obvious fact of being overcharged because of it. The termites had to live and they had their uses. When he entered the main line railway station he was unaware that the Metropolitan Police Headquarters was only a block away. It wouldn't have worried him anyway.

Vence had an uncanny knack of homing on to the point he had to find as if he was completely familiar with the layout. It was a primitive talent that had rarely failed him. He could read none of the notices, yet he cut through the evening rush hour crowd almost without hesitation. The strange thing was that he noticed very little as he went. Danger signals were different; they invaded him with his eyes closed. But as he hurried through the station it was doubtful if he had conscious knowledge of which city he was

94

in despite ethnic and dress differences. He had no interest in anything but the job in hand and when that was over he'd get out quick.

He found the property boxes, checked the number he wanted with the tag on the key he took from his pocket, opened the box, took out the package inside and went back to the main entrance leaving the box door open with the key in it. Due to the crowds he had trouble getting a cab back to the Hilton and he showed his first signs of irritation. When he finally reached his room his mood was ugly. He didn't like being hampered.

He undid the package and laid out the items, taking them in order of importance to him. The automatic was a .45 Colt Commander, a lightweight at 25 oz. for such a big calibre. He had no quarrel with the choice, had fired most makes of gun in his time. There was a spare box of rounds and a lightweight belt holster with a spring clip. Okay. Next. Photographs of Jimmy Bustillo leaving the restaurant that morning. The guy was distinctive but dressed like a bum. Stooped a bit, but big enough to make a good target. Fine. No problem. There was a slip of paper with an address and instructions on several methods of getting there. Times for each alternative were roughly given. There was also a telephone number, a street map and another separately parcelled package which he now opened. Twenty-five thousand dollars. He sat in an easy chair and laboriously counted, having to do it twice after an initial mistake. Satisfied he placed some notes in his wallet and the rest in two long envelopes which he sealed, printed his passport name on with the room number.

After that he examined the gun in detail, stripping and reloading it. He clipped the holster to his waistband and inserted the gun. His suits had always been made to accommodate a gun without its being noticeable. The photographs and the instructions he put in his jacket pocket, leaving the street map on the writing desk. He telephoned the number, not asking or caring who answered. "Is the bird at roost?"

"It's flown but hobbled. We'll give you a call when it's back on its nest."

He hung up. Now he felt tired after the long flight. He looked at his watch. Eight p.m. Dark outside. He rang room service and ordered a meal to be brought to his room with a couple of cans of beer for the ice box. He might get thirsty in the night after the hit. It was the only way it took him.

Back in the easy chair he again studied the photographs. He

thought he'd seen the face before. Somewhere. Some time. It didn't matter. There was one more thing to do and then he must remain in his room. He went down to reception and deposited the two money envelopes in the hotel safe.

* * *

Graham Leach stood in the shadows, gloved hands tapping each other, topcoat collar turned up. It was not excessively cold, particularly for an Englishman, but he'd been standing for some time and his circulation had never been good. The area was hardly fashionable but it had been his own choice. As he moved his feet he was already aware of waiting for fifteen minutes and he began to believe he'd been let down. He'd hang on longer because much depended on it. While he waited he considered Chieko's unspoken protest.

She was gravely unhappy. The last thing he wanted was for any of this to reach her father. If it did, more than a business arrangement might collapse. If he could finish it quickly they'd get back to normal in no time.

A voice whispered in his ear in an accent from the north of Japan. "Sorry you waited for so long. Unavoidable delay."

All Leach could see were teeth seemingly huge in the dark, and an impression of someone his own height but incredibly thin. He said, "Where can we go that's private?"

"Many places. You want instruction on gun?" There was no effort to hide incredulity.

"And some other supplies. It shouldn't take long."

"It will cost you money."

"Of course. Can we move from here? I'm frozen."

"Come with me."

The contact had a small Toyota parked less than a block away. Leach was unaware that the car had passed him twice already, the driver puzzled by the need of such a meeting. They drove some distance to the fringe of the city, the driver instinctively avoiding main thoroughfares but whether for Leach's benefit or his own was never clear.

The distance suited Leach. He felt safer. He said, cramped in the small car, "You understand that I must not be seen. I'm European. People will remember."

The teeth widened in the gloom. "I understand."

They didn't speak again until they stopped outside a wooden dwelling, one of a row in a wide, deserted street. Clearly un-

96

fashionable, Leach governed his sensation of distaste. It was suitable. All that mattered.

Inside there was little concession to western encroachment. A low table indicated that meals were eaten cross-legged. Through an open door Leach saw a rolled mattress. A rush carpet covered most of the floor. It was spartan, but scrupulously clean. Two fine blue and white early vases stood in opposite corners.

Leach was able to see the man better in the artificial light. He was as he'd thought, all teeth and bones, western clothes, like his own, out of place in this undemonstrative sanctum of old Japan.

"Does anyone know I was coming?"

"I wasn't sure myself. What is it you want exactly?" The cavernous face hardened.

Leach drew out the gun with thumb and finger. His obvious distaste of holding it even so delicately raised curled contempt from the lips of the gangly man. "What's the best way of aiming?"

"You want to kill someone?"

"God forbid. To protect myself."

The man took the gun, removed the magazine, pulled back the breech. "There are several ways of aiming. One-handed, bringing the gun down slowly to your target. Squeeze the trigger. Two-handed, feet apart, taking direct aim. It is a matter of personal preference."

"And yours is?"

A slyness crept into the hooded eyes. "I never use one. If I did I would aim instinctively. Where is the gun pointing now?"

"At my chest."

"Exactly. Yet I am not sighting. Keep the lower arm and gun in one straight line and do not bend the wrist. Do not jerk the trigger. That is all you need to know. The rest is practice."

"I see. And the safety-catch?"

"This is it. When forward the red dot shows. It is ready to fire."

"Thank you. I would like a silencer and some more bullets."

The man stared at him, doubtful if this strange white European could hit anyone. Business was business. He left the room and was quickly back. He screwed the silencer on.

"This makes gun most inaccurate. If you intend to use it get as close as possible." He produced a small box of spare ammunition from his pocket. "That will be eighty thousand yen. Silencers are difficult to find."

97

Leach nodded, pulled out his wallet, carefully counting off the notes. A hundred pounds. He was being done. It didn't really matter. He unscrewed the silencer, feeling its weight.

"You've been very helpful. I'm sure we can do business again. Do you want to double your money?" He held out his hand for the magazine.

The narrowed eyes flickered, suspicion and greed combined. "How?"

"I'm trying to trace a friend of mine. He might be in trouble."

"Another Englishman?"

Leach kept his hand steady as he slapped home the magazine. He supposed it was inevitable. The man was sharp. "An American. Tall, with long fair hair, named Warton."

A long-fingered bony hand snaked out to turn the gun aside as Leach held it awkwardly while pulling back the breech. "Never point a gun like that. It is dangerous. Keep it down."

"I'm sorry." Leach pointed the gun at the floor, fiddling with the silencer. "Do you know of anyone who could help me find him?"

"Warton. That's strange. That's the second American of that description I've been asked to look for in the last twenty-four hours. I suppose there are a lot of tall fair-haired Americans."

"Do you know his name?"

The long fingers dexterously produced a slip of paper from a pocket. "Bustillo. A difficult name for us."

"Have you seen him?"

"No. Not personally. I know someone who has."

"If you were looking for him you must have had a fuller description."

The man described what he'd been given; open-necked shirt, cardigan, ruckled trousers.

Leach was still, his mind racing. Bustillo. Warton. "Where is he?"

The teeth showed again. "Oh, no. I don't know but if I did I couldn't tell you. Is it the same man?"

"I don't know. If I know where he is I can check. How much?"

"It's too dangerous for me."

"Who wanted him found?"

Fear overcame greed. "You want me killed?"

"Who's going to know? How much?"

"You haven't enough money."

Leach reached for his hip pocket. "Four hundred thousand yen?"

The greed was back but the expression was uncertain.

"I can't tell you. That much wouldn't save me."

"All right. The same amount for just telling me where the American is."

"I don't know. I told you."

Leach riffled the high denomination roll. "Eight hundred thousand."

The eyes narrowed still further. Uncertainty, fear, greed, cunning all there.

If Leach was short on gun practice he had abundant experience of human nature. "Don't try what you're thinking with this in my hand." He waved the gun carelessly. "And you'd better remember a mutual friend arranged the contact. If you want this money you earn it. What risk can there be to you?"

The tongue flickered, eyes now on the notes, one long finger rubbing the side of the flat nose. "When must you know?"

"Now."

"And you'll give me eight hundred thousand yen?"

"I've already counted it out." Leach stood with the gun in one hand and the notes in the other, the small surplus held in between spare fingers. "That's one thousand pounds in my currency. A very great deal of money for such little information. After all," he added persuasively, "I'm not asking you to withhold it from whoever employed you. Presumably he has it already. The information is already shared."

"I must ring a friend. It is better that you don't hear."

"Naturally. Shall I go in here?" Leach went to the bedroom and closed the door. There was no chair to sit on and he paced the room restlessly, making no attempt to listen at the door. He wasn't there long. The door opened surprisingly quickly. He went back into the living room. The man held out his hand.

"The money."

"The address."

The man handed over a slip of paper. Leach read it abstractedly holding out the notes which were hastily snatched. He looked up smiling. "I'm really most obliged to you." He placed the slip in his pocket. The gun still dangled from his other hand. He looked down as if suddenly realising it. The man was standing against the wall counting the money.

"You know, I had almost forgotten why I really came. Keep the forearm straight like this?" He pointed the gun at the door. "This contraption screws on like this?" He turned his head but the man barely nodded, still counting. "But only use it if close up. Like this?" He swung the gun and fired.

8

THERE WAS A MOMENT of suspended animation while the man's arms were spread upwards as though belatedly capitulating. His mouth was open, lips curling back over the long teeth. The eyes were at their widest, surprised, unblinking. Partially screening this image were the notes, scattering upwards then fluttering slowly to the floor in time with the buckling legs as the man slipped down with his back against the wall, his jacket ruckling up to his waist. He sank to the floor with a long sigh his eyes still on Leach.

"You were right," said Leach conversationally. "You do have to be close. I didn't make too good a job of that." He stepped nearer as the man tried to scream but the bullet had pierced a lung and all he produced was a froth of blood and a gurgle. The terror in his eyes, which Peter Vence had seen so often, came as a new experience to Leach and he marvelled at it as he leaned nearer to fire again. The man's hands reached for the gun all too slowly and the bullet passed through one of them before entering the heart. The head fell forward and Leach noticed for the first time a balding patch in the jet black hair.

Leach squatted on his heels in front of the man, surprised at his own impassiveness. He hadn't known what to expect but his satisfaction verged on controlled elation. If Bustillo would prove as easy. He unscrewed the silencer, applied the safety-catch and pocketed the gun. Quickly he collected all the money making sure that none was left. A few notes had taken the first bullet. One had actually adhered to the man's jacket with a hole near its middle.

The man's knees were up, legs bent. Leach straightened them, not out of compassion but because he had to search the body and they were in the way. His good looks disfigured with distaste as he went through the pockets. He had no objection to what he was doing but he didn't like the blood and was careful to avoid it. Finally he stood up, keys dangling from his fingers. He put on his gloves and crossed to the bedroom door, wiping its handle both sides. Even now he didn't know the man's name. There had been no identification on him. A careful man. Not careful enough.

At the door Leach paused to study the broken doll figure against the wall. He was beginning to feel a little shock. A slight trembling of the hands. He clenched them. But no remorse. None.

He stepped into the tiny hall and cautiously opened the front door. He could hear no one. See nothing. It was as if the district was expressly designed for stealth. He stepped out, closing the door behind him. When he was in the Toyota he felt safer. He switched on, pulled away, leaving his lights off, until he was further down the street. He drove the car to within a hundred yards of the Nippori main line station, leaving it in a side street. He caught a train to Oji where he'd left his own car.

Chieko knew something had gone wrong as soon as he entered the house. He was late and angry.

Leach allowed a little softness to show as he greeted his wife. He kept his topcoat on as he kissed her on the cheek, noting its coldness.

"What's happened?" Her demand was illustration of her distress. She would never normally be so firm.

"Chieko, I'm sorry, my darling. Will you ring your friend and tell her nobody turned up. I'm frozen from waiting and very, very angry."

Her face lightened. "Perhaps it's as well. I didn't like the idea of you seeing this man in the first place."

"And you were right. I should have listened."

"I'll ring tomorrow."

"No, my love. Please ring her now. I want her to know how I feel now, not tomorrow. And tell her I'm not making another appointment. The fellow doesn't know the meaning of the word."

"Let me take your coat."

"Not yet. I'm so cold. Unbelievably cold." He didn't want her to detect the extra weight of the silencer and ammunition.

"Then go in here while I make the call." She opened the door for him but he insisted on going to their room to put the gun in the top drawer of a lacquered tallboy. He would tell her it was there. In the bottom drawer he hid the ammunition and the silencer under some sweaters he rarely wore. He returned to the drawing room, still with his topcoat on although he was warm from the car heater. When Chieko came in she stood before him quite assertively, small hands clasped.

"I told her how angry you are. How much time you wasted. She was apologetic but explained that these sort of people can be unreliable." Chieko was clearly delighted that the meeting hadn't come off.

Leach put his arm about her. "We've certainly learned that much." He kissed the top of her ear. "Thank you, my love. I'll pay more heed to you next time." He could tell from her reaction that he'd acted well. But then he'd been acting most of his life.

★   ★   ★

Jimmy Bustillo took his tail back to the apartment as painlessly as he'd drawn it to Tadashi's. The difficulty was how to get out without being seen. These were apartments in a small block. One fire escape for all of them. It would assuredly be covered. He reasoned that he'd be kept under wraps until the hit man was ready to burn him. That would be night time not early evening. But he had to get out somehow or be a sitting duck.

He found the bottle, annoyed that it was half empty and that he'd been too preoccupied to remember to bring another one in with him. He didn't trouble to get a glass but sat on the edge of the bed, bottle in hand, wondering whether it was all worth it.

★   ★   ★

Peter Vence had fed well. The dinner trolley had been taken away and he lay on his bed dozing, shoes and jacket off. The phone rang. He made no visible effort of waking, his hand going out to the receiver almost at once. "Yeah!"

"The bird's nesting."

"Okay." He looked at his watch. "Can you get me a car round here at eleven?"

"It will be parked on the east side."

"Gimme the number." Vence propped himself up to make a note.

"He's been no trouble all day. Doesn't know what's happening."

"That right? I'll ring before I leave. I don't want your boys around from that time on. Okay? Not one. This guy's alone there, I take it?"

"Until later."

"I getcha. You do what I say when I ring." He rang off. He

103

glanced down at his watch again then lay down and fell into a light sleep.

*   *   *

Drink in hand Graham Leach leapt to his feet. "Good God. I've forgotten my appointment."

Chieko was startled. They had finished a late dinner and had only just returned to the lounge. "Appointment?"

"I told you, darling. The computer engineer." He moved over to the door. All through dinner he had mentally rehearsed how to get out of the house again without arousing Chieko's suspicion.

"But you told me of no appointment apart from the one with that horrid man."

"It's that damned fellow who's caused all this. Put it out of my mind. Your father will be furious."

The telephone was in the light, spacious hall. He left the door open so that Chieko might hear. He put down his drink and kept a finger on the cradle while he dialled a random number. He waited, gazing at a fine Japanese silk print on the wall.

"Mr. Suma? This is Graham Leach. How can you forgive me? No, I was quite unavoidably detained." A short wait. "I'm dreadfully sorry. I can come over at once if you're agreeable. If you feel it too late we can ... You don't mind? Good. I should be there in half an hour." He walked back into the lounge, wiping his forehead. "I think I got out of that rather well. Had that been me I'd have been furious."

"Will you be long?"

"I shouldn't think so. But I dare not appear in a hurry after forgetting to go. I was supposed to be there at seven-thirty."

"Where is he?"

"The other side of town but the traffic's not thick at this time. I'm sorry, darling. I really am. I've messed up the whole evening for you."

After he had gone Chieko sat on the edge of an easy chair, features drawn, eyes blank, fingers clasped. Her hands untwined and her fingers came up behind her head deftly to untie the silk at the back. It had taken her a long time to arrange her hair in the high sweeping Yuiwata style. Strictly speaking it was an old style for young maidens but it was one her husband favoured. She had done it specially for him, with the help of her daily maid. She had wanted to get his mind away from its present unhealthy occupation. He hadn't even noticed. Nor the special meal she had pre-

104

pared. The long hair fell around her shoulders as she shook it out. She went to the telephone and called her father.

For some moments they went through the ritual formalities of polite enquiry and then, inevitably, he asked if Graham was there.

"He's gone to meet a computer engineer. A Mr. Suma."

"Ah. He must be a new one."

"You don't know him?" She was careful to keep her anxiety down.

"No. Not that name."

"I really thought you knew everyone in the business."

Her father chuckled. "So did I, my dear. But I am getting old."

After the call she went upstairs. The gun had gone from the top drawer. She searched the other drawers and found the box of spare ammunition. She had only brought the gun back from her friend.

She went to her dressing room. In one corner was a small altar richly covered in the finest embroidered silk. The smiling Buddha was of pure gold, a present from her family. She sank to her knees and held her hands in prayer. With lowered head she prayed to Mahayana. She knew that suffering is inseparable from existence, that the principal cause was desire the suppression of which in turn reduced the suffering. Yet all she desired was the restoration of her marriage, as it had been up to only two days ago. Was this too much desire? Must she suffer so much because of it?

*   *   *

Jimmy Bustillo found no solace from the now empty bottle still clutched in his hand. He'd come up with no answers and time was running short. The building, so far as he knew, had no more than a dozen apartments, two to each floor. There was only one small elevator of the open grid type, one exit plus the fire escape. As a hideout it left much to be desired in escape routes. The sensation of the pincers closing was too strong to ignore. He'd suffered it before.

With sudden resolve he got off the bed, put his front door on the latch and took the elevator to the sixth floor. The twin apartments on each floor were side by side, their front doors on the same corridor but well separated. Stairs ran down at each end converging in the ground floor hall. Exactly in the centre of the corridor was the elevator. Each floor had the same simple layout. Bustillo called at each apartment in turn asking for a Miss Houston, an American lady he understood to be living there. By the time he reached the ground floor he'd discovered that all apartments were occupied. Only at one had the door bell not been answered but he'd heard loud music through the door. The possibility of breaking into an empty apartment was dead.

He went back to his own lounge. Ten o'clock. They'd wait until the streets were clear. The district was normally quiet. Apart from the restaurant round the corner there was virtually nothing in the way of entertainment. The few shops closed late and after that there were few people about. He kept the light on because for the moment it was his safety valve, suggesting that he was still up and about. Stuffing the gun in his waistband he hung around with nothing to drink, his nerves fraying with the passing of every minute. He rang Nikki but there was no reply. Then he tried Tadashi but the number was still unobtainable.

At eleven he went into the darkened bedroom and peered obliquely into the street, barely pulling aside the net curtains. He could see no one even after staying there for some time. They were there somewhere. It was already very quiet down below. Neon signs glared outside two of the shops. Over one of them the blood red Kana script was flashing on and off. The ideographs were a work of art in themselves. With nothing better to do he watched the signs for some time until they affected his sight and he had to draw back.

A little later one of the signs cut off with a time switch. The second sign, pale blue and advertising a wine, snapped out as he watched. He pulled the main curtains across then switched on the bedroom light.

For a while he kept on both lights before finally switching off the lounge light. In the bedroom he allowed his shadow to fall across the curtains knowing that from the street the perspective would be too misleading for a shot. Eventually he switched on a bedside light and turned off the main one. He checked the gun. He gave it another ten minutes before dowsing the last light. Leaving the room, he closed the bedroom door and silently crossed the lounge, sorry now that the neons had cut out; their reflection would have given him some visibility.

At the front door he slipped the key from the lock and went out into the corridor. He already knew his next-door neighbours to be in but when he crept along the corridor the light strip under the door had gone. Going back to his own door he turned the key to lock himself out.

*   *   *

Peter Vence was already waiting outside the hotel when the car arrived. He saw the lights switch off and the driver climb out and disappear. Vence went over, climbed in, switched on the map light.

In the door pocket he found a street sketch of how to reach Bustillo. It was an illustrated version of the first instruction he'd received. No street names, he wouldn't have understood them. It was all done by numbers and again with alternatives. He studied it for some time before setting off. A sense of direction was complementary to his prowess at executing. Before moving off he checked the pocket for a second item.

At first he took the shortest route to Bustillo's, memorising as he went and having little difficulty in finding the place. He had been informed that the apartment was opposite two small stores and when he passed them their neons were still on. Parking further down the street he walked back with hands in raincoat pockets. He didn't feel the cold too much but topcoats had their uses. He located the small terraced block. On the opposite side of the street he looked up. His information was that the living room was the one with the light still on and the darkened room was the bedroom. He didn't stop but walked past quite slowly.

Further up, he crossed the road and walked back again, his tread inaudible in the quietened street. The occasional car went past with dipped headlights. At such times Vence merely slipped in the nearest doorway with face averted. When he reached the apartments he tried the only door. It opened easily into a badly lit hall. One elevator; stairs. Too small for a porter. Too ordinary for entry phones. Not bad. Not good. He didn't linger there. The bedroom light was still not on. He went back to the car, sat in it for a few minutes. During that time three people passed on his side of the street and one on the other. There was time yet.

He drove off again, following the other routes, familiarising himself with the district, homing on the Hilton. As it neared midnight the traffic thinned. There was no problem except for the centre of the City and he could avoid that because the Hilton was west of the part they called the Ginza and which he thought of as eastside. Having lived in New York for some time it wasn't difficult for him to think of the Sumida River which flowed into Tokyo harbour, as East River. It was an apt, simple substitution and one he understood. At first he had found it strange driving the wrong side of the street which was another reason he kept moving. No problem with the automatic gears, though. By the time he was ready to return to Bustillo he was satisfied with his knowledge and reluctantly impressed with the traffic system and the streets, having passed under overhead expressways and the monorail.

He glided into the spot where he'd parked before. He switched off, waited. No movement now. None. Not even cars. He switched on the courtesy light and pulled out a small bunch of skeleton keys from the door pocket. He'd seen guys on the movies open any door with one little gadget. That was okay for belly laughs. He waited a while then climbed out risking leaving the driver's door unlocked, crossed the street and walked up it. It was almost impossible to see him as he hugged the building line and certainly impossible to hear. As he approached he slowed, hardly moving at all. He stopped. The neons were out and so were Bustillo's room lights.

*   *   *

Graham Leach drove quite fast. He was tackling the job amateurishly, but he was aware of it. It would be different when he got there. Meanwhile there were other considerations. He had to satisfy Chieko on the time factor when he got back. There was some distance to go. Fortunately he knew the topography of Tokyo well and had more than a rough idea of the position of Bustillo's hideout. Bustillo. He wondered where the name came from as he overtook a string of cars on the expressway. Once tonight was over he'd breathe again. My God, he would. Bustillo. He had to be Warton and he could only be here for one reason. He found himself speeding as his mind wandered. Braking, he pulled in behind the eternal string of red lights chasing through a tunnel of darkness.

Leach filtered off the expressway and slowed considerably. As he negotiated the city traffic he began to have qualms. Not at what he intended to do, he had already proved himself capable of killing, but about his adequacy to reach Bustillo. He was ill prepared. He really wasn't sure how to set about it yet he accepted that it had to be done quickly and at night. He could conceive of no possibility during daylight. At no time did he consider turning back.

He parked in the street near the restaurant where Bustillo had eaten his breakfast. It was well before midnight. He'd have preferred it to be much later but his deception of Chieko was almost as important as this. Compromise was second nature to him. There

108

was still a little activity on the streets. Sound, rather than visual movement. He went to the corner and passed along the street where the American was supposed to live. After a few moments of indecision he walked along. When he reached the front door he checked the number. Bustillo was one floor up. He went into the hall.

A great believer in minimal physical effort he took the elevator to the floor above Bustillo's. When he stepped out he closed the gates and went down the stairs on tiptoe, quietly furious that he should have to be doing this himself. It really wasn't his line. He reached Bustillo's door, standing outside it. He put his ear to the wood. It was so quiet in the room he wondered if anyone was there at all. Drawing away he listened for any sound above or below him. Somewhere, someone had a radio on too loudly. Pulling out his gun, silencer already attached, he held it ready and with his other hand put pressure on the door.

He hadn't expected it to move yet he'd had to try. He knew that he couldn't unlock the door, wouldn't know how to begin. He leaned against the wall weighing the risk of ringing the bell. At this time of night it could warn the man if he was expecting trouble. There was nothing else he could do. He turned to the door, reached for the bell and stopped with his thumb actually touching it.

There was someone in the entrance hall below. Leach didn't hear movement but he heard the main door close. Just faintly. The possibility of being caught in the enormity of what he was doing sent a quiver through him. Yet he kept his head. Slipping the gun into his pocket he went to the stairhead and listened. The door opened and closed again. Faintly but there was no mistake. He crept down the stairs, aware of his limitations in the game of stealth but achieving a fair degree of silence.

When he flattened himself against the wall at the bottom and peered round the corner the hall was empty. The elevator was two floors up where he'd left it. Someone had been in and out without calling at an apartment, for there was none at ground-floor level. He waited another minute or so before stepping outside. Remaining in the protective shadow of the shallow porch he looked up and down the street.

It was a little while before a car started further down the street. He couldn't see it until it pulled out then he could see only its red tail lights going away from him. The experience unnerved him, the more so because his whole future hung in getting rid of the

American. He crossed the road, noted that there was only one room of the apartment lit. Footsteps. Leach pulled up his coat collar and returned to his car, sitting as Vence had sat but far less sure of how he should continue.

He was still sitting there well after midnight. Chieko would be worried, yet he couldn't go back to her until this was over. Somehow he had to get into that apartment or draw Bustillo out. Afraid to run the engine to warm the car for fear of being noticed, he sat shivering, hands in topcoat pockets, feet playing with the pedals in an attempt to keep the circulation going. In the end he couldn't stand it. He climbed out and shuffled his feet. He had to go back to Bustillo. At least it was quiet now. The district had died.

Walking to the corner, he stopped. The street was much darker. The neons were out. Above the slit of the street stars were visible as the earth glow diminished. Christ, how was he going to tackle it when he got there? An approaching car made him draw back. It went past Bustillo's and pulled in a little further down. He waited for someone to climb out but all he saw was the lights being dowsed. The street went completely silent. Leach waited, wondering.

The car door opened. Had it not been so generally quiet he would have missed it. Afraid to move he continued to wait, half his face exposed round the corner. He heard nothing more. Not a thing. But because his eye was so close to the wall he noticed a shape, a darker patch in the shadows. It was moving towards him. Leach instinctively felt for the gun, his hackles rising involuntarily.

The shape disappeared into what Leach was convinced was Bustillo's front doorway. The same person must have returned. Once certain the figure was inside, Leach crept round the corner and crossed the street, moving into one of the store doorways. Bustillo's lights were all out.

Because of the totally professional stealth of the man, Leach was ready to believe that his luck was changing. Could this be the other party who wanted to know Bustillo's location? Was the job going to be done for him? It was too good to be true. He would wait to find out.

★   ★   ★

Vence took to the stairs. He wasn't happy. Rushed jobs were risky. That's why he was being so highly paid. He didn't lack confidence, he simply disliked the sensation of being half blind. He'd never run into a situation he couldn't handle but he'd prefer to get the guy in the open or a confined space of his own choosing. He was uneasy.

Although there were night lights he used a small torch going up the stairs. Reaching Bustillo's door he put an ear to it then examined the lock. Quite without warning he straightened and turned towards the upper stairs where Bustillo was standing breathlessly, back to the wall.

Bustillo drew back from watching with one eye just as the gunman turned. He couldn't be sure that he hadn't been seen. What he did know was that sweat burst suddenly from his pores. His reaction was slow but he made up for it by taking the stairs two at a time with the noiselessness of an animal.

Vence had received a danger warning. Nothing to pinpoint, just an intense feeling. Maybe it was because he hadn't had time to prepare. He'd be happier with more light about the place, yet the semi-darkness could work for him. With silenced gun in hand he went to the stairs and climbed up as silently as Bustillo. Above him Bustillo had stopped simply because his breathing had become heavy and audible. The place was as quiet as an empty church and he struggled painfully to breathe soundlessly. He was now just above the third floor landing afraid to look round the corner for anyone approaching head on must see him.

Vence, too, was winded with the climb but not so much as Bustillo. He reached the third floor and stopped. Physical action had eased his qualms some but he was still not entirely satisfied. He walked along to the continuing stairhead and peered round it and up unaware that Bustillo had just risked moving to the half landing above. He mounted the stairs, stopping halfway. This could go on all night. He could finish on the roof. He waited for perhaps two minutes, listening, unmoving. Then he descended as quietly as he'd come.

Bustillo didn't know what to do. His nerves had been stretched to almost unbearable length. The last thing he wanted was a shoot out. There had to be a moment of risk when he peered round the corner. Nothing. He went down in stages, using every corner as a careful observation post until he reached his original position. Reluctant to take another sighting of his own front door he barely caught the faintest of clicks. He wiped his face and then his gun hand on his trousers before taking a grip again. He peered round. Vence was picking the lock.

Bustillo pulled back against the wall relying solely on hearing. The tumblers clicked quite loudly. He risked another look and almost gave himself away. Vence had backed against the wall close to the door, gun raised. He was facing Bustillo but was concentrating on the door. He stood still waiting for any reaction to the noise of the lock from anyone inside. Swiftly he crossed the doorway, his back now to Bustillo, leaned forward and gently pushed. The door swung inwards a few inches.

He went in low, crouched in an awkward position but moving quite fast. Bustillo stepped into the corridor and produced the key. He too moved fast. On reaching the door he saw the torch, held low, sweeping from side to side, caution all the way. The beam swung on to the bedroom door as Bustillo edged forward, arm outstretched to pull the door. The man was opening the bedroom door just as he was closing the front one. When it was almost closed he knelt to insert the key, half turning it so that he could use it to pull the door the remaining inch or two. He heard the inner door bang and guessed that the gunman had found the bedroom empty. Time had run out.

Caution didn't matter any more. Bustillo tucked himself against the wall and turned the key. It was still in the lock, his fingers still on it when the wood holed and splintered and bullets cratered the plaster and brickwork of the opposite wall. It was uncanny. There was no sound of firing but the rending of wood created its own strange noises. It was a minor miracle that Bustillo's hand and wrist had been missed. The sudden savagery of it lost him seconds as he gazed, fascinated by the damage and the accuracy of the shots. Strength came back to legs that had temporarily deserted him and he ran for the stairs as the door was being pulled.

9

Bustillo had almost reached the lower half landing when the door opened. He had to make a split second decision and made the right one. He backed on to the wall and faced up the stairs as Vence emerged. He fired, the roar of the shot becoming a ragged volley in the echo chamber of the stair well. A shot from Vence's silenced gun was drowned, the bullet scything the wall above Bustillo's head.

Vence's gun hand half dropped, his other hand going to his side as he staggered but still kept his feet. The look of cold hatred he fastened on Bustillo was tinged with pain as he tried to raise his gun again. Bustillo didn't wait. He hurtled down the stairs two at a time and out into the street, turning right. All he wanted to do was to get away. The sound of the shot would rouse everyone in the building and many outside. But sleeping people took time to react. As he ran for the intersection he saw someone cut obliquely across his path from the side of the street. Two of them! For Chrissake.

Bustillo slowed but the man in front heard him, turned his head while still running, faltered, then continued down the intersection. It was the way Bustillo had intended to go. To turn back was to head towards Vence. He now decided against taking the intersection. Quickening his pace again he crossed the corner, heard the plop and the whine and felt the slipstream of a bullet just in front of his eyes, so close that he instinctively closed them.

He threw himself forward and rolled in the open street, vaguely aware of the tinkling of glass. His roll carried him behind the doubtful protection of a car and he raised himself to crouch behind the bonnet. A man was standing at the corner as though stunned.

Bustillo raised his gun. The last thing he wanted to do was to fire in the street, to face a brush with the police. He had to avoid that at all costs.

The other man was staring across but even in the bad light the face seemed familiar to Bustillo. Before he could concentrate the man ran. The footsteps stopped, a car door slammed and a car pulled out, speeding away from him with terrific acceleration. Bustillo rose and broke into a jog-trot, heading in the same direction. His breath started rasping after a few yards but he kept going, stopping now and then, but always to move on after a few seconds.

★   ★   ★

Peter Vence's first reaction to being shot was revenge. His target had fired fractionally before him but even so he'd come close to nailing him. But a miss was a miss. Following so close on his first reaction that it almost ran parallel with it was safety. Some bastard would raise the cops because that stupid fink Bustillo hadn't used a silencer.

He was losing juice. His hand came away from his side with bloodied fingers. The bullet had taken him just above his waist-band holster. Tucking the gun away he made an agonised descent of the stairs, using the wall for support. The whole action had taken no more than a couple of seconds but he had to get out quick. Just one floor down. Well, that was something.

When he reached the street he made no effort to locate Bustillo. If the guy had wanted to burn him he could have done it on the stairs. He didn't understand why he'd been let off the hook but he did understand that he'd have to reach his car fast. The bullet in him and the increasing loss of blood slowed him down but he made the best pace he could.

He reached the car with difficulty leaning against it to gather strength to climb in. Jeeze. He winced with pain. His guts were burning up. The slug must've been poisoned. He collapsed on the the driver's seat as the first siren sounded faintly. Closing the door was an effort. Getting the key into the ignition was a little easier. He managed to wind the window and he tried to locate the direction of the siren. He switched on. The car hadn't been left standing long enough for the frost to film thickly on the windscreen but he couldn't see too clearly through it. The whole balls-up hadn't taken long. Switching on the heating booster he pulled out, staving off threatening waves of faintness.

Vence now reaped the benefit of his earlier reconnaissance. He took a circuitous route back to the Tokyo Hilton. He lost more blood by doing it and there were times when he thought he couldn't hang together but by so doing he avoided the police converging on Bustillo's borrowed apartment. He parked where he'd first picked up the car, leaving the keys in the ignition. He slipped a folded handkerchief under his shirt to cover the wound, holding it there. For some seconds he sat building up the mental resolve to take the next step.

He climbed out, clinging to the car, gathered himself, then walked slowly round the corner to the main entrance. Every step was a knife in his side. He kept going, into the subdued night lighting of the lobby. There would only be night staff on at this time. No guests about. It took enormous effort to cross to the elevators and he staggered a couple of times. Okay, so they'd think he was bombed out of mind. At this time, why not? In the elevator he was able to lean back and display his pain. It came as some sort of relief. He was almost bent double on the way to his room but he got the door open, kicked it shut behind him and sank on to the bed reaching for the phone.

Everything takes longer at night. It seemed hours before the operator came on to take his number and when she did Vence's demand was a pain-filled growl. Then the phone rang for ever the other end while he bent forward with one arm across his middle, a hand keeping the blood-soaked handkerchief in place. Eventually a voice, irritable and sleep-filled answered.

Vence said, "I'm hit. My guts are hanging out. Get me out of here fast."

"Someone's on the way."

Vence dropped the receiver on to the cradle, fell forward to the floor and passed into a semi-coma. It was half an hour before there was a rap on his door but time had ceased to operate for him. The need to survive brought him round as the tapping registered. He crawled to the door. It wasn't gonna be room service at this goddam time of night, and he reached up to unlock the door.

A bustling little bald-headed man came in with a bag. He had to push Vence back with the door but once in went straight to work propping Vence against the wall where he was. He got Vence's coat, jacket and shirt off, ignoring the curses of pain. He opened the bag and produced gauze pads and bandages.

Vence eyed him mistily. "You a doctor?"

"No." The English was hesitant even in monosyllable. The small hands worked fast.

"I hope you know what you're doing. I ain't gonna croak."

"I stop bleeding. Bandage. Get you to car. No more."

It was not easy. Vence had to call on tremendous reserves to rise again, let alone face the walk to the elevators and across the ground floor lobby. He closed his mind to it. Practical as ever he figured that once he got to a doctor and had some more blood pumped into him he'd be okay. He had a courage some of his victims had lacked. He hadn't thought about it too often but he did now as the pain increased with his physical effort. Some day he'd get his. He accepted it as part of the pattern. This was not the day. Somehow he straightened. At least he had help. Funny little guy, now packing his things away. But he was someone to lean on.

*　　*　　*

Leach drove dangerously at first. He'd overlooked the icing and had scraped only the tiniest runnel from his windscreen before diving into his car. Once round a corner he had stopped, climbed out and used a de-icer before hurrying on. He was completely bewildered. Everything had gone wrong. The sound of the shot, even from inside the building, had made him jump almost from his skin. At first he'd stayed, needing to know who had been shot. Then he'd realised the dangers of staying and had run for it. The other footsteps behind him had shaken him and when he'd looked back he couldn't believe his eyes.

Warton. His gaze had gone straight to the man's face. The light was poor but sufficient. There was no mistaking the bone structure, jaw line and general build. His own shot had come close, he knew that. Almost got Warton. When it finished up through someone's window it had unnerved him. He'd seen no future in a street gun battle so he'd fled. He would have to return. The man who now called himself Bustillo must have shot the other one. Must have been waiting for him. What mattered immediately was to get home and to spin to Chieko a plausible yarn of discussions long into the night. It helped take his mind off the nerve-racking fact that Bustillo was still alive.

*　　*　　*

Jimmy Bustillo went from doorway to doorway when he heard the police siren. When it cut out it became even more dangerous for there was no hint of the direction from where the car was coming. He rightly guessed that an over zealous police driver had been instructed to cut the siren off. Who needed it at the dead of night with virtually no traffic about?

With nowhere to go he kept moving, feeling half dead from exertion. At least the movement kept him warm. He avoided the main streets which diminished any hope of picking up an all night cab. When he finally took stock of his position he realised that he was not far from his own studio room. Like a homing pigeon he had subconsciously beamed on to its direction. Right now was it any riskier than anywhere else? He went there because there was nowhere else to go. Nikki's place was too far without some form of transport. Stakeouts wouldn't resume until news of his escape reached the right quarters.

It wasn't much of a street. Short, grey and neglected. So far as he knew he was the only foreigner living in it. Which was a danger in itself. He unlocked the front door, went up the creaking stairs, no longer caring, opened his room door and tried to take stock in the dark. He didn't want to put the light on, to advertise that he was there, even at this hour. The curtains were drawn back so that the barest grey light crept in. By touch, memory and sheer necessity he went through drawers and cupboards and crammed clothes into a grip.

*   *   *

Susumu did not show his anger. He hadn't explained to his waking wife why he had to leave her in the middle of the night. If the matter was ever raised by the wrong people he knew she would swear, with natural timidity, that he had been with her all night. And now he paced a room in a wooden villa well outside the Tokyo suburbs and watched Vence who made no effort to conceal his feelings.

Vence was in a deep armchair, feet raised on a stool, blankets around him to ward off shock. The bleeding had subsided but he was weak and in pain. He held a glass of brandy in one hand. "It was a set-up," he insisted. "The guy was waiting for me at a time he should've been collaring a nod. He must've had a buzz from someone."

Susumu came round the chair to face him, his expression bland. Like that he was at his most dangerous.

"No one has warned him. Certainly he anticipated it but there must be more to this man than we realised."

"You can say that again. When the boss hears about this there'll be hell to pay. You gave bum information. That guy can use a gun.

I'm burning up so much inside it's like I've got the belly habit. I was lucky I wasn't busted with the cops coming in like that. Say, when's this doctor coming?"

"He lives some way out. He'll be here."

"Yeah, well, when he's been I'll have to do a Houdini."

"We have a safe place for you to convalesce."

"Don't give me that high jive. I'm finished for the job. The contract's busted. I'm off to the main stash."

Susumu considered it. Since he'd arrived here he'd been thinking of nothing else. He gazed down thoughtfully at Vence giving nothing away. A simple job had been bungled. He accepted no blame. Obviously that brash young fool Kenji Miyoto had communicated his intention to Bustillo. But any competent hit man should have known what to do once he realised he'd been expected. Instead, Vence had shot his way out of the room like an amateur. Perhaps he was past it. Done too much and had grown careless through success. Susumu rang a wall bell. A servant opened the door, stood there.

"At nine, I want you to settle this gentleman's account at the Hilton. Go to his room, pack and collect his things and bring them here. If anyone asks, he has gone to stay with friends."

Susumu turned to Vence. "It will help if you can give me your room key."

Vence struggled painfully. He had insisted on keeping his jacket and his gun. He produced the key, white face screwed. The brandy had helped. Just as well he hadn't been hit in the breadbasket. He couldn't make out the fat Jap but he recognised authority. This guy was a big wheel; he had to be if he could call on the boss for a hit. Yet there was too much about him that he didn't understand. Too good to be true. Quiet. Sort of correct in what he said and did. Too much of it though, like a big con. Animal instinct played a part as he groped beneath the blankets for his gun. He didn't like the way Susumu kept prowling about like a big fat cat still looking for a meal. He didn't intend to take any crap from him, that was for sure. Jesus, if only the goddam doctor would show to take some of the pain away.

Susumu was fiddling about at a desk somewhere behind him when Vence said: "You'd better ring Frisco. Tell 'em what's happened. They ain't gonna be too pleased with the crap you fed 'em."

"I was just working out the time differences. We don't want to rouse anybody in the middle of the night."

Vence forced a grin. It hurt but it was worth it. Fatso was worried. "You'd better let me talk to the boss. I'll tell him what happened."

"I thought you might suggest that." Susumu came up behind Vence, gun in hand. "I find you an embarrassment, my friend."

Vence's reflexes were incredible. His gun was out and he had twisted round before Susumu had finished speaking. What beat him was his wound. The sudden twisting of his body was agonising, slowed him down a fraction. Susumu, cunning as always, had approached at a very difficult angle for Vence. He fired through the back of the wicker chair. Vence gasped and jerked forward. His gun hand dropped but he still wasn't dead as Susumu came slowly round to face him. The two pairs of eyes locked, their expressions vastly different.

Vence felt terror for the first time in his life. It wasn't supposed to be like this. Not this way. Not now. The fat bastard was gloating over him behind that smug expression. Jesus, he could feel himself going and it wasn't time. Not yet. The pain was crucifying him. He tried to raise his gun and Susumu dispassionately fired the final shot.

Incredibly there was a soft knock on the door and Susumu called, "Enter." The servant stood politely in the doorway. "I heard shots, sir." As if someone had called for tea.

"I'm all right." Susumu pointed to Vence. "First get rid of this trash. There's chemical in the outer shed. Bury the blankets with him but dispose of his gun elsewhere. Then burn the chair. When you've done that, clean my gun, reload it and return it to the drawer."

"Yes, sir." The servant stood, wooden faced, then retreated at a nod from Susumu who buttoned his jacket across the ample belly. It would be better to return to his home while it was still dark. He had absolute confidence that the two servants who ran this emergency retreat would adequately cope. His difficulties had grown and by so doing had created fringe problems, not least of which were the Miyotos and his own San Francisco connection who was a man of some magnitude, bigger even, in aspect, than Susumu himself. And the Bustillo contract had to be reconnected. As he drove back to his villa, none of this worried him but he gave it constant thought. For the short time he allowed himself from what was left of the night, he slept extremely well. His restless wife was astute enough to ask no questions, a capacity that was prematurely ageing her.

Wearing a light topcoat Jimmy Bustillo, the fuse to the bomb being built up around him, faced the early morning chill feeling better than he had for days. He was in no way underestimating his dangers. They were worse now, but he had a short respite. A cold shower and change of clothing had restored self-respect. Carrying his grip, he travelled openly but observantly. They would soon be out looking for him again but it would take a little time for them to regroup. The cloudlessness of January was still holding good, the sun parrying the crisp air with shafts of warmth.

Nikki was a wreck when she finally opened the door to him and it was obvious that she had just dragged herself from bed. She fell into his arms, crying and trembling with the joy of company, someone to cling to who might understand. He ran a bath making her get in and combing her once pretty hair while she sat upright in the water. Afterwards, with make up, she looked quite different and he suffered the usual pang of sadness when he considered her future. He had to walk away while she took a fix but he made no effort to stop her. That should have been done by someone else long before he'd met her. At times like this he felt like shopping the Miyotos, but that would only expose himself and cut off Nikki's supply.

Once she was dressed Nikki wanted to undress at once, to seize the fervour of his company to help him forget whatever it was that bugged him and to live for each culminating second. His response was half hearted and, after the shot, she was steady enough to see that his mind was occupied elsewhere, so she produced a bottle with over-bright eyes and a devastating smile. But even at drinking he had lost impetus and she was quick to notice it but slow to see the tiredness of him.

"Jimbo, you look as if you've seen a ghost."

"I have." He didn't elaborate.

She came to sit on his knees, stroking his face, eyeing him uncertainly. "Why don't you tell me about yourself?"

He smiled wearily. "I'd have to know myself to do that and I know myself less each day."

"Have they—had a go at you?"

"Last night. I shot a man."

Nikki leaned back to see him better. "You killed him?"

"No. You haven't a newspaper?"

"News is for the living."

"I wondered what happened to him."

"So you're still in danger?"

"For the moment. I think I'll have to leave Tokyo for a bit."

"Take me with you."

"It's too dangerous."

She laughed, prettily at first then verging on hysteria but she checked it in time. "Dangerous? Of what matter is danger to me?"

"Life can be sweet, Nikki, however short."

"Shit." She was so vehement that there were tears in her eyes.

He had heard her break into swearing and coarseness and profanity before. It was usually in moments of truth and self pity when she saw herself without blinkers. "Don't give me that crap. Not you, Jimbo. I've always had truth from you."

She meant that she relied on him. "I'm sorry, honey, but I can't put you through what faces me right now. Don't you think you have enough?"

"Oh, God, Jimbo. I thought you understood. A bullet would be better."

"Come on, now."

"I want to come with you."

"No way."

A look of cunning crossed her face. "Where are you going?"

"Specifically? I don't know. General direction Osaka, Kyoto. That way. South."

"They'll find you. It won't take them long."

"Maybe. I'll play it as I see it."

She kissed his forehead spontaneously, then his lips with increasing passion. Drawing away, her lips barely parted from his she said: "I know a place in Kyoto where they'll never find you. *Never*. But you'll have to take me because I won't tell you where it is."

*   *   *

Chieko Leach listened to her friend on the telephone with sinking heart. "Have you read this morning's paper, Chieko?"

"Some of it. Why, what's happened?"

"Now I know why your husband waited in vain. Naoni was shot last night."

"Shot? Dead?"

"In his own house. There was another shooting, too, in the Taito-Ku district. At a woman journalist's apartment, but she's away so someone must have been using it."

Chieko was hardly listening after the first sentence but she caught the gist. Out of politeness she asked: "Was anyone hurt?"

"They don't know. When the police arrived nobody was there."

Her despair was rising. Why? Why? She never talked about things like this, now she was clinging to it. "You should stop mixing with these people."

"You may be right." Her friend was matter-of-fact. "And you should stop making silly bets. It could have been awkward for your husband if he'd seen Naoni."

Chieko studied the silk print above the phone. What was happening? In the space of forty-eight hours. Less. Why couldn't she remove the doubt? The dreadful, churning doubt that she wanted to tear from her mind with the long polished nails that crept to her temples. Had Graham seen the man Naoni? Late, after he'd left the house to see a computer expert her father had never heard of? For sanity's sake she would have to get away for a while. It was going to be difficult to explain to Graham why she must go. Lying was foreign to her. He would see through it. And how would she explain her absence to her father? Yet if she stayed her dignity would dissolve. It would be impossible to keep up an act of belief. She wanted to believe. What then was preventing her? The pain inside her was real, as if she had committed hara-kiri and the knife was still there but she was still living.

* * *

The call to San Francisco came through to Susumu's office. In the circumstances the call itself might suggest something wrong to the American end. The sparse, curt greeting was not unexpected. Susumu came to the point.

"Your contractor had a bad accident on site. I'm sorry."

"How bad?"

"Fatal. He underestimated the job."

"That don't sound like him. You sure *you* didn't?"

"He was fully briefed. No one forced him to do it. He was perfectly satisfied with our help."

"Did his friends arrange the burial?"

"Fortunately. They were notified first. We were lucky."

"So he's got a wooden kimono. I don't like it. Guys like that are difficult to replace. Someone's gotta pay."

"His fee wasn't on him, otherwise I'd have forwarded it to his widow."

"He must've stashed it. That could be dodgy."

There was a long pause so Susumu put in quietly, "I must remind you that the profits from such a contract are exceedingly high. The potential through the take-over I have arranged is enormous. This man made an elementary mistake whatever his experience."

"I can't go along with that. He could cover all spots. There's something grimy about this. Someone pulled the carpet."

"I understand your feeling. Please understand mine. The job is left undone. We both have a lot at stake in it being completed."

"I haven't forgotten. It it's that urgent you'd better take care of it yourself. There's no time to raise another top adviser."

"I understand. But how he tackled it was left to him. He was the expert." Susumu left it hanging.

"Okay. Keep me in touch. But we've gotta straighten. I'm left short-handed."

"When this is finished the fee will look like petty cash. A matter of tossing a coin between us as to who pays."

"You'd better be right or *your* water'll be on the boil. So long."

Susumu was satisfied with the warning. He hadn't shot Vence without being certain of the necessity. Vence could well have caused a breach between San Francisco and Tokyo and that was the last thing Susumu wanted. He had put too much planning into an enormous potential to have liaison disrupted by the groans of a wounded gunman. All he had to do to restore relationship was to kill Bustillo and clinch the remainder of the deal with the Miyotos. His men were already scouring Tokyo. There was one more source he could try. He dialled a local call.

"Anyone watching Nikki Miyoto's yet? Good. Keep them there. You remember my orders about her? Cancel them. Send some persuaders to see her. Ask her where Bustillo is? If there's the slightest suspicion that she's lying you know what to do. But don't go all the way."

When he put down the phone he was still unaware of Graham Leach's involvement and would have been more worried had he known.

*   *   *

The Miyotos both read the newspapers avidly over breakfast. They found the account of the shooting of the minor gangster Naoni and of the strange shoot up at the woman journalist's place, but nothing at all that concerned the death of a white American. They looked at each other, checked each other's feelings.

"He didn't guarantee it for last night," mollified Fujio. "There might have been complications."

"Complications my ass. That loud mouthed fat bastard has balled it up."

Fujio winced at his son's language; he was growing wilder, more uncouth.

Kenji grabbed the telephone. He was shaking. He turned to his father before he dialled. "Whatever the rights or wrongs of this we're now in it up to here." He drew a line under his chin. "And we can't get out. It's already cost us a fortune and damn all's happened."

Susumu answered as if he'd been expecting the call, but his gush of oil failed to quell Kenji's restless waves of rhetoric.

"What went wrong? After all the smooth talk what happened?"

"I refuse to speak over the open telephone and so should you." No heat, hardly an admonishment. A suggestion really but it didn't allay Kenji. "I'm on my way round and you'd better have some answers."

"Do you think that wise? In daylight? A clandestine meeting would be preferable, don't you think?"

Kenji was almost beside himself with fury. He turned helplessly to his father who showed no surprise. At no point had Fujio underrated Susumu even though he'd been outwitted by him; he shrugged. The warning signals buzzed in Kenji's head. He simmered. "When and where?"

"Tonight. As before. Don't worry. I keep my bargains."

*   *   *

They were well into the first bottle. Both knew that they'd be in bed before it was finished. Bustillo was drinking for sustenance and to keep Nikki quiet. Nikki on the other hand was still planning to change his mind. She would suggest going away again when she was sure he was sufficiently weakened by the alcohol. Both were surprised by the ring at the door. Bustillo bustled from the chair, grabbed the bottle and glasses and rushed them to the kitchen, warning Nikki to stay silent as he passed. When he returned he had the gun in hand.

Nikki stared at it, sobering instantly. She'd never seen a gun close up before but it was immediately clear to her that Bustillo was completely familiar with one. She noted the forefinger along the trigger guard, the ease with which he held it as if barely conscious of it.

The bell rang again. Nikki looked to Bustillo for instructions. He put a finger to his lips. She remained seated, eyes now on the door. Bustillo had taken up a position behind it. Unaccountably Nikki wanted to laugh. It could be anyone: postman, delivery man, even a friend. A giggle started to bubble from her lips but Bustillo's glare was so cold that she stopped at once. He was now signalling her to get into the bedroom but that was ridiculous. Nothing was happening. Bustillo placed his head nearer to the door and she heard the faint scratching. Someone was trying to get in. She looked again to Bustillo but he was now concentrating on the door. She'd better get into the bedroom like he'd said. Yet when she tried to stir her legs wouldn't move. She was scared. The door started to open and she couldn't take her eyes from it. When the real need to flee struck her it was too late.

Bustillo could have cracked the man's head as he came in but he suspected there would be more than one. Two quite small men seemingly in no hurry. They saw Nikki at once. As her mouth opened one of them said, "One scream from you, Miss, and I'll cut your windpipe." A short bladed knife was already in his hand. The other drew a gun and he was half-hidden from Bustillo by the partially opened door. They stepped fully into the room and the one with the gun closed the door, at the same time seeing Bustillo.

10

BUSTILLO WAS ALREADY MOVING as the man turned. He crashed his gun down on the head of the nearest man, catching him by the jacket, holding him like a shield. The knife had dropped. The gunman was taken by surprise and he was now facing a muzzle protruding from under the armpit of his unconscious colleague. "Drop it." Bustillo was tense.

The gunman reacted quickly, swinging his weapon to point at Nikki. Bustillo heaved the inert body at him. It was enough to make him stagger and Bustillo's gun was at his head before he recovered. He reached round and took the other's gun away from unresisting fingers. "Get something to bind them with, Nikki. Tear some sheets. Anything."

With Nikki's help he bound and gagged them both and carried them into the bedroom, dumping them on the floor one each side of the bed. Nikki was trembling. "He was going to shoot me." She couldn't believe that it had happened. She hustled to the kitchen and brought back the glasses and bottle, drinking as she came back.

Bustillo took a mouthful from his glass. His pulse rate was up, his breathing heavy. He finished the liquor but refused to recharge.

"What are we going to do with them?" Nikki was filling her glass with a shaking hand.

Bustillo sat down, rubbed his face. "They would probably have tortured you, Nikki. To find out where I am. I've really landed you. I'm so sorry."

"What are we going to do with them?" she repeated.

"Leave them here."

She picked up his meaning. "Does that mean I can come?"

"You can't stay here now." He thought for a while. "It'll get worse. I've rubbed their noses in it twice in quick succession. They won't like that. Do you still want to be with me? You could go to your safe hidey hole on your own."

"As long as you're with me I'll be all right, Jimbo."

"Don't think it will be as easy as that was. I had the drop on them. Luck. Nothing more."

"Shouldn't we tell the police they are here? They should be put away."

"They should. But I can't afford to be mixed up with the police, honey. I'm between the devil and the deep blue sea. I can try to ride it out or I can split. Go some place else. I don't want to do that. I have a strong motive for staying."

"And that isn't me."

He smiled. "You wouldn't believe me if I said it was. What are you going to do? Go it alone or risk getting your head blown off?"

"I can't go it alone, Jimbo. Even if I wanted to. I need support."

His voice softened. "They're pretty grim terms I'm offering, Nikki. It might get agonisingly rough. It could be tough alone but not so tough as this might turn out to be. Think carefully. I've already created a situation that's forcing you out of your own place."

Bustillo crossed to pour himself a small drink. Nikki noticed it.

"You've hardly wet the bottom. Now I know it's serious. I'll stick, Jimbo. I'll take my chances with you. You'd be a nice person to snap out with." She had spoken quite seriously and he felt for her again. Her options were so limited.

He looked at her thoughtfully, hesitated before saying, "You only know half the story, Nikki. I think you should know something of why I don't want the police involved. I don't want you taking blind risks."

"I'm not that blind that I can't see that if you stay here Kenji will get you."

He smiled at her concern. "I was working for the U.S. Government in Chile. I didn't like what I was involved in. But I'm American and loyal I hope. So I volunteered for a job that was twice as dangerous. I finished in Cuba still working for the Government. I guess I was sort of mixed up a bit. I could see shades of Chile again and my system couldn't take it."

"You sure you want to tell me this? What would I know about moral issues? Is that why they want you? Is that what you want me to know?"

"That's part of it . . . There's . . ."

"Jimbo, sweetheart. Let's get out of here. Kenji won't hang around while you're explaining."

He shrugged. "Okay, pack some things and include that letter I gave you. I'll fix it so these characters can free themselves." He went into the bedroom.

One man was still unconscious, the other had wriggled to a sitting position against the bed. Bustillo untied the gag. He reached over to pull a pillow from the bed. He placed it against the side of the high bones, sullen face and rammed his gun against it. "It'll cut down the sound," he explained. "I want to know who sent you. If you don't tell me in five seconds I'm going to blow your head off."

Sweat beads formed on the high brown forehead. The bloodshot eyes widened. Bustillo started counting slowly. The man's mouth opened but he didn't speak. Fear had dried it and he was using his tongue. At five he closed his eyes and screwed up his streaming face.

Bustillo accepted that the fear had not been of him. The man had weighed the odds and he had taken his chances. "Okay. I'll settle for your name."

"Shoji." It came out as a breath of relief.

"And who's the guy out front?"

No answer. Bustillo held the head and pressed the gun savagely into the pillow. "*His name*."

"Jumata."

Bustillo retied the gag and examined the second man. His hair had parted and a blue black suppurating bruise had risen like a volcanic eruption. The one who'd just given his name had almost passed out from shock. But he'd make it to the kitchen. There were knives there, including the short bladed one Bustillo had picked up from the unconscious man. It would take time but they'd get out.

Nikki had crammed clothes into matching suitcases and she'd hurriedly climbed into a neat blue pastel suit as if she was going on honeymoon. Bustillo said, "Ring the porter. Tell him to go outside and find a guy called Jumata. He won't be far. When he's found him, tell him to say Shoji wants him up here. Get the names right, Nikki."

When she had phoned he took one of the cases and his own grip and they took the elevator to the first floor. They got out, sent the elevator down to ground level and went down the stairs half a flight. When they heard the porter return with another man and then an elevator start to rise, they scurried down. The surprised porter saw them go, but Bustillo thought, what the hell, the two monkeys upstairs were going to talk anyway. So long as nobody knew *where* they were going.

They hadn't looked up train times and at Tokyo Station there was a good half hour's wait for the next Tokaido Line express to Kyoto. It gave them an opportunity to book first-class seats and for Bustillo to make some telephone calls. He persuaded Nikki to stay in the waiting room rather than prop up a bar and she reluctantly promised. He found a kiosk and telephoned the British Embassy.

"Extension three one eight, please."

"Donaldson."

"Hi! Jimmy Bustillo."

"Good grief. Where on earth have you been?"

"Right here in Tokyo. Under your nose."

"We'd given you up. Concluded that you extracted a free fare from us."

"Wadderyer know. You figured I was that sort of guy?"

"Frankly, we don't know. You could be any sort of guy."

"It didn't stop you using me."

"Is that what we've been doing? I've seen no signs as yet."

"Okay. I'll level. You were right in assuming what you did. I was sort of desperate."

"I can understand that. Do I detect a change of heart?"

"Not so much of heart as circumstances. I may be able to stick to the arrangement."

"Agreement, rather. What changed your mind?"

"I've had sight of the quarry."

"You have my undivided attention. Are you sure?"

"Sure enough. He almost blew my head off last night."

"Really? Not the apartment affair?"

"Outside. I'm kind of caught between two parties. *He* came nearest to supplying me with a harp."

"Or a spade, as the case may be. He has no reputation for violence."

"Maybe someone should tell him. He's one helluva lot to lose."

"Indeed. It would seem that he intends to hang on to it. Do you know where he is?"

"No. But he knew where I was and that worries me."

"How will you trace him?"

"As I've no idea where he's holed up I'll have to get him to come to me."

"Once you have him located you need only tell us."

"I know. At the moment I'm in the bush without a compass."

"Do you need help?"

"Yes. But I can't see you giving me the sort of help I need. Right now I need a ring of half a dozen heavies round me day and night."

"We dare not create a situation here. Relations with Japan are too good. I'm afraid that's out."

"I wasn't banking on it. I thought you ought to know."

"Who's the other party pestering you? Your old firm?"

"Pestering?" Bustillo laughed. "I heard you English were masters of understatement. It's not tied up with the other and it's not the old firm. Forget it. It's just another headache for me."

"Where can I contact you?"

"I wish I knew. In any event it's better that you don't know. Leaks do occur and your boy had some contacts in his day. He might still have them."

"People in glass houses . . ."

"Okay. I'll keep you posted. Just wanted you to know."

"Good man. Take care."

"If it goes wrong there's a letter you might want to hand to the Japanese police. It's not your baby but you'll know what to do. So long."

Bustillo tried Tadashi's number and was delighted when the journalist answered. "Tashi. So they fixed your phone. How are your—wounds."

"Do I hear you laughing? You think I've left the field clear for you?"

"I wouldn't laugh about a thing like that, Tashi. Can you get out yet?"

"By tomorrow, I think. Weals heal and memory fades. Where are you calling from?"

"Tokyo Station. I want you to do me a favour. It's not a set-up. No come-backs. Can you write a piece about me under my real name? As the C.I.A. man Warton? Say anything you like. New rumours. Information from reliable sources. Anything to hot it up. Most of all I want you to add that he was known to have been in Kyoto. That it is believed that he has friends there. Implant the impression that he's got interested in the Nara Temples. Gone religious."

"Warton isn't news. Not on his own. I have to persuade an editor. That won't be easy."

"Will it make it easier if you tell him that behind the story is another that will take over the front page in the biggest banners of every paper in the country? He will be the first to have it."

"Are you serious? My job could be at stake."

"I know that. Look, Tashi, you set me up to get a story. Okay. No hard feelings. I've been used before. I'm being used now. The story I'm going to give you will hit every newspaper in the world. That is a promise. If I survive. Will that swing it?"

"Can't you give me a hint? Something to tell the boss?"

"No chance. It's not a matter of trust, or of being sure. It's a matter of my own neck. I'm not risking a leak. You may be okay but what about your editor and anyone he cares to tell to blow up his image? It could kill it stone dead. Once I've done what I intend to do you'll be the second person to know and the first one isn't a newspaper man."

"I'll try."

"And Tashi. Tomorrow morning's edition. Later might be *too* late. Grab what space you can without overdoing it."

"I know what to do. I won't ask you where you're going."

"You don't have to. But exactly where, I don't know myself."

The Tokaido Express came in like a white, blue streaked bullet, its red nose splaying the air. Called the 'bullet train' it was a name it had earned in sleek good looks and speed.

Bustillo and Nikki pulled forward the cushion foot rests so that they could relax in the wide seats on the three-hour plus journey. To Bustillo it was an enforced and welcome rest—perhaps the last he'd enjoy. But Nikki couldn't settle. She wanted to drink and because Bustillo was afraid to let her go to the bar on her own, where she might get out of hand, he went with her shaking off the need for sleep.

When they walked down the train snow traces were already flecking the fields. The undulating white range of mountains to the west showed stark natural beauty. Nikki wasn't at home outside Tokyo. A city girl. Accepting the dire necessity of moving out meant insisting on the concession of enjoying some city comfort. The train couldn't be more comfortable, so Bustillo understood her need of liquid comfort.

The bar was lengthways down the coach, tables and chairs in front of it. Bustillo shrewdly decided to stand at the bar. He wanted to ensure Nikki's sobriety and her legs were always the first to go. He'd keep an eye on her. They ordered saki and it automatically was served warm. His eyes switched to the clock-sized speedometer above the bar door. The needle had already crept up to two hundred and thirty-five kilometres an hour. It hardly seemed they were moving.

*　　*　　*

Susumu listened patiently to Kenji's outburst. He continued pouring the drinks with great solemnity, passing them round, his huge hands holding the glasses with exceptional delicacy. He then sat in his favourite chair, raising his glass to Fujio Miyoto in a silent toast as if Kenji didn't exist at all. When Kenji finally ran out of steam Susumu politely addressed Fujio. "Mr. Miyoto, you must really keep your son in order. There is no respect these days. Not even here in Japan where the old traditions matter."

Fujio saw the gross hypocrisy of it. Coming from Susumu of all people. Yet he saw, too, the underlying truth. And the warning. Because he had sufficient percipience to know that Susumu could neither agree nor condemn he said, "We have adopted too much from the West. Since the war some of the old ways have gone; the new ones are too brash."

Kenji was furious at being ignored and, once again, at the way he had handled Susumu. He had bounced straight off. When he'd set out with his father that evening he had been intent on playing it cool. Being more subtle. Yet confrontation had changed matters almost immediately. Susumu had a way of getting under his skin. It was almost as though Bustillo wasn't important any more. Right now he was feeling dangerously angry and his father wasn't helping matters by obliquely sniping at him.

Susumu continued to address Fujio. "I had an expert flown in from San Francisco. A highly experienced man. There should have been no problem. It was quite a simple straightforward job. Yet Bustillo was waiting and ready. Our man was shot dead. Only by the greatest good fortune and, in due modesty, aided by an enormously efficient organisation, were we able to reach him before the police. What does that suggest to you, Mr. Miyoto?"

"Obviously, Bustillo was warned."

"Of course. But by whom? When you and your son were here two nights ago I specifically posed the question whether either of you had given Bustillo cause to think his life was in danger. I was told, no. From you it was easy to believe. You are indeed a level-headed man. The same cannot be said of your son. I believe that

132

your son gave Bustillo ample reason for thinking himself to be in danger."

"That's a lie. I said nothing to him."

At last Susumu's gaze swept over to Kenji. "That might be true. You did not precisely say, 'I am going to kill you.' You wouldn't have to. Your expression would be enough. Just as it's enough now to tell me that you'd like to kill *me*." He turned back to Fujio. "I say again, Mr. Miyoto, exercise greater control over your son. He wears his feelings like an advertising board."

Fujio knew it to be true but it was family duty to protect his son right or wrong. "That doesn't answer for the astuteness of Bustillo. Nor his apparent capability with a gun."

Susumu nodded. He raised his glass again, this time including Kenji in the silent toast. His magnetism was such that Kenji immediately calmed, lifting his own glass before he'd realised what he'd done.

"You've raised a valid point," agreed Susumu. "Just who is this man Bustillo? You considered him to be a danger, yet he has had ample time to create problems for you. As far as we know he hasn't done this. An attempt is made on his life yet my information is that he has not reported to the police. Nor has he tried to blackmail you. I feel he creates a danger of a different kind. He must be killed. That is an absolute necessity." He didn't mention that his men had broken into Nikki's apartment earlier that day. And that Bustillo had been there, once again to deal with a potentially dangerous situation with the efficiency of the well trained. Nor did he add that Bustillo's death was now as essential to himself as to the Miyotos. Bustillo knew that he'd only wounded Vence. And Vence had disappeared from the face of the earth with bullets from two different guns in him. The situation was highly volatile. He had already widened his scope of enquiry far beyond the bounds of Tokyo.

Kenji might have found a certain satisfaction had he known the qualms stirring in Susumu's fat belly.

*   *   *

Graham Leach always read the newspapers carefully. All his life it had been part of his stock-in-trade and had played a part in his profession. It was still important to him if for a quite different reason. He located Tadashi's article in the middle pages. It was quite small but well headed, difficult to miss. IS THE AMERICAN DEFECTOR WARTON IN JAPAN? Well, he knew that he was but it seemed so did a newspaper man. Kyoto? Pilgrimages to the Temples of Nara? He had been in Tokyo. Which didn't mean he lived there.

Chieko was sitting quite silently at the other end of the table drinking a small bowl of jasmine tea. She had taken the usual care in her personal appearance. It would be almost impossible for her not to do so. The beautiful image of her was no less impressive than usual. She chose her kimonos so well, the colours always blending with her skin. Had Leach trusted himself to look more openly at her these days he would have noticed the dimmed restlessness of her eyes and the eclipsing of the half moons under them.

He knew she was worried. All he could do was to ride out the storm. The last thing he wanted was friction between them. It was one of the trickiest situations he could remember and he'd had a few. Yesterday had been hell. A complete day of not knowing what had happened to this fellow who now called himself Bustillo. He'd read about the shoot up. Luckily nobody had *seen* anything. Except those involved in the play. No news even of the other chap. That *was* strange. He read the article again. He folded the paper, lowered it. He steadied his nerve to face Chieko who carefully avoided his gaze.

"Why don't we go away for a few days?"

She looked up sharply then, her expression guarded.

"Look," he coaxed. "I know you're concerned about this fellow Warton. We both are. It sickens me to see you worrying so much on my account, yet what can I do? It's no use pretending the man doesn't exist. It's no use pretending that he doesn't want to kill me. Chieko, darling, perhaps if we go away he will just disappear. Go back to wherever he came from."

It was the most hopeful thing he had said during the last few days. Her thoughts kept vacillating over the murdered man Naoni. Graham could lead her away from suspicion but only by doing the right thing. "Where will we go?"

He gave a practised smile. "Does it matter? Not terribly far. South a bit. The parks are beautiful at this time of year. What about a visit to some of them? And the shrines; I know you'd love that. Nara, Kyoto or Osaka if you want to do some shopping. I could get you some more pearls. They're better down there. We could go to a silk factory, get some kimonos, Happi-coats. We'll give him time to go from our lives. Then I can throw the gun away. What do you say?"

It was a wonderful suggestion. The thought excited her. She loved old Japan, preferred it to Tokyo where the business affairs of her husband and father kept her bound. She belonged to the old ways, old courtesies and strong principles. Age had nothing to do with it. She loved the infinite delicacies of the beauty her country could produce. Modern advance represented only convenience to her. She well remembered the encouragement she'd received when she had joined the Tachibama Ballet School. It was there that she had been attracted to western classical dance and music and had veered from the individual dance traditions of Japan. While her roots were still firmly embedded in her own country her scope had widened. She recalled the party after a performance of the 'Nutcracker' ballet when she had first met Leach. It turned out to be one of many interests they had in common. Getting away from Tokyo could restore those interests, take their minds off the dreadful tangent their lives had taken.

Leach saw the hope flitting over her face. And he subtly exploited it until she was smiling, looking forward to the break she was convinced they both needed. While she was still in a happier frame of mind he prepared to leave, as he left most mornings, for a series of meetings designed to launch a computer manufacturing business that incorporated some unusual designs. It took time, money and effort. She understood this and knew that great steps had been made. What she didn't understand was why he was taking the *Nippon Sun* with him. He always left it for her to read. It was still tucked under his arm as he was leaving the villa.

She called after him. "Darling. The newspaper. You've forgotten to leave it."

He smiled back at her. "There's a special article I want to read. Do you mind? Just this once?"

There was nothing she could say, but for some reason it stirred fears she was just beginning to discard. She didn't know why. There had been nothing furtive in the way he had acted or spoken. She was churning again. Inexplicably. Unpleasantly. She waited until he had driven off then took the small Honda to the nearest conglomerate of stores and bought a copy of the *Nippon Sun*. It sat on the seat beside her like an unexploded bomb, her gaze intermittently fleeting to it as if it contained secrets she really did not want to know. She took it into the villa, feeling like a pariah. Spying on her own husband. Yet she couldn't stop herself.

She laid the newspaper on the floor of the lounge and knelt before it as if she could atone for her misdeed at the same time as committing it. She spread the pages and found the article. Warton. That was the name of the man her husband had told her about. She let her body sag, her face held in her hands. Graham had lied to her. The only truth she had left to cling to was the point that Warton was clearly a defector. Graham had at least told her that much. When she was sufficiently recovered she took the newspaper to the incinerator hidden behind a decorative wall in the garden and burned it. When she returned to the villa her feet were wet from the melting frost on the grass, but she hardly noticed.

*   *   *

Graham Leach made the telephone call from the small office Chieko's father had lent to him until his own premises were ready. But first he locked the door. As he'd been given a permanent outside line he had no need to go through the operator. He called the *Nippon Sun* and asked for Tadashi Fujuda under whose by-line the article had appeared. The journalist was sick. No, they couldn't give his home telephone number but it was listed. Leach had spoken in Japanese with a simulated American accent throughout. He dialled again.

"Mr. Fujuda? I'm sorry to trouble you at home, sir. Sorry to hear that you are sick. Nothing serious, I hope? I'm speaking from the United States Embassy here in Tokyo. I noticed your very interesting article in this morning's *Sun*. I wondered if you could give me a little more information."

Tadashi, used to dealing with Americans, immediately picked up inconsistencies in the accent which he couldn't place.

"May I have your name, please?"

"Why, surely. I'm Ed Harper. I don't want you to get the wrong impression, Mr. Fujuda. I mean Mr. Warton no harm. On the contrary. If I can find him I can do him a power of good. Yes, sir. He's a much maligned man but I guess that's by the way. Where exactly in Kyoto do you think he might be?"

"I don't know, Mr. Harper. And you must understand that if I did I wouldn't tell you. However, my source *is* reliable. I understand that he was there, and was a frequent visitor to Nara, whether for religious or cultural reasons I cannot be sure. He may have moved on, of course. I can't go beyond that."

"Sure. Ethics. I understand. It's a nice change to see some, if I might say so. Well, I guess that's as far as we can go. I'm indebted to you, sir. I hope you are soon well again."

136

It had been a try. At least Fujuda had confirmed the article. These journalists got their information from all sorts of people.

Meanwhile Tadashi telephoned the United States Embassy and asked for Ed Harper. He was not surprised that there was no such person. The accent puzzled him. It had floated between the north and southern states and then sometimes it was hardly anything at all. The sensation of a news story struck him hard. He felt it in his bones. Jimmy Bustillo hadn't exaggerated; he'd bet on it. Just then he'd have given almost anything to have been able to identify the caller. He moved about the room to see just how far he could cope with his incapacity. He rang his office and told his editor that he was going south.

*　　*　　*

The luncheon was at the United States Embassy. It made a change from dinner. For a start it was shorter and varied, if only marginally, the evening cocktail circuit of western Diplomatic Missions. They knew each other almost as well as their own families; some, with clandestine liaisons, better. Today it was the Americans. Next week, perhaps, the French, who always laid on a good show. There was a friendly competitiveness about it that staved off boredom.

Brad Dacy stood, back against the wall, watching the arrivals, with a dry Martini in his hand that he hadn't touched. Luncheons always left him so tired afterwards. On the other hand they might leave the evening free which meant more time with Cherril and the kids. He was a tall, thin, relaxed man, eyes half closed as if almost asleep. He was the Commercial Attaché. On paper. His actual job was chief of the Central Intelligence Agency section in Japan. Everyone knew it. As long as they didn't know his operatives he was willing to bear the focus.

Not so Jock Donaldson who approached Dacy, carrying his gin and tonic low down as if it was a hand grenade. He would have stuck out his blue chin and gone to the grave denying he was anything to do with London's M.I.6. Everyone knew his connection too but it was a matter of pride not to acknowledge it.

"Hi, Jock."

"Hello, Brad." Donaldson managed to gaze up at the taller man without raising his head. It made him appear slightly inane but neither man was that. "I read rather an interesting article this morning. Just a shortie. About your man Warton."

137

"Saw it myself. A load of bull." Dacy's eyes were sweeping the arriving guests over Donaldson's head.

"You really think so?"

"I hadn't heard he was in Japan."

"No?"

Dacy took more interest. No man he knew could put so much into one word as Donaldson. The whole thing lay open to question before him. More than that. "What's on your mind, Jock?"

"How seriously are you looking for Warton?"

"We're looking."

"Why not give it a rest for a while?"

Dacy became aware of his drink, sipped it. His eyes were still half closed, but sharper. "Are you serious?"

"Oh, absolutely. Leave it for a bit and I might be able to help you."

"Help me what?"

"You know. Land him."

"For old time's sake?"

"Why not? It wouldn't be the first time we've helped each other."

"I'm puzzled by your interest. I may not be able to help you. Folks back home like to see justice done."

"Oh, come. He can't be that important to you. And you won't lose him."

"You can deliver?"

"When the time is right. If you help me now."

"Call off the heavies?"

"If you have any. For the time being."

Dacy viewed his friend narrowly. "You're a bastard, Jock. How long have you known and what are you doing with him?"

"I might be a bastard at that. My lineage goes way back to the clans, and they were pretty rugged."

"If I'm to help I need an answer."

"If you do help you'll get one. I'll promise delivery."

"Does *he* know that?"

"I should hardly think so."

Dacy didn't reply. Donaldson added, "You think I'm using him then, setting him up; that it's poor reward?"

"Aren't you?"

"Only under pressure from you. If you'll call off your dogs as a purely personal favour to me I don't need to."

"Touché. Okay, Jock. We'll ease off and you deliver."

Susumu Takana read the article without it conveying anything to him. He wasn't interested in Americans unless they could show a profit for him. He used part of the morning working out how he could smuggle drugs through the use of legitimate freight consignments handled by the Miyoto Travel Company once he had full control. He also saw interesting ways of using the passenger side of the business to the same end. All that stood in his way was one man, after which control would be complete.

Later that morning two of his men produced a third between them and bundled him into the back of the car where Susumu was waiting. The man was a fringe employee of Susumu's own organisation although it was unlikely that he even knew it. When he saw Susumu he thought his last day had come. He was well aware of the vast importance of the man although he'd never before met him. He'd seen photographs, heard countless stories. If he crossed him he was dead. What had he done?

"You supply Nikki Miyoto?"

"Yes, sir."

"She's left her apartment. Where's she gone?"

"I don't know. She's rich. Buys a lot at a time."

"When will she be due?"

"Two weeks. Three weeks."

"You've no idea where she is now?"

He couldn't win. Not this one. His lips wouldn't frame an answer.

"Make out a list of all the places you know she visits. And any you think she might. In Tokyo or outside. If you forget one, you're dead."

*　　*　　*

Kenji didn't see the article and if he had his reaction would have been negative. He was too busy studying the financial columns and share index and working on his utter dislike and distrust of Susumu. But even he accepted that the matter of Bustillo was better in Susumu's hands, that there was really nothing else they could do. How his life had changed over the past few days. There'd be no more real enjoyment until they traced and killed Bustillo.

*　　*　　*

Fujio did see the article. He didn't at once associate it with Bustillo, there was no obvious connection, but it made him think again of Bustillo—not that he was ever far from his mind. He had the advantage over Susumu in that respect; he had actually met the American. There was no doubt at all that Bustillo was no ordinary man. His actions weren't ordinary. His failure to use the power Fujio believed him to possess wasn't ordinary. Taking the job in the way that he had when he clearly had higher qualification wasn't ordinary. Nor, if Nikki was to be believed during her earlier association with Bustillo, was his relationship with her. His apparent handling of the gunman wasn't ordinary. Which added up to what? Someone beyond understanding. Yet everyone had a motive for what they did. Like this man Warton in the article. He must have had a motive if only for money. And what more powerful one than that? It was the nearest Fujio came, at that stage, to connecting the two names.

*   *   *

Jimmy Bustillo himself read the article. His mind was split on it. On the one hand he would be keeping an obligation. He didn't like doing it but it rankled that he hadn't. On the other he was not blind to the repercussions of what he'd done. When he considered it in detail he might just as well use his gun on himself. More than the Englishman would come after him and this time better prepared. It was a matter of time only before one of them got him. He was so mentally weary that he was almost resigned to dying. He was so tired of running. He just hoped that he wouldn't die entirely in vain. But he could see no way of avoiding it. Somehow he must ditch Nikki. Before he was betrayed which was only a sideline of the issue. He read Tadashi's piece again. Just sufficient. Not overdone or underplayed. It was like reading his own obituary.

11

As they lay in bed he could see the blue southern tip of Lake Biwa through the hill folds, and a little to the west the snow-crest on Mount Hiei. The villa lay on wooded slopes on one side of a small valley just north of Kyoto, the ancient imperial capital of Japan and of whose name Tokyo was an anagram. Beside him, Nikki lay in an exhausted sleep, her prematurely grey-tinged hair spread over the pillows like stained candy floss. A near empty bottle of bourbon was on her bedside table.

It was almost midday. Bustillo had crept out of bed early, motored into town, using the car that was apparently always garaged there, and had done a little shopping. On his return he'd made some coffee, and because there was little else to do, had climbed back into bed. Nikki hadn't changed her position from the time he'd first got up.

Her hand crept over him while he was still reading the *Nippon Sun*. It was the first indication that she was awake.

"You've been out."

"Yep. You want some coffee?"

"We can have the paper delivered. It comes late but it does come."

"And have everyone know that we're here?"

Her hand stopped exploring with the realisation of why they were there. "I'd forgotten."

"That's something you must never do. Not for one second. You want me to split? I can look around. It'll be safer for you."

"But not for you, Jimbo." Her voice was still dreamy and her hand started to move again.

"Not now, Nikki."

"Why not?"

"It's not the right time."

"It's always the right time. What are you reading anyway?"

She struggled up on her elbows, peering over his shoulder, body pushing against his. He smiled involuntarily. "You never give up, do you?"

"I'll have to one day." As he tried to turn the page she stopped him. "I want to see what interests you."

He didn't try to stop her, keeping the pages open for her scrutiny. She held his wrists and he noticed the tremors of her fingers. She scanned the two pages, taking her time, using the excuse to touch him.

"Do you know this man, Jimbo?"

"Who?"

"Warton. The American defector."

"Would it matter? I'm not a defector."

"Is that why you let Papa and Kenji tread all over you?"

"That'll die down."

"Not with Kenji it won't. If he sees you as a threat to the Miyoto empire he'll get you. He has to prove himself all the time. Who else are you running from?"

He almost told her then realised she might worry. He compromised. "The only real enemy I had was a man I met in Europe. He was with NATO. Now *there* was a defector for you. He nearly sank the Western Alliance and almost permanently ruptured Anglo-American relations."

"Why should he be your enemy?"

"Because I know where he went. But that was a couple of years ago. God knows where he is now. You know, the person I'm really running from is myself."

Bustillo turned to look at Nikki. "It doesn't seem to worry you who I am?"

"Oh, Jimbo, how can I pass judgment on anyone? I don't care who you are so long as you're here."

He put his arm around her, pulled her head under his chin.

"I sometimes think you have more right than most people to pass your judgments. You can do it to me any time you like."

"Okay. You're a lousy lover."

He grinned but it faded as she shivered. "I need a fix." She broke away to go to the bathroom. Because he could not stand the silence while she took a fix he called out, "You sure your father and Kenji won't want to use this place?"

"Not at this time of year." Her voice came through the open bathroom door. "I told you. Using Papa's villa is the safest place of all. He'd never think of looking there."

★　　★　　★

Chieko sat in a window seat of the Tokaido Express. She had rallied her reserves and had fallen back on an inner strength she knew to have its limitations. Pride would not permit her to take her problem to a father who had really been reluctant about her marriage to a foreigner. Without the guidance of her mother, her father's original objections, it had seemed to her, had been traditional. He had accepted Leach's charm and wealth and industriousness as excellent qualities but he could hardly keep the pure Japanese strain of the Kitas going. There had been sound commercial reasons for allowing the marriage to go ahead and he certainly had raised no personal objections to Leach himself. Nevertheless, the objections, though largely tacit, had been clear enough. There was no question of her seeking his counsel.

The passing scenery was something of a balm. The further south the nearer she came to those things she loved and understood. Whereas Nikki had stood at the bar for three hours Chieko did not move, marvelling at the ragged snowlines, at the white fields, and then when they were green again. There was an inner pull as though she herself was being drawn in by a length of cord against which she made no resistance. It was some compensation for her unshed tears at losing sight of what life was about and the bewildering loss of understanding of the husband by her side. She closed her eyes for a while to feel the gentle tug that was carrying her to the heart of a gently spinning top as though her ancestors were gathered round it. In the darkness behind her lids the top gathered speed until she was swirling frantically in a vortex. She opened her eyes as her heart thumped louder.

The Leaches checked in at the Miyako Hotel in Kyoto that same afternoon. To soothe Chieko, knowing that he was walking on hot cinders, Leach chose the Japanese inn style annexe of bungalows set in a traditional garden. Around the huge hotel were sixteen acres of landscaped gardens positioned on eastern slopes almost facing the same way as the Miyotos' villa.

Leach's immediate need was to find Bustillo. The only clue he had was Nara but if it was accurate it pinpointed one area. Chieko would want to get to Nara, the shrines, the Old Palace. It was a haphazard way to start a search but until he came up with something better it was all he could do. One man stood between him and complete freedom in the western world.

*　　*　　*

Jimmy Bustillo stirred sufficiently to start on his defences. They were not so much to save his life but to prolong it in order to trap Graham Leach. It was of little use luring Leach, to find himself on the wrong end of a bullet before he could contact Donaldson. And always in the back of his mind was Kenji. How long would it take him to produce a new killer and to pick up the scent again?

The ground below the villa fell towards the serpentine valley road in a series of haphazard terraces. Some were huge rockeries, creviced and shrubbed with a wildness that gave the illusion of nature's own pattern.

He emptied cans of perfectly good food and searched for pebbles to put into them. With green gardening twine he set up a series of crude alarms through the shrubberies and trees of the Miyotos' gardens. He had neither the twine nor the number of cans to do a perfect job but he studied the approaches both below and above the villa and worked out strategic spots. Nikki, at first watched him with some humour, then wanted to help, but he'd have none of it. He knew exactly how and where he wanted them and it was almost sundown before he was finished.

He went round his traps, reasonably satisfied but knowing that he needed more supplies. Because of the limited noise pebbles in empty cans will make, all had been placed fairly close to the villa which was raised on stilts to cope with the slope. He had kept three cans back for use inside the house. Amongst the tools in the garage separated from the villa, he found shelf brackets which he fitted to the front, rear and kitchen doors so as to suspend cans from them.

By this time Nikki was no longer amused. "You think they'll find, us don't you?"

He was screwing the last bracket on. It was after nine and long since dark. "Not *them*. Someone else."

"Who Jimbo?"

"He won't be after you."

"Not unless I see him killing you."

Bustillo was standing on a chair, screwdriver in hand. "I couldn't leave you in Tokyo. Those men would have mangled you."

"And this one?"

He didn't answer. He'd always found it difficult to lie to her as if to compensate for her own spasmodic stream.

She went from the room and came back with the morning's newspaper. "Is this what it's about?"

Again he didn't answer. He turned his back and continued screwing.

"You bastard, Jimbo. This is to draw someone else here, isn't it? Not Kenji's mob."

He climbed down off the chair. "This one won't torture you. Your only danger is if he gets me. At the first warning get down under the house. He won't know you're here."

"If you take care of him, he won't know. If you don't, what's he going to believe when he sees my clothes? Think you've been running around in drag? And what's he going to think when he sees my junkie kit? Think it's yours? Oh, Jimbo."

He was used to her fluctuations but it was true that he hadn't told her he intended to use the villa as a trap. Yet had he told her he knew she would still have come.

"I thought you wanted to be with me regardless."

There were tears in her eyes. "Sure. But I trusted you. You are the only one I ever trusted. Now I find you're no different from the rest. I thought you were running from Kenji. Now there's someone else. You're using me."

Bustillo held on to the chairback. He was gazing blankly at her, deeply disturbed by her assessment of him. Had he really put her in danger from Leach? He had banked on trapping Leach. But Nikki was right; it could so easily go the other way. His grip tightened on the chair and he stared at the liquor bottles and glasses on the table. To hell with it. He poured out two stiff ones, handing one to Nikki with a slightly apologetic air.

"I've been pretty stupid. I can't tell you who's involved."

"Because I'll blab?"

"You're too intelligent to blab in all normal circumstances. You've worked this out on your own completely accurately."

"But if I can't get dope I'll tell everyone. Is that it?"

He shrugged. "You know it's true."

"So that gives you the right to lure someone here while I'm here?"

"No. No, it doesn't. I'm sorry." He swallowed some liquor fast, his face muscles contorting. "I guess I have used you. Inadvertently. Believe me I didn't see it like that. It was your idea to come." He finished his drink, wiping his lips with the back of his

145

hand as he peered at her. She had a way of making him feel more wretched than anyone. It centred round her own helplessness; she was so reliant on him. And he'd let her down.

"Is it the man you spoke about? I mean, why would you mention him? You know where he is, don't you? *And he knows it?*"

He nodded reflectively, more to himself than in answer to her surmise. "Look, I'll move out tomorrow. I'll take down the alarms before I go."

"*No.*" She was holding her drink in both hands held out to him. "Don't leave me."

"Look, honey, you can't have it both ways."

"I'll take it your way. Anyway as long as you stay. I love you, Jimbo. You're the only one I ever have." She was crying now. "I know it's not the same for you. I know it can't last forever. But what we have going for us is something special. It's the one thing that props me up."

He gazed at her helplessly, moved by her plea. "Do I prop you sufficiently for you to give up the needle? The bottle?" He waved his hand towards the table.

She stared back at him, scared and yearning. Raising the glass she tried to hold it steady as she drank but it rattled against her teeth. She made an effort to get hold of herself.

"Sure. I can do it. With you I can do it."

It would never work. It was written all over her. Her tone lacked conviction. Her frightened eyes said, NO.

He crossed over, put his arm around her shoulders and she turned her head to bury her face against his chest. He gently stroked her hair while she quietly sobbed. When she had quietened he murmured above her head, "It's best we split, Nikki. It came as a shock to find that I'm just like the rest. But you're right. The irony is that I'm in my present situation because I thought I was different from the rest. The oddball. I guess we never really know ourselves."

"I know that you've got guts, Jimbo. I know that about you."

"You're kidding yourself. Don't confuse guts with simply not caring."

"Stay, Jimbo. I was only upset because you didn't tell me."

"I know. It doesn't change it though. You're my mirror and I don't like my own reflection."

"Let's get bombed and go to bed."

He laughed. It was half humorous, half tragic.

"Nikki's cure-all."

She looked up wiping her eyes. "It's not so bad, is it?"

"It's great. While it lasts."

"And you stay on?"

"Maybe. For a day, anyway. Tomorrow I'll take you to Nara. You can say hello to the sacred deers."

"That'll be wonderful."

It was her endorsement of a strong need for him. She hated going round parks, museums or whatever. He gave her a little squeeze and turned to make sure that he'd finished fixing the ungainly door alarm.

*　　*　　*

The Nara Deer Park covered twelve hundred acres. In spite of its size there were certain parts where almost all visitors were bound to go. A hub where they revolved. As Bustillo drove with a subdued Nikki by his side he was aware of possible disaster from his action. He must put himself on show near the temples. Similarly, Leach, if he had seen the article, would be reduced to starting his hunt in the same way. For Bustillo it had to be done as quickly as possible, for he was also putting himself on view for Miyoto's men. There was no other way. He was in trouble whatever he did and he hadn't Nikki's faith in the safety of the villa.

He took a long route round, wherever tourists might gather. They passed the Great Buddha Hall and then the five storeyed pagoda of the Kofuruji Temple in Nara City before parking the car and walking round the park in the bright morning sunshine. The sacred deer were immediately upon them so they bought fruit from the gaily decorated stall of a pathside vendor. In winter, mid-morning, the wide paths through the park were sparse of sightseers. Nikki took Bustillo's arm as the deer nudged them with wet noses.

Further into the park Chieko and Graham Leach were acting similarly. They had been there for some time. Chieko had bought some oranges for the deer but she knew how to feed them to make them show proper respect. Holding an orange high out of reach she would bow gracefully from the hip and the deer, once realising that food depended on it, would place one foreleg out and bow back, head sweeping down. It was a tradition that some foreigners didn't understand. While she was doing this Leach was scanning the park. If it was true that Bustillo came here he would find him. It was difficult to equate with seeing Bustillo in Tokyo but that might have been a brief visit. Anyway, there was no other course, no matter how futile it might prove to be.

It was almost two hours before Leach saw Bustillo coming down the main central path with a youngish Japanese girl on his arm who was dressed in a short Western skirt with a long sleeved jacket. He was restless and tired but remembered thinking her legs were nice and that she was agitated, before he saw the American. Immediately he turned his face. His pulse rate rose. Now what? He would have to follow and that meant coping with Chieko. He started mentally to examine some plausible lies when Chieko straightened.

His action had not been lost on her. His own behaviour forced her into untypical stealth. She almost despised herself as she surreptitiously glanced where she had seen him look before he turned so sharply away. *Nikki Miyoto*. It had been three years since she'd last seen her. They had both been on the social circuit. Then Nikki had dropped out. There had been a scandal about a couple of years ago. Drugs, she recalled. It was about that time that her own father had dropped the more than nodding acquaintance he'd had with the older Miyoto. That had meant nothing to her. She was used to the jealousies and back-stabbing of businessmen.

Chieko's immediate reaction following her initial surprise was to do what her husband had done. She wasn't a snob. Moneywise the Miyotos were wealthier than her own family. But the drug scene frightened her. She had only to look at Nikki now to see how it had ravaged her. She felt sorry then but they'd never had much in common. Nikki had never cared for the old traditions; she wasn't true Japanese. More than half American. About to obey her impulse she noticed the tall man with her.

There was something about Bustillo that arrested her and then she belatedly realised that it was he whom Graham had noticed, not Nikki. She turned to her husband who was tickling a deer's ear and studiously facing the other way.

"I've seen an old friend. I must speak to her."

He followed the direction of her eyes and when she turned back she couldn't believe that he could lose so much colour in the time.

"She doesn't look your type, Chieko, we really haven't time."

Chieko had dreaded confirmation of her surmise and he'd just given it to her. "She's seen me. I really must speak to her. Come I'll introduce you."

"No. Chieko, don't go."

He was pleading. He had never done that before. For reasons she could not explain, Chieko went forward to meet the couple.

Jimmy Bustillo had spotted them both before they had seen him. He gave no sign, said nothing to Nikki, and he was surprised when a little later Nikki was waving to the exquisite beauty in the peach coloured kimono. She came towards them with the grace of an empress, length of pace restricted by her dress but so straight, head held so well. She smiled, giving a little bow when she'd almost reached them. Bustillo felt the tired Nikki straighten beside him and noticed she inclined her head with a dignity she may once have worn well.

The two women gave a perfunctory embrace and Nikki introduced Chieko to Bustillo. He felt exposed as Chieko's warm eye encompassed him. There was more than normal interest in her quiet examination and he wondered if Leach had told her anything. She had the same effect on him as she'd had on Nikki. Suddenly he was drawing himself up from an easy posture as if her image would shatter if he didn't. Instinctively he knew that she would always draw the best out of people. Concurrent with the thought was the almost certainty that she was immensely vulnerable.

The women talked of old times and Bustillo was aware that Chieko was dragging it out deliberately. One thing emerged: Chieko was married to her escort and their name was Leach. As they chatted it became clear that there was little between them, yet Nikki, too, was willing to prolong the contact; she had virtually no real woman friends outside of drugs and sex. It was a temporary life line, a link with what might have been. He stood and listened and the deer gathered round trying to snatch the bag of fruit Nikki still carried. Without looking directly at him Bustillo noticed that Graham Leach had found refuge in a bunch of deer. He well understood why Leach hadn't joined them. Why had his wife come over? The answer came at an unexpected moment.

At last one of the deer got sufficient grip on Nikki's paper bag to tear it. The fruit dropped out and started to roll away from her with the deer chasing. In a reflex action she laughed and ran after a solitary orange with two deer chasing her. Chieko turned round to Bustillo and said in English, "Why do you want to kill my husband, Mr. Warton?"

Bustillo was so startled that he couldn't reply. He shook his head, trying to find the right words and before he could sort them out Nikki came running back having lost her fight for the orange. It was a cue to break up. He couldn't answer her with Nikki there and Chieko seemed to realise it. Instead he said, "Perhaps you and your husband will have dinner with us one evening. Where are you staying?"

Chieko smiled. "That is kind of you. I'm not sure how long we'll be here. Perhaps we can give you a ring?"

Bustillo appreciated the neat twist. He had betrayed himself by making no reply to her. Nikki helped him out. "We're moving around too much, Chieko. But if we both stay on here we're bound to meet up again."

Chieko inclined her head. Bustillo could see she wasn't happy. Protecting her whereabouts was a giveaway, just as their own had been. As they watched her move off Nikki said bitingly, "You can't take your eyes off her."

"If I told you why, you wouldn't believe me." He took her arm, leading her slowly forward after Chieko.

"Try me."

Bustillo shook his head, wondering what to do. "You know her. Where would she stay?"

"Is she more your type, then?"

"Cut it out, Nikki. She's a married woman."

She looked up at him in disbelief. "That sounds real corny coming from you. The bottle and bed man. Since when have you had scruples?"

He took his hand away from her arm. That's what the whole gig was about: scruples. "Where would she be likely to stay?" he insisted.

"Not a doss house. Her daddy brought her up properly."

"Don't sneer, Nikki. You blew your chance." He hadn't meant to be so cruel. "I'm sorry, but I don't like bitchiness."

"At one of the best hotels. I don't think her father has property down here but it's three years since I saw her. It was strange that her husband didn't come over. Is he American?"

"I don't know." He wondered at the lie.

"Why are we following them?" Jealousy disguised the obvious.

It was a subconscious action. He had to find out where they were staying. He stopped. There were other ways. "I didn't realise we were. Anyway this is the main route to the shrines."

"Oh, she'll love that. Very traditional, our Chieko. Jimbo, let's go home. I've had enough of this place."

It might be better if they did. Leach might expect him to follow. "Okay." They turned off. "How did a girl like that marry a punk like him?"

"It seems to worry you." Nikki was bitter.

"It does. But not in the way your jealous little mind is figuring it out. What would someone like that do with someone like me except to dump him on the garbage heap?"

She turned on him furiously. "Is that where you are when you're on top of me? On the garbage heap?"

People turned as he tried to pacify her. "For Chrissake, I wasn't equating you to me. Stop twisting my words. Cut it out."

They quarrelled all the way back to the villa. It was not until she cooled down that Nikki wondered more about Chieko's husband.

*   *   *

Leach was furious at Chieko going off. It left him alone and embarrassed and ostensibly bad mannered in not going with her. He dare not meet Bustillo face to face. What on earth would they say to each other? Equally, when Chieko had returned to him he had somehow to arrange to follow Bustillo, get his car number, track him down in some way. Chieko seemed calm as she rejoined him. Then straight out of the blue she said, "That's the man Warton."

It was like an explosion in his head. He had split seconds in which to make a convincing answer.

"What on earth made you say that?"

"I saw you looking at him. I called him by that name."

"*You what?*"

"I asked him why he wanted to kill you."

He looked round. Bustillo and his girl had branched off. He sat on a bench and Chieko joined him. How did he start? "And what did he say?"

"I surprised him too much. Before he could reply Nikki had come back from chasing an orange."

"At least you had the sense not to say it in front of the girl. How can you think he is Warton?"

"He didn't deny it."

"Chieko, darling, what on earth has come over you?"

"Do you imagine I don't know why you didn't join us; why you didn't want me to go?"

"I don't know what you're saying. I don't understand any of this, least of all you." He twisted on the seat. Bustillo and the girl were still in sight. "If you're sure of what you say I must follow them. I must find out where he's hiding."

"Why? I thought we wanted to get away from him."

151

"He's *here*, don't you see? If you're right he must have followed us."

"But you didn't recognise him."

"I wasn't looking. I can see now that you must be right. It must be him."

"I think you knew he was here. That was why we came."

He stared at her, astounded. She'd been thinking it all out while he thought he was fooling her. "What a monstrous suggestion. From you of all people. My wife."

She had gone so far she couldn't retract. Chieko was numb. She was on her own and she was challenging her own husband. It was almost too much to bear. "I don't know, Graham. I am beginning to think there is much I don't know."

"I've explained all that. There are things I can't tell you. I thought you understood." If he didn't move soon he'd lose Bustillo. He hadn't handled Chieko too well. Not this time. "Look, Chieko, I must get after him. It will help to know where he's staying. I might find out how long he's likely to be here."

She had one more surprise for him. "There's no need. The Miyotos had a villa here. Nikki is the sort of girl who must have privacy. She's a drug addict; not inclined to stay in hotels, I think." She wasn't sure why she told him or where it was all leading but she had to see it through now. One way or the other she had to get the truth no matter how painful it might be.

"That's splendid. Why didn't you tell me?" It was difficult to see her angle; one moment accusing, the next, helpful.

She turned round in the direction Bustillo had taken. They were no longer in sight. It puzzled her that Bustillo wasn't trying to follow them. "He didn't strike me as a man who would kill," she said.

Time to lay it on again but not too thickly. She was more astute than he had imagined. "Don't let that fool you," he said listlessly. "Looks don't mean a thing."

She gazed thoughtfully at him, numbed and upset, and considered with some difficulty that he might be right.

They continued with their sightseeing with little communication. Neither particularly noticed the absence of conversation, both were firmly tied to their own disturbing thoughts. When they finally returned to the hotel he asked the question he'd been dreading to ask. "You didn't tell him we're staying here, did you?"

"Oh, Graham. With the man threatening to kill you?"

He wasn't sure how she meant it. While she bathed before

dinner he turned up the Miyotos' telephone number, made a note of it and the address of the villa. He had to get Bustillo tonight before he himself was located.

*   *   *

"Is that the man who's looking for you? *Chieko's husband?*"

"There was no point in holding out. "Yes."

"Then why didn't you say so, you bastard? Did you think I'd laugh about it? Be glad that a snooty bitch like Chieko had landed a bum?"

"*Cut it out.*" He was angry at himself for ever mentioning Leach to her at the same time accepting that she had a right to know. He wanted to find out where Leach was staying. Yet first he had to suffer a drinking jag with Nikki to quell the friction between them which it failed to do. Nikki had gone morose on him, perhaps having seen something of herself that was beyond recapture on meeting Chieko. She still resented his appraisal of her. At heart it was because she was beyond competing, could only grow worse quickly and he tried to be gentle with her. He had to wait until she was sleeping it off before he could use the telephone with safety. With a directory by his side he rang every important hotel in the area asking if the Leaches were staying there. He wanted to send some flowers. They wouldn't give a room number, promised to deliver if he would address them c/o the hotel, but he did discover that they were staying at the Miyako.

He'd been going easy during the drinking session. Now he poured himself a good slug, took it to the bedroom door to make sure that Nikki was all right. She was still sleeping, face relaxed, almost innocent in repose. He was baulking. He knew it. All he had to do was to ring up Donaldson at the British Embassy and that should take care of Leach. When it came to the point he couldn't do it and he couldn't convince himself why. He remembered how Chieko had looked. What would it do to her? It mattered. There was also the problem of where he would go from here. What Donaldson would do. There was a possible way out. He crept into the bedroom, opened a drawer, and took out his gun. Compromise could go only so far.

*   *   *

There was no compromise with Graham Leach. He bluntly told Chieko after dinner that he was going out to check that Bustillo was at the Miyotos' villa. He refused to take her on the ground that she would be in danger. A husbandly touch spoken

153

with conviction. When he left in the car they had hired she was aware that he'd taken the gun with him.

In the solitude of their suite, Chieko produced slacks and shirt. She rarely wore Western clothes of any description. They slimmed her down after the kimono showing her narrow hips. She put on a jacket against the cold, then rang down to reception for a taxi. She resented strongly the circumstances that were forcing her into such furtive action. Yet truth was all-important. Peace of mind had to be sought and at the moment she was suffering mental anguish. She might ruin their marriage or save it. At the moment it was disintegrating about her through lack of trust.

She went through the gardens to the front of the hotel where the taxi was waiting and instructed the driver to take her to the Miyotos' villa. She had one advantage, she knew precisely where it was.

12

"Nikki's gone." Kenji Miyoto glared at his father as though he was personally responsible.

"You've called round to tell me that, my son?"

"Bustillo was with her. I did some checking. I'm losing confidence in Susumu. Not that I ever had much. Anyway, the porter saw them leave yesterday. With baggage."

"Hadn't you better tell Susumu?"

"I did. He already knew but what annoys me is that he didn't tell us."

"His only obligation to us is to get rid of Bustillo."

"He should have had Nikki's place staked out."

"I believe he did until Bustillo was first located. He expected Bustillo to be killed that night."

"Yes. Well, there's something else he hadn't told us. Some characters visited Nikki yesterday morning. They didn't leave until well after Nikki. They looked flustered, angry and ran out of the building."

"I'm not certain that I see your point."

"I reckon they were Susumu's men sent to shake down Nikki. Bustillo was already there. Now either they didn't go into Nikki's or Bustillo took care of them. Susumu wouldn't want us to know a thing like that. Beaten twice by a man he didn't rate."

"You can't be sure, Kenji."

"Sure enough, Papa."

The older Miyoto stirred. "I'm sorry we ever entered into this. I think Bustillo told you the truth when he said we had nothing to fear from him."

"No. We were right." Kenji pulled a letter from his pocket. "I went through Nikki's place trying to get some idea of where they might have gone. I found this. It's addressed to the British Embassy and there's enough information in it to rate a full-scale Government enquiry into our affairs. This could destroy us completely."

"Why the British Embassy? Written by Bustillo?"

"I guess so. I don't know which is his right name." He passed the letter over. "It's signed 'Warton'."

"Warton?" Fujio read the list of notes, stunned by the shock of what he saw. Kenji had been right. Bustillo had spied. Why to the British Embassy? Donaldson? Had he met the man at any of the functions? He couldn't recall. Warton came more easily. He rose slowly, reaching for the *Nippon Sun* in its bamboo rack. His intensity froze Kenji who sensed that he had touched something off.

"Warton. Read that if you haven't already." Fujio passed the paper over with shaking hand.

Kenji read, then crumbled the newspaper into a ball and threw it down. They stared at each other in silence. It was Kenji who said, "It answers a lot, Papa. All the inconsistencies."

"There was always something odd about Bustillo. Now we know he was telling the truth. He couldn't have betrayed us without giving himself away. We were safe and couldn't accept it."

"He could have blackmailed us."

"But he didn't."

"We were right to go for him," Kenji insisted strongly.

"Yes, we were. Though for the wrong reasons. If this man is caught here he will use this knowledge on our own authorities as some form of defence or deal perhaps to seek asylum. This letter proves it." Fujio waved it, then put it carefully in his pocket. "You realise we are not the only ones after him? We had better be the first to reach him."

"Kyoto. Where would they stay there?"

"Where would you stay if you were Nikki?"

"The villa? It's somewhere to start."

"Ring Susumu. Tell him what we think."

"To hell with Susumu. Let's handle it ourselves."

"Kenji, listen to me carefully." Fujio had raised his voice unusually high. It was so unlike him that Kenji waited.

"We have already paid Susumu half. Why dirty our own hands? Let *him* take the risks." Fujio bent to pick up the ball of newspaper. "There is a much better reason even than that. This article was written by Tadashi Fujuda. Tadashi is a friend of both Nikki and Bustillo. We now think Bustillo is Warton. Do you think Tadashi would betray his friend so blatantly?"

"What are you suggesting, Papa?"

"The article was put in for a purpose. Let us go by all means. But as spectators, not executioners. There is more to this than we realise. Ring Susumu and tell him where we think Bustillo might be. No more than that."

"Okay. I'll ring the airport to get the Cessna ready. I'll fly us down to Osaka tonight." He was better when active. He picked up the telephone and turned to see his father toss the ball of newspaper into a basket. "I'll tell you this much, Papa. If we're right about Bustillo being at the villa we're not going to give the second lot of shares to Susumu."

His father did not answer. It was impossible to judge whether his present attitude of deep concern was due to Kenji's last assertion or to the dreadful state of their affairs.

*   *   *

Bustillo was eating a snack meal at the time he heard the car coming up the long winding drive. Nikki was up but in a strange mood and she would not eat with him. Bustillo heard the increase of revs as the driver changed down. He signalled Nikki to get back into the bedroom. She went as far as the door while he turned the main lights off, leaving one side lamp on. He signalled Nikki again but she didn't fully obey him until he drew his gun and backed against the wall by the window. She wanted to tell him to take care but her moodiness prevented her.

Whoever was approaching was making no secret of it. Bustillo circled the window to avoid his shadow falling on it then slipped into the darkened hall. He pulled back the letter-box flap and peered through it. It was completely dark outside but he saw something of the treeline, and, below, filtering through the foliage, full beam headlamps. As the vehicle rounded an upper bend the lights flashed across the front of the house. Bustillo drew back but kept the flap open.

The car swung in front of the house and pulled up. Someone climbed out and fiddled with money. Bustillo clearly heard the rustle of notes and the clink of coins. It was too dark to distinguish anyone except that the shadowed figure was small. The car then drew away to complete the erratic circle of the drive and Bustillo's hand crept up to the porch light switch. He was still bending, looking out gun in hand. The figure turned to ring the bell as Bustillo pressed the switch and eased his gun into the aperture, eyes just above it. The narrow face that sprang into the light was startled but if he was armed he made no move.

Bustillo swore. Tadashi. He bawled through the letter box, "You nearly got your guts blown out." He opened the door and the journalist came in slowly.

"You're touchy," Tadashi said, noticing the gun. "I couldn't have arrived more openly."

"You might still have blasted me. Come in, Tashi. See if you can get some sense into Nikki."

Tadashi preceded Bustillo into the lounge, immediately noting the bottles and glasses. The scene surrounding his two friends hadn't changed much, only its venue. Nikki rushed out to greet him, flinging her arms round his neck and kissing him hard to punish Bustillo.

Bustillo, understanding, smiled faintly. "How did you find us?" he asked as Nikki broke away.

"Where else would you be? I've known about the Miyotos a long time. If you're down here with Nikki this is number one try."

Bustillo poured them all a drink. He put the gun back in his hip pocket and remained standing up as the others seated themselves. "What do you want, Tashi?"

"That's no way to speak to a friend." Nikki was still trying to get at him.

"I thought I might help. Seeing you waving a gun convinces me that I can."

Bustillo went to the side of a window, trying to see out into the grounds. "You *can* help," he said. "Get Nikki out of here. Keep her away for a day or two."

"She's in danger?"

"So are you if you stay."

"I'm not leaving. This is *my* family house." Nikki defiantly poured herself another half tumbler of spirit.

"Tashi, if you found us so easily so will the others. I'm saying no more, so don't try to jump a story until I'm ready."

"If you're killed, the only story I'll have will be murder."

"If I'm killed Nikki can give you a letter to pass on. The contents partly concern the Miyotos but it's addressed to a man who might give you another story, the big one, if you try hard enough. I'm stretching a point for you. But in return get her out of here. If you don't we might all be killed."

Nikki looked up strangely, then rose and went into the bedroom taking her drink with her. When she returned her glass was empty and she replenished it quickly. She looked sick and worried.

"How important is the letter, Jimbo?"

Her tone made him uneasy. "Have you lost it?"

"I can't find it. I think I must have left it at my apartment."

He wasn't angry with her. What was the use? He'd remember some of the detail if he tried. "Nikki, you'll have to go. Leaving the letter makes it imperative. Someone will find it and it will lead them here. Don't ask questions, just pack a bag and go with Tashi."

Tashi rose. "There's a small hotel at Otsu where we'll get in. Where's the phone?"

"No. I'm not damn well going. This is my home."

Bustillo crossed the room and snatched the drink from her. "Pack a bag."

"I'm staying here. Why don't you tell Tashi someone else is after you?"

He restrained his rising temper, pleaded with her with his eyes to keep her mouth shut. Her obduracy was partly due to not wanting to be separated from him and partly caused by drink and drugs. He had to get through to her quickly. Behind him Tadashi was already telephoning. Bustillo pointed to him. "Do you see Tashi arguing? You know goddam fine that I'd clear out if it would help. It might've done earlier, but now it's too late. This is where they'll pitch up and if I'm not here they'll pull your finger nails out to find out where I've gone."

"Or worse," said Tadashi feelingly over the top of the phone.

Still not convinced Bustillo bawled at her. "Listen, you silly bitch, you left the letter for them to find. It makes all the difference."

Nikki backed to the wall, screaming at him. "Why don't you fight them instead of always running away? We could get help."

He tried to grab her wrist but she pulled away. "Is that what you want? Go out in a blaze of glory? Get it over quick?"

"Fight them. Stop running." She stood against the wall, fists clenched tight in front of her face as if to ward him off.

He softened his tone. "I'll tackle it my way. Be a good girl. Pack a bag before it's too late."

"Oh, Jimbo, you're committing suicide, do you know that?"

"Come on, Nikki."

"Are you ashamed of what you've done?"

"I'm not ashamed of anything I've done. It has no bearing."

159

Tadashi had finished his call and was listening carefully to their exchange. Bustillo was aware of it, careful not to say too much.

"Don't make me go, Jimbo. I can help you."

"You already have. And you can help some more by going with Tashi. Just for a day or two. I'll follow." He turned to Tadashi for help.

Tadashi said, "They've already tortured me, Nikki. It wasn't pleasant. You're not strong enough to stand it, believe me. Jimmy knows what he's doing."

"If you hadn't come he wouldn't have got rid of me."

There was truth in it. Bustillo knew that if she'd gone alone she would have returned. He reached for one of her wrists.

"Come on, honey. I'll help you. I'll be along."

She allowed him to take her into the bedroom and between them they packed a bag.

Tadashi said, "I suppose you have transport here?"

"There's a car in the garage." Bustillo tossed over the keys. "Look after Nikki."

"Haven't I always?"

"I've landed her in this. Just keep an eye on her for me. And Tashi, thanks for your restraint. It'll pay off."

Nikki left the bedroom with a case which Tadashi took from her. She had combed her hair and applied a little make up but she had failed to hide the pinched flesh under her eyes. Bustillo kissed her lightly. "Look after yourself. And don't worry about me."

"Don't let them walk all over you, Jimbo. Ring us if there's trouble." Tears were trickling down her face.

When they'd gone Bustillo was grateful for Tadashi not seizing on Nikki's slip. The journalist had made no serious attempt at obtaining information and that was a measure of friendship difficult to assess to the full from a man whose sheer professionalism must have been crying out for answers.

Bustillo unhooked the cans from the door. With Nikki gone he could change his tactics without having to worry about her. He did a quick check of the villa, locked all but the front door. He made some coffee and found a vacuum flask in a picnic basket in the kitchen. He humped pillows under the bed blankets to give an impression of a body, took the top blanket off and draped it round his shoulders like a cape. He left the house with the flask and his gun.

For a few minutes he stood in the porch. The air was as sharp as

160

iced water, clear and tangy, catching the back of his throat. His vaporised breath formed a diaphanous cloud in front of his face. There was a moon low down, giving the distant mountain snow a metallic tint. Between the trees the black cavity of Lake Biwa lay still, with a solitary light moving slowly across it as a boat came in. The cold purity of the dark scene cleared his head.

He went silently down the wooden steps. Moving over to the grass edge of the drive he walked along it, feeling the strain in his legs after a while as he resisted the pull of some of the more acute slopes. It would be easy to allow himself to break into a run but momentum would be difficult to stop.

The villa was well isolated by virtue of its huge grounds but there were other dwellings around on the slopes both sides of the valley and at times he could see their distant lights cutting out and re-appearing as if *they* were moving and not the foliage in a stiffening cold breeze.

It was a long walk down to the drive entrance. There were gates that were kept permanently open and Bustillo wondered why they had been installed at all. At this lower level the light on the lake had disappeared and the trees had grown taller, towering over him, whereas before he had been able to see the sky strip above their heads.

He turned left at the main earth road at the bottom, following the serpentine line of the perimeter of the grounds until he found a satisfactory observation post. He made himself as comfortable as possible against a rising shrubbery which concealed his back and left him unfettered in front. He sank against the earth banks, pulling his blanket closer and curling his feet under him for warmth. The real quietness of the night struck him then. First making certain that he could see the gap at the gates, a streak of grey against the black, he unscrewed the flask and poured himsef a steaming coffee. He had no idea how long he might have to wait, but it would happen tonight. As he sipped the coffee he wondered at the change in him that had suddenly preferred it to hard liquor. Perhaps, he reflected, even tawdry lives were worth an effort.

The car came up the main road, feeling its way as it slowed then accelerated again. At first Bustillo heard rather than saw it, sounding like a tank approaching in the clear air. The noise reminded him of Chile, of the tanks and arms and bloodshed he'd seen there; of his part in it. He was sickened as he briefly recalled the days of murder and double cross. Sight, smell and sound.

They could all play their part in vividly triggering a memory and just for a second or two, a labouring car engine did that to him. He clutched the blanket, swallowed what was left of the coffee in the flask lid then screwed it back on.

The dipped headlights floated in the gloom. They shadowed the hollow of the road, exaggerating its surface into unmanageable craters. The car came straight on, the driver using his gears badly as he took the rise towards the drive entrance. Bustillo pulled his gun out then folded the blanket round him again. The car was about a hundred feet away, partially screened by trees and shrubs olive green under the lights. It passed the gates by some yards, then pulled up and reversed back to the drive entrance. There was the murmur of voices. The car used the drive entrance to reverse into then sped back towards Kyoto.

Had anyone got out? Bustillo hadn't heard a door bang above the rough edge of the engine. He pushed himself forward on to his knees to get a better view. All he could see were the twin rear lights of the car before they sank into a dip of the road. The breeze was faintly rustling leaves but he could hear nothing else. Slowly he straightened until he was standing, knowing that the height of the terrace behind him would conceal his shape.

Someone was standing in the middle of the driveway. It was just a small dark shape and at first he thought Tadashi must have returned. The figure was too distant to identify and in the darkness he couldn't see all its outline. It started to move up the drive treading so lightly that he couldn't hear the footsteps. When it disappeared round a bend he left his post and cut through the shrubs. He came out onto the drive behind the figure because it was sticking to the middle of the drive.

An unlikely killer. The thought flashed into his mind. Yet the movements were furtive if uncertain. He followed, keeping close to the edge ready to dive into the bushes. The distant sound of another car reached him and the figure ahead stopped. Immediately Bustillo dropped into a crouch. The figure turned, looked back down the drive then dived into the shrubbery. Bustillo turned off the drive and followed the sounds.

As the car drew nearer it covered all other sounds. Bustillo kept moving, speeding up as he took advantage of the overriding noise. He could no longer be sure whether the figure was moving or stationary so he halted every few seconds, trying to pick up a trace. Bustillo judged the car had reached the gates when it stopped. He could see the milky spray of headlight reflection but no more. The tick over of the engine was quite clear and he cursed it as it drowned everything else.

Again the drive was used as a turn round, the change of tyre crunch quite distinct between the road and the drive. The car moved off back down the hill then stopped. The engine was switched off and the silence was hard on the ears. Bustillo stopped moving and, it seemed, so had the figure ahead of him. There was the slightest sound of a footfall below him but it wasn't repeated. With sickening realisation Bustillo saw that he was now caught between the two of them.

He started to move again in the direction of the villa but to circle round to home on where he thought the first person to be. The alarms he had set were further up but it was something to bear in mind as he climbed the slope. The soil under his feet was hard from the descending frost and the moon was creating diamanté patterns as crystals formed on the upper leaves. He continued with the intermittent approach of a few feet at a time. He saw vaporised breath like a miniature cloud long before he saw the figure.

It came up like a puff of steam from a cactus just ahead of him. He was crouched at the time and it was sheer luck that there was a triangle of sky visible through the leaves and that the breath had filtered into the gap.

He was too near. Yet he couldn't see the actual person. He had to move to get sight of him. He worked his way round in a difficult, stomach cramping crouch. It had been a long time since he'd done this and a good many bottles of bourbon had passed his lips meantime. He had to stop when his breathing became too heavy. When his breath was steadier he pulled the blanket from his shoulders and pushed it carefully under a bush. The cold stung him but he could move more freely. He continued on at a snail's pace. Only a few feet separated him from the hidden figure near the driveway.

He edged sideways like a baboon on all fours, head held high, nostrils dilated. He was about to move again when he saw the figure by a bush. It was so still that he wasn't at first sure. Then it moved, an arm coming up slowly, and he could just see the paleness of a face. He appeared to be sitting on his haunches.

Bustillo looked around, found a spot where he could lose himself in the shadows, and squatted behind the other. Keeping his head down he waited.

The second figure came up the edge of the drive, half bent

from the effort but it gave Bustillo no satisfaction to know that his hunter was little better conditioned than himself. As he stood catching his breath, his outline fairly clear, Bustillo was satisfied that it was Leach. He pushed the safety-catch of his gun forward and crept a pace or two nearer the first figure. As Leach moved off again Bustillo saw his gun as his arm came forward. If Leach stuck to the drive he would avoid the alarms. An amateur's approach but it could work for him.

The figure in front of Bustillo moved to follow Leach but Bustillo moved faster and silently. He placed his gun against the back of the head and murmured, "One move and you're dead."

The intake of breath was so sharp that he quickly placed a hand over the mouth. Leach stopped. He had heard something. Bustillo, his arm round the figure, hand over mouth, gun to head, whispered right into the ear. "Keep absolutely still." The figure was trembling, the jaw juddering with fright. Under his forearm he could feel a softness that could only be a woman's breast. Jesus. He had to wait for Leach to move off again before he could force the head round. Two terrified eyes stared up at him. Chieko Leach. *Operating with her husband?*

"Keep still," warned Bustillo again. "I'll only harm you if you're stupid." He had to keep his voice so low that his lips touched her ear. Her tremor had quietened. She occasionally juddered but he still kept his hand over her mouth and the gun against her. She hadn't struggled at all. The shock had probably immobilised her but she was coming round fast. He whispered, "If I take my hand away will you promise not to scream? Nod if you agree. If you scream I will have to shoot you. You understand?"

Chieko nodded. Bustillo carefully removed his hand. He had been holding her very tightly over the mouth to prevent her biting him. She rubbed her face while he took the gun away from her head but still pointed it at her. "I'm sorry." It was ludicrous. "I thought you were a man."

She nodded again as if understanding but her mind was on her husband. Turning away she scanned the drive. Leach was barely visible as he still hugged the verge, but he was higher up now.

"We've got to move," said Bustillo. "Keep nice and quiet and just ahead of me. I'll be watching you all the way."

"Why do you want to kill him?"

He barely heard her. "Kill him? If I'd wanted to kill him, I could've picked him off when he was outlined just now. You've got it the wrong way. Now move. Be careful."

Chieko moved off ahead of him, low as she had been before. Her jacket caught on a spine of a monkey tree, she pulled, instead of falling back to unhook it. The resultant noise was loud enough to make Leach spin round and fire. Bustillo flung himself at Chieko but she was already falling as he struck her.

13

IT WAS DOUBTFUL IF she recognised the plop of the gun as a shot. But there could be no mistake about the rush of a speeding bullet through foliage. It was like a scythe moving at fantastic speed, tearing, rupturing and finally smashing into the sap of a huge cactus.

Bustillo couldn't tell whether the girl was hit or not. She lay panting, face down under him and he eased his weight away. Another shot ripped the leaves over his head. He called out, "Leach. For Chrissake, your wife is here. You might have hit her."

Two shots sliced through as Bustillo rolled. Chieko was still stretched out and he reached for her ankles, gently pulling her towards him. As quietly as he could he dragged her further into the shrubs while he heard Leach running lightly down the drive.

When he considered it safe to pause Bustillo eased the girl against the bole of a tree. "Are you hit?" She didn't reply. Her breathing seemed normal. "You sure you're okay?"

"He fired at us," she spoke listlessly, finding it impossible to believe.

Bustillo had pulled her up the slope at an angle to fox Leach. It would be a helluva job finding anyone in these grounds at night. But they couldn't stay there.

"He shot at us," Chieko repeated.

"Yeah. Well, maybe he didn't believe the bit about you being here. Did he know you were here?"

"No." She shook her head and Bustillo saw the reflection of tears.

He put his fingertips to her face. She was silently crying. Noticing her hand holding her side he slipped his own under her coat and felt the warm stickiness of blood. He had to get her out of here. Which was impossible with Leach roaming around with a silenced gun he was all too ready to use. He padded his handkerchief, lifted her blouse and placed it where the blood seemed thickest. "Hold it there. It might stem the flow."

She nodded again, not looking at him. She couldn't get over the shock of her own husband shooting her.

"I don't think it's too serious," he whispered.

"Are you leaving me here?"

"I've got to. Only for the moment."

"You're going to find Graham?"

"I must. Before he kills both of us."

"If I call to him he'll know that I'm here."

"He'll wonder what the hell you're doing with me. He's in no position to take chances."

She faced him then, unable to comprehend. There was no time for explanations. "Stay here," he said gently. "Don't try to move because he's not gonna know who it is and he'll fire. Okay? I'll be back."

He moved further away from the drive before cutting down hill. What the hell was she doing there anyway? He used his advance and pause technique, giving a little time at each listening post. Then, incredibly, he heard Chieko calling:

"Graham." Her voice floated over the trees, descending to the valley basin with hypnotic clarity. Again. "Graham. This is Chieko. I'm hurt."

Jesus. Did she realise she was setting him up? Bustillo got ready to follow any sound of Leach moving towards his wife.

After each call there was nothing. It was easy for Bustillo to see Leach's dilemma.

"I'm wounded, Graham. I'm bleeding. I'm alone but this man won't hurt you. He could have killed us both already."

The naïvety of it was incongruous in the darkness of a cold night with two armed men on the prowl. It was an appeal for purity of thought and motive. Bustillo was touched by its innocence and dismayed by its hopelessness. The effect on him was to listen intently for any move Leach might make. After two or three minutes of agonising waiting he started to crawl back up the hill aiming to get above Chieko's position.

The higher Bustillo went the nearer he was to his own alarms. To maintain essential silence his detour had been wider than he first intended. He took stock, tried to get his bearings then crept down to where he thought Chieko should be.

The only opportunity to listen was when he wasn't moving himself. A night flight took off from Osaka heading north-east, directly over their heads. Bustillo saw the pulsing wing and tail lights and the long golden bar of the cabin windows. Still low, he used its full throttled roar to cover a lot of ground. He wanted to finish on the higher ground above Chieko so that he might see Leach approach. When he stopped he realised he had lost direction.

He remained still, figuring it out, listening. Either Leach was not moving at all or he was doing so with skill. Bustillo reckoned the drive was to his left as he faced downhill. With its many twists and turns he couldn't know just how far. It was his only chance of sorting out direction. He took his time, making silence the main essential. Leach wasn't going to leave without killing him.

Direction in total darkness is impossible. It took him much longer than he had reckoned to reach the driveway. When he did he almost blundered on to it, the shrubbery just there, thick and crowding the edge. He flattened himself and crawled forward. Poking his head round a bush at ground level he saw that he was on the bulge of a wide bend. He saw too, the crouched figure of Leach on the fringe, some forty feet lower down.

It was movement that betrayed Leach. But Bustillo gave him full marks for silence. Bustillo watched. The difference between them was that he needed Leach alive and Leach wouldn't be safe while Bustillo was alive. It was an unfair equation with all the advantages with Leach who needed only one accurate shot.

There was little Bustillo could do while Leach was facing his way. He continued to lie flat until Leach, at last, moved into the bushes, for the first time making a faint rustle. Bending low Bustillo crept along to where he'd seen Leach disappear.

Bustillo was never more sensitive to a situation, never more careful. He was on all fours again, moving painfully slowly and straining every sense. Looking up, he could now identify the overhang of the tree where he'd left Chieko Leach must surely be there by now. The hairs on his nape rose. He stopped.

A move had to be made yet every instinct warned him to stay there. Gradually he flattened then stretched a hand towards a small cypress tree until his fingers touched the rough trunk. Keeping his head down he pushed. He didn't want to make a noise but to display movement. A sound like the soft withdrawal of a cork from a bottle came from his right. The whine of the bullet was just in front of him. He gave an audible groan withdrawing at once.

Chieko, who had quickly learned the sound of a silenced shot, called out, "Graham. Is that you?"

She had no place in any of this. Completely out of her element Chieko was complicating the death game between the two men. Leach didn't fall into the trap Bustillo had set. Maybe he thought there should have been more noise. A dead man would collapse without regard for silence and a wounded one would involuntarily move on impact. All Bustillo had done was to confirm that he was there. Leach didn't waste another shot and they were back to the waiting game.

Bustillo cursed himself for underestimating Leach. It had reverted to a game of nerves. Sudden death or the remainder of life in prison. Neither had reasonable choice. Yet it had to end for one of them. Bustillo moved in the direction of the shot. Leach wouldn't be there now but it was all he could do. His knees were sore on the hard, scoured earth and his hands lacerated by roots and brittle shrubs. It must be the same for Leach. He kept going up and round and then finally down towards the tree again.

The sensation of imminent danger returned as he neared the tree. He stopped using his gun hand as a fourth leg and managed on three, the gun ever ready to fire. He saw Chieko first, just the dim shape of her against the tree as he'd left her. Her face was turned away from him, facing Leach who was part hidden by the tree and partly by Chieko. At first sight it seemed that she had two heads, two pale blobs on the dusky curve of her shoulders. He could risk getting a little nearer.

He couldn't threaten Leach with Chieko there. He'd have to get round the back of him. As if reading his mind Leach moved round to face Chieko, making his first apparent mistake with his back now turned to Bustillo: his head was close to his wife's, seemingly whispering to her as Bustillo had done. She was shaking her head in rebuttal.

Bustillo came down slowly, emerging into the small clearing around the tree. Chieko saw him and Leach was quick to notice that she had. Instead of turning to fire he swung round partly, using Chieko as a shield. He fired as Bustillo hurled himself across Chieko's front to create a blind side to Leach. And then Chieko was struggling with Leach's gun, crying out as she gripped the hot muzzle and from the pain in her side as she twisted.

Bustillo scrambled up and rushed forward raising his gun to

slam down on Leach. As Chieko still struggled with her husband Leach sensed his danger and rammed his wife's arm against the tree. As she screamed her legs thrashed out, tripped Bustillo who fell hard on his knees dropping his gun as he tried to save himself.

Bustillo quickly groped for his gun. Leach guessed what had happened and raised his own gun.

"Don't shoot. Graham, please don't shoot," Chieko screamed at him as Bustillo saw the end.

"Stand up." Leach was now holding the gun outstretched with both hands.

Bustillo scrambled up, accurately interpreted Leach's hesitation, and said bitingly, "Are you going to kill me in front of your wife?"

"Shut up, Warton, or I will."

"Then you'll have to kill her too."

It was clear then that Leach had already considered it. Without dropping his aim he said, "This man wants to kill me. I must finish him."

"No. He could have killed you before. He could have shot you a moment ago."

"If I don't kill him he'll destroy me one way or another." The whine of self justification was a vocal thread through the assertion.

Chieko looked up painfully at Bustillo. "Is this true?"

Bustillo shrugged. But for her presence it would be over now. They were two misty figures against a patchwork of varying dark hues. It was impossible to see clearly but he knew that Leach had sufficient outline of him not to miss from the very close range. "His death is the last thing I want. His destruction is a matter of terminology. *I* can't destroy him. I can merely put him in the way of justice."

"What has he done?"

"Open your mouth, Warton, and I'll fire. I won't have you telling her your filthy lies. Chieko, I must finish this." If he killed in cold blood he knew that it would be over with Chieko. He would have to kill them both. It was the only reason for the ridiculous exchange. He had to think it out.

"You're asking my permission?" Chieko had her hand at her side now. She started to get up slowly, using a leverage on the tree. The effort hurt her and her sharp breath was like a punctuation on the bizarre tableau.

"I am asking for your understanding. There is nothing else I can do."

"How can I understand cold-blooded murder, my husband?"
She had become icily formal with him. It was a pity at that time
that she hadn't a trace of his own deviousness for her tone probably
decided him. He had one more try.

"The issue is simple, Chieko. It's him or me. All I ask is your
silence."

"I cannot give it. It would be the end of us."

"Then it's the end of us anyway."

"If you shoot him I will fire this thing." Chieko held Bustillo's
gun out unsteadily. It was sufficient to shock Leach but he had to
make sure that she had the gun. What surprised both Bustillo and
Chieko was the way in which Leach swung round taking his gun
in an arc.

As he dived at Leach's legs, Bustillo thought, Christ, he's going
to shoot her. Leach fired as Bustillo smacked into him. There was
the crack of a shot from Chieko like the breaking of a rotten
branch. The flash from the unsilenced gun was the only colour in
the black scene. Bustillo kept his grip round Leach's legs and they
rolled down the slope crashing into bushes and mangling the
smaller shrubs.

Leach was trying to bring his gun down on Bustillo's head
which was tucked well in. They were stopped by a rockery which
jarred both men hard. Bustillo, knowing it was life or death
grabbed frantically at Leach's gun hand and caught the wrist. He
was taller and stronger but out of condition and Leach fought like
an alley cat, using nails, knees and elbows in a totally unprofessional
way that had Bustillo trying to cover himself from all angles.
Bustillo, who hadn't cared much whether he lived or died, found a
gallantry that was based on protecting Chieko. If he died, she
died. And all for this bastard who was trying to wrench his gun
hand free. Leach displayed the strength of his motive in the mad
way that he fought. He had never suffered physical combat before,
yet it was impossible to believe as he tried to gouge Bustillo's
eyes out.

Bustillo concentrated on getting the gun. Leach was moving
like a snake, continuous and viperish. He bit Bustillo's hand.
Bustillo brought his knee up sharply and was partially successful.
He closed his eyes as finger nails raked his face and then he
smashed Leach's hand against the rocks. It was good enough. A
disarmed Leach was a different proposition. Still holding Leach's
wrist he jerked back, pulling the two of them away from the area
of the gun. They rolled again and then Bustillo waded in with

both hands. Leach's retaliation faded as Bustillo got on top and it was a while before Bustillo realised that he was punishing an unconscious man. He straddled Leach, lifted his head by the hair and hit the jaw, letting the head fall back.

For some time he was stooped over the body, head bowed, lungs rasping, one hand rubbing at his chest trying to quell the internal fire. His knuckles felt as if they were broken, the pain agonising. When he tried to rise he slumped down again, falling across Leach whose breathing he could barely hear. His knees hurt as he tried to crawl away and his shin was burning where Leach had run his instep down it. Even now his paramount thought was the gun. He could handle a disarmed Leach. He crawled away, groping, collapsing on occasion, and starting all over again. Searching around the earth by the rockery he found Leach's gun, rammed it into his waistband, then collapsed on to his back, sucking at the cold air, staring at an impartial moon and aware of a piquant scent rising from the shrubbery. He didn't want to move again.

The cold began to cool him before he moved. He started to shiver, his teeth chattering. He needed a drink. A bottle. When he heard someone moving he thrust up on both elbows dreading that it might be Leach again. He doubted that he had the stamina to go through another struggle.

It was Chieko. She was roaming aimlessly, the shock of what had happened almost too much for her. She stumbled, recovered and started to wander away.

"Over here," called Bustillo. It took an effort to raise his voice. "It's okay. He's out." He tried to get up and his legs would barely hold him. It was difficult to believe that he'd let himself go so much. He wanted to retch but somehow restrained himself in an old-fashioned regard for the girl. He staggered towards her and her own condition was little better than his. He could feel the tightness down his face where the runnels of blood had dried under the styptic chill of air. The cold was really cutting through him now.

Chieko came towards him in a daze and he put out a hand to steady her, noting the blank expression of shock. "Is he dead?" she murmured, and even after what she had suffered it was clear that he was still important to her.

"Unconscious only. I've got the gun."

She lifted a hand and he saw that she was still carrying his own gun. Gently he removed it from her fingers.

"I'll have to bind him. If I leave him to come round he'll come back at us somehow."

She made no sign of understanding. He held her shoulders.

"Stay here. I won't be long." Chieko, too, was shivering now but whether from cold or shock he didn't know. Taking his thick cardigan off he draped it round her shoulders. "Sit down."

Without the cardigan it was like being naked to the waist. Somewhere, within a hundred yards in any direction from where he stood was the blanket. There was no hope of finding it. It took him longer than he'd allowed to find Leach but when he did the Englishman hadn't moved. Bustillo ripped off Leach's tie, already half off, rolled him over roughly and bound the hands behind his back. He searched the pockets, found the spare clip for the gun and two handkerchiefs which he tied together and then bound the ankles.

Chieko was standing where he'd left her. The cardigan had fallen from one shoulder but she had apparently not noticed. She stood with hands clenched in front of her, trembling from head to foot. He readjusted the cardigan, put an arm round her shoulders and said, "Come on. Let's get you back to the villa. We've got to get a doctor to look at that wound."

"No." The suggestion had been like a slap in the face to her. "No doctor."

"Someone's got to see it."

"It's not bad. You can do it. No doctor."

He didn't raise it again then. He knew the form, had suffered it himself. No doctor. No police. No publicity. So that her shame would remain her own. She was suffering much more than a flesh wound.

They found the driveway and started the slow, long haul up to the villa, pausing now and then for breath and because Chieko was feeling the pull of her wound. Bustillo made no objection to the frequent halts, he needed them. He helped her up the steps, into the lounge, flicking on the main lights as he passed. He helped her into a chair and she lay back, deathly pale, with eyes closed.

He poured a stiff brandy, taking a quick swig from a bourbon bottle himself. Before he could give her the drink he had to make sure it wasn't a stomach wound. "It'll be better on the bed with you lying flat." Time was important yet somehow he couldn't rush her.

She opened her eyes fractionally. "I must look at the wound," he said. He held out his hand and helped her up. She barely knew

173

what she was doing and he suspected that part of her was trying to shut out what had happened. She simply didn't want to face the overnight wreckage of her life. He helped her on to the bed, left her there while he quickly searched for a first-aid box, eventually finding one in a bathroom.

He thought she had fallen asleep but when he undid her shirt her eyes flickered not in alarm but in a bewildered attempt to recall what had happened, why a virtual stranger was pulling up her shirt. She made no effort to resist.

"I'll try not to hurt. You'll have to trust me." He had raised the shirt no more than was necessary in an effort to gain her confidence. The small breasts were left covered.

Chieko gazed up at him. Trust? Where had trust got her? Who was this man her husband wanted so desperately to kill? He was concentrating on her wound; the handkerchief had stuck where the blood had congealed.

"I'm sorry." He saw her wince, guessed some of what she must be thinking and was pleased that concentration on him was diluting her trauma. He swabbed the blood away from the wound with spirit. When it was cleaned up he could see the damage. "Can you turn on your other side?" He helped her over and he cleaned up the exit point. "You've been lucky. Straight through. Not much more than a graze." He smiled. It took an effort. All he wanted to do was to fall asleep on his feet. "I'm going to give it another cleaning then dress it. It should be cauterised. You really should see a doctor."

His accent was dissimilar to Graham's. Sometimes a turn of phrase struck her as different. When he had finished bandaging he pulled down her shirt, tucked it into her slacks. Then he bunched the pillows behind her and gently lifted her up. He handed her the brandy. "Better than a sedative. You need a lift not a knockout drop."

She sipped and spluttered and he apologised because the movement pulled at her wound. "What will you do with Graham?"

"I'm going to fetch him now. I can't leave him out there, he'll die from exposure."

"You really do want him alive."

"I don't want him at all. I'm saddled with him."

"And when he's here?"

"I can't let him take his time over another crack at me. I'll inform certain authorities and he'll be handed over."

She took a bigger sip of her drink and pulled a face as it stung her throat. "Why does Graham want to kill you so badly? What has he done?"

He was at the door looking back at the slim form of her. Curiosity and the brandy had raised some life in her eyes but she had been hit very hard. All she was now trying to do was to find a little sense in the tragedy that had struck so violently.

"When I get back I'll try to give you an answer." He closed the bedroom door behind him because there was a phone call he had to make first. He checked his watch; one-thirty a.m. Time had stretched out unbelievably. He rang the British Embassy in Tokyo. The number buzzed out but there was no response. He tried twice more holding on for long periods. No answer. He was so angry then that he almost threw the telephone across the room. There had to be someone on night duty. He cursed the inadequacies of the embassy staff and of Donaldson in particular. There was no other known way of contacting him.

Grabbing his cardigan he went outside. The girl complicated everything. Having got rid of Nikki he was now landed with Chieko. He had to get her out but Tadashi had taken the car. He had previously searched the villa for a flashlamp but had found one with dead batteries. He went out into the dark with pistols in his waistband and a box of matches in his pocket.

It was easier going downhill but reaction had set in and he was nervous of every shadow. By the time he swung into the shrubs he was reluctant, almost decided to leave Leach there to survive if he could. He made no effort to conceal his approach and it was the mistake of a weary man.

Leach, who had come to with a swollen and aching jaw, had wriggled towards the rockery and was already rubbing his wrists against the sharpest stone he could find. The movement helped with his upper circulation and took his mind off the cold. He had planned and schemed and cheated for far too long to let one man destroy him. There was no limit to what he would do to safeguard himself. There never had been.

When he heard Bustillo he worked harder, then realised that he would not be free in time. With sheer strength of desperation, aided by a pathological murderous intent, he pushed himself up the rough face of the rockery until he was almost standing, then rolled and twisted so that he was on a higher terrace of rocks off ground level. With a similar effort he gained more height. His fanaticism pushed him far beyond his normal capability. The sound of the approaching Bustillo was all he needed to go yet

175

higher again. Then he was sick and could only lie still, for the moment defeated.

Bustillo's directional sense was fairly accurate. He reached the point where he'd left Leach and searched around, difficult even with night sight. Finally he had to use a match and had the sense to close his eyes as he struck it. The tiny flame gave surprisingly good range but beyond the bowl of visibility the blackness was more intense. There were signs of struggle, leaves and earth scuffed and scarred.

Leach had moved. There was no doubt of it. And a mobile Leach, even if hindered, was a dangerous man. Bustillo took his gun out. He searched, he struck matches, knowing that each time he did he was giving away his position. In between he reverted back to his silent routine and listened. He retraced his way back to the rockery, used more matches, but by this time Leach was prone on a higher terrace, hidden partly by height and rock shrubs.

Bustillo searched for twenty minutes, widening his circle and getting nowhere. Finally he went down the drive to the gates, out into the road and downhill for a hundred yards. Leach's car was still there. No keys. That meant he was still around. Bustillo didn't like it a bit yet there was no further point in searching. It could take hours and he needed light. He hid near the car and waited for another fifteen minutes.

He gave up because Leach was cunning enough to know this was all that was left for Bustillo to do. Chieko was still in the villa and Leach might make his way there. The odds were crazily against Bustillo again. Right now Leach held the initiative. With fading reserves Bustillo tried to run for the villa, sick at the thought of the danger to Chieko. Uphill all the way he kept moving, eventually losing himself in the pain of effort. When he staggered into the bedroom he leaned against the door frame barely able to get his breath.

Chieko was still on the bed, the only indication that she'd moved at all was the brandy glass still in her hands but now empty. "He's gone?"

Bustillo nodded, unable to speak. He came into the room like an asthmatic, sat on the dressing table stool. His breathing slowly eased. He managed, "He's still in the grounds. His car's there. I don't like it." His bloodied hands were resting on his splayed knees, his mouth still open for air.

"It's as well." Chieko twisted the glass round, looking at it as she added, "If you had brought him here I would have freed him at the first opportunity."

"*You'd have done that to a man who tried to kill you?*"

"Yes. It would be my duty. He is my husband."

"He would then have killed us both. He's still out there figuring out how he can do it."

"I would have held a gun on him. But I would have let him go."

"And if he had tried to take your gun?"

"I would have killed him. Then I would have killed myself."

Bustillo gazed at her. That was exactly what she would have done. Thank God the pain had gone from his chest. "He's not worth it," he said bluntly.

"Perhaps not. You've yet to tell me why."

"Yeah. Well, give me your glass. One thing we must do is to stay awake."

"I want nothing more to drink. Thank you."

"If I help you, do you think you can make it down to the car? We must get away from here."

"Graham knows you have the guns. He won't try anything with the odds so much against him."

"I wouldn't bank on it. It's only fair to tell you that there may be other visitors."

"Trying to kill you?"

"More professional than your husband. Look, if it's difficult I'll go down again and bring the car up. It's locked and the keys aren't in it or I'd have brought it back with me. There must be some tools in the garage that will help me force it open. Once open I can start it."

"You think it's too dangerous to stay here?"

"Much too dangerous."

"I don't want to go back to my hotel."

"You dare not. I think I know a place where you'll be safe until this is over."

"I will walk with you."

He helped her off the bed and took her into the lounge, seating her while he went down to the garage to find something with which to force the car window and a wire to short the starter to get it going.

Before they left Bustillo insisted that Chieko took one of Nikki's topcoats to keep the chill out. She didn't say anything but looked curiously at him, wondering at their relationship. He did not explain. They went down, keeping to the centre of the drive so that they would have at least a minimum of warning if Leach tried to jump them.

They didn't speak. Their pace was slow because Chieko couldn't hurry. She had gone into herself again, perhaps because of the possibility that her husband might be watching them at this moment and planning their destruction. Perhaps she saw no point in going anywhere. Bustillo, who knew a good deal about a lack of will to live, was desperately sorry for her. There was nothing he could say, no reassurance he could give. Her world was dead but not yet buried. The problems facing her were still ghastly and real. They wouldn't go away with the closing of eyes and the blessing of sleep. When she awoke they would still be there, unsolved and unthinkable.

He took her arm when she stumbled but she gave no sign that she was even aware of him as though the darkness was a backcloth to the events that had taken place and she could see it all again. As they neared the spot Bustillo tried to get her to move a little faster but her apathy was almost complete.

It didn't matter. The car had gone.

14

"WHERE WOULD HE GO?" Breath rose between them in two vaporous clouds. "*Chieko*. Where would he go?"

"I don't know. I thought I knew something about him. Now I realise I know nothing."

"He wouldn't go back to the hotel?"

"Not if he thought you would tell the police."

"He knows I won't tell the police. So he might go back? To collect some things?"

"You seem to know about each other very well." It was the only part of what he said that interested her. "I must know what he's done."

"I can't stand here and tell you. We're in a lonely spot without transport; patsies set up for target practice. You can't go back to the villa."

"It doesn't matter where we go."

"Can you continue walking? It's downhill most of the way."

"I'll do what you say. There is nothing else for me to do."

"Come on. It'll keep the circulation going."

The road flowed like a river taking the easiest course through a descending valley. There was high ground on either side, rising steeply on their left and more gradually on their right. The river effect was heightened by the moonglow on the frost-speckled surface.

They kept to the right hand side, their footsteps rising off both banks and multiplying into tiny echoes. Bustillo had no preconceived plan. The arrival of Chieko had thrown him. He couldn't leave her to walk on her own. The town was miles away. There would be other villas but they both had good reason for maintaining privacy. As they walked Bustillo remembered Nikki's words. "You're committing suicide. Just waiting to be killed." It was true. And he would have to go back. The running had to stop one way or the other. The loose ends couldn't flap indefinitely, they had to be tied, even if round his own neck.

"You can tell me now."

"Tell you?" He glanced down at her beside him, slight, lost, seeking answers to a nightmare. The regal beauty who still walked like an empress, still held her head high while she was falling apart internally.

"Where you met my husband?"

"In Brussels."

"What happened?"

"Do you want it straight?"

"Do you think the truth is worse than uncertainty?" It was the nearest she had come to flaring up.

"Okay. I guess you won't like it but you're entitled to know. Graham Leach is Colonel Harvey Sutherland. Does the name mean anything to you?"

Chieko frowned in the darkness. "I can't recall it."

"He was a British Military Intelligence officer with NATO. Eighteen months ago the whole western world heard of the name when he simply disappeared. Nobody knew where."

"*He's Graham?* That's impossible."

"They discovered that he'd been feeding information to the eastern bloc for at least two years. The whole of western strategy, strength, weaknesses, was blown sky high. Worse; many western intelligence men behind the curtain disappeared. For a certainty many were killed."

Chieko slowed, her hands coming up to cover her face. "No. No. No."

"I'm sorry. Leave it there."

She gripped his arm fiercely. "I must know it all." She didn't query it again. The way Graham had reacted to Bustillo and herself was enough.

"Can you walk a little faster?"

She tried but her pace slowed again and Bustillo started to worry. They would get nowhere at this rate but he didn't want to hustle her again with the pain and the problems she already had.

"Please go on."

"I'm concerned about our progress. I guess we've taken on too much. Would some of these villas be empty in winter? Perhaps we could hole up in one."

"Most of them around here will be empty. It's not residential."

The dwellings were widely separated, mostly out of sight in their own grounds but identifiable by gates and name posts.

"I'm all right. I can keep walking," Chieko protested.

"I know you can but there's no need."

It was another two hundred yards before they reached the next set of gates. It meant going uphill again and Bustillo suggested to Chieko that she wait at the gates for him while he explored but she wouldn't hear of it. The suggestion turned out to be a drastic form of therapy but it forced her thoughts outside herself. They were lucky. The villa was not so far up the hill as the Miyotos. And it was considerably smaller. There were shutters over the windows, which looked hopeful. Bustillo went round it while Chieko huddled on the wide porch. Once satisfied that it was empty Bustillo broke off one of the rear shutters by perseverance and sheer brute force. He smashed a window, unlatched it and climbed in. The outer doors were all mortice-locked so he had to help Chieko in through the window with the aid of a chair.

So much had happened to her in the last few hours that Chieko could see nothing strange in any of it. They were breaking and entering, a crime that would normally have appalled her but life had changed overnight and the transition was still continuing. Using matches Bustillo tracked down the fuse boxes and switched on, so that they at least had light which they restricted to one back room. He found blankets in a closet and they huddled down in easy chairs. He studied Chieko from across an open fire grate for which there was apparently no fuel. She was just a pale oval face stretched by fatigue and shock and cocooned by blankets.

"Why did Graham want to kill you?"

"That's better than the way you phrased it at Nara. He has to kill me because I'm one of the few people outside the Communist bloc who knows who he is. I could be the only one. The second time we met was in Havana. I didn't recognise him for some time but later it was clear that he'd had a face lift, he certainly looks younger, and had changed the colour of his hair. We got to know each other quite well, attracted by a joint gift for languages and a mistaken belief that each had gone over."

"Gone over?"

He studied the fireplace, fingers intertwining. "I was in the American Central Intelligence Agency. I was in Chile and dis-illusioned with the part we were playing there. The murder and treachery and pillage turned my stomach. As paymaster, I was organising the finance for a good deal of it. My options were limited. I wanted out but couldn't desert my colleagues. So a compromise was reached. I was rigged as a defector and finished up in Cuba broadcasting condemnation of the U.S.A. All by arrangement of the C.I.A. Where I went wrong was in failing to operate the other side of the arrangement. Once there I saw shades of Chile, the whole thing starting again. Not so easily perhaps but that was the ultimate intention.

"So far as Leach is concerned I can only guess. I'm convinced he spied for money and not for ideals. In return he had an arrangement not to flee behind the Curtain, as many who have done so have since regretted it, but to have protection and time for him to rehabilitate in a place of his choice when safe to do so. Cuba was a safe halfway house and a good jumping off place."

"But Graham is a computer man." Chieko was clutching desperately.

"He was involved with computers a long time ago. Perhaps originally to interest himself on military retirement. That's how he got the information out. Second-hand computers were sold to the Russians from London via Brussels and Prague. The information was fed in during transit."

Chieko pulled her blankets closer. Bustillo saw her dismay and guessed at part of it. "Is he in computers here?"

Instead of answering she asked, "How can you be sure that it's the same man?"

"I can't reassure you, Chieko. You want me to give a measure of doubt. As we got to know one another we practised languages, Japanese in particular." Bustillo hesitated, then realised it would have to come out sooner or later. "He had a photograph of himself, a woman and two boys in his wallet. It was a link with the past. It fell out one day when he was pulling out some notes. I retrieved it and handed it back with barely a glance. But it was enough. I remembered him then, not at once, but gradually. I think he knew. It didn't matter too much so long as he thought we were on the same side."

Chieko didn't cringe but her lids drooped in anguish, her hands balled into small white fists. She made no reference to the possible invalidity of her marriage. "There seems little difference between you."

Bustillo had gone over it uncountable times. "I didn't betray anyone. I simply opted out of what they wanted me to do."

She looked up. "Yet you must have come here looking for him."

"I couldn't get out of Cuba on my own and I couldn't expect C.I.A. to help me when they had taken such pains to get me in." Bustillo gestured helplessly. "Leach disappeared months before I finally made it. The British got me out. They do a fair trade with Cuba, businessmen passing through. They knew about me. I'd worked in the East before and they believed that Sutherland had gone to Japan. They could use me without embarrassing themselves. I knew how he looked. Too many big ones had escaped the net from Britain. It would be good for morale to land one; show that their security network wasn't as sterile as the newsheets had claimed.

"They arranged my escape and funded me for a while. They had rigged me a work permit. Then I ducked out from under again. I just wanted out from all of them. They'd have found me soon enough but the chances are that they'd cut their losses or maybe had more faith in me than I had in myself."

Bustillo suddenly cocked his head, listening. He rose, went into the front room. When he returned he said, "A car. Racing up the valley. It's gone past." He moved to the shuttered windows, still listening. He looked round at her wryly, shrugged.

"I didn't see your husband until he shot at me a few nights ago. It was only then that I knew he was definitely in Japan and that I'd better tag him before I got a hole in my head. I knew for sure then that he knew that I could finger him."

"He shot at you?" It was barely a whisper.

"He missed by a fraction."

Chieko was staring at Bustillo as if transfixed. "I know the night it happened. I feel I should die from shame."

"Because he deceived you?"

"You have both deceived. Each other. Your employers. Graham is willing to kill me to continue a deception. You want him alive because the British might then help you to rehabilitate and perhaps persuade the Americans to leave you alone. You have something to gain from it, Mr. Bustillo. You are little different from him."

It was like a grenade exploding in his guts. This pale slip of a girl who had probably never had a devious thought in her head had now confronted him with his own problem. How could he explain the dirtiness of the game he was in, or justify it? He couldn't even justify it to himself. With dry mouth he tried: "My guilt was in not giving up something that became abhorrent. It's not a job you simply resign from. But I harmed no one. I broke a contract but nobody suffered because of it. I would have left your husband alone had he done the same for me. I had the bottle and I had Nikki to see through her difficult times. I guess I have too many reservations about too many issues."

"You have not struck me as being indecisive."

Bustillo shrugged. "I've got to get you out of this and Nikki, too."

More gently she said, "Would it have helped had you not had the bottle?"

"Don't knock the bottle, Chieko. When there's no way out, particularly from yourself, it has its uses."

"I'm sorry. The job you do seems—unsavoury." She shuddered. "Deceit, deceit all the time. Even with those one is supposed to love. I can't help but wonder that if killing Graham could produce the same result as delivering him whether you would have fired last night when you saw him?"

"I'd have run from the situation. That's what it's all about. I don't want to kill anyone."

"I believe you, Mr. Bustillo. I don't like what you do but I do believe you."

"Anyway, he's still loose. Dangerous."

"He's a clever man. I've always known that much. I respected his cleverness. I didn't realise it was rooted in evil." She covered her face. The blanket slipped from her shoulders. He went across to adjust it and saw the tears escaping between her fingers. She didn't move or make a sound, which somehow made her misery worse. What have we done to her, he thought. In Christ's name what have we done? He placed a hand on her shoulder and she made no resistance or gave any sign that she was aware that he was standing beside her. He doubted that she knew. Her hands were quite wet and he guessed at what it cost her to give way in front of him. Yet it was better that she cried. He was reluctant to leave her but it would be better for her if he did. He caught the sound of another car and went into the darkened front room.

There was the sound of more than one car. Two certainly. He leaned close to the window. They were coming up the valley road at speed. They went past and as they rounded a long looping curve of road the sound of them was lost behind the intervening rise of ground. Four o'clock. Could any night pass so alternately fast and slowly. Bustillo went back to the rear room. Chieko had taken the opportunity of his absence to tidy herself. She had stopped crying but there were tear stains under eyes that were still wet. In the harsh light it made her more beautiful.

"I'm so sorry," she said. "To break down like that was unforgivable. I'm so ashamed."

"Ashamed? To show your feelings? I wish I had your fortitude. Perhaps, if I had I'd have solved my problems and avoided the mess I'm in."

"I'm in it too."

"Yes. It would have been better if your husband had never seen me."

"So that we could continue to live a lie? No. This had to be, whatever the pain."

"Don't stand in judgment of him, Chieko. Of any of us. No one really knows what motivated him."

Her head tilted sharply. "I don't judge him for what he's done to others. I now know that I'll never hear the truth of that from him. But I must judge him on what he's done to me and his need to kill me. I cannot believe what's happened yet I shall always live with the sight of the gun pointing at me and his unloving eyes as he decided quite cold-bloodedly to fire."

"How's your wound?"

"Burning a little. No more."

"You'll be safe here. I want to find out if those cars have gone to the Miyotos' villa."

"For you it's not over. You are still in danger. Stay here. If it's safe for me so it will be for you."

"It's got to end. You've condemned me for running. So does Nikki."

"It does not matter what I think. Get the police, some help from somewhere."

"I just want to see what's happening." He checked the two guns. Leach's magazine was empty. There was one round left in the breech. Removing the empty magazine he pushed the full one in. He handed his own gun to Chieko. "Just in case."

She cringed away from it.

"You would have used it earlier."

"To stop *him* from killing. I don't want it."

"Okay." He put it on a table near her and the other in his waistband and folded his blanket neatly. "I'll be some time. If I'm held up there's a telephone in the other room. You can call a taxi soon after it's light. And perhaps the police too if I'm not back by then."

"Who are these others who want to kill you?"

"There's no time. It doesn't matter."

"Committing suicide will end your problems, but it won't solve them, Mr. Bustillo."

First Nikki now Chieko. "You think that's what I intend to do?"

"I think your despair is greater than you've shown me. You might see it as an honourable way out for mistakes that do not warrant it. Please don't run *all* the way. Have you more emptiness to face than I?"

He paused by the door. Leach must have been mad to want to hurt her. "What made you marry him?" He didn't think she'd cry again. Not in his presence.

"I loved him."

"And now?"

"I still have a duty to him."

If only his own logic could be as simple. "Don't make it a blind duty, Chieko. He has a duty to you too." He gave her a wave and left, closing the door quietly behind him. He climbed through the same window as before and found he couldn't see a thing after the bright light of the room. He stood outside until he could distinguish the lighter and darker shades and then set off across country. By bee-lining to the Miyotos' he would save a great deal of time and also avoid using the road.

It was a difficult journey. He had no compass but he had an acute sense of direction and if he got lost he could always fall back to the road. The ground was uneven and hard. Apart from open patches of lawn there were dense growth areas whether natural or cultivated it was impossible for him to see. He went for speed while the early morning air was like ice particles in his lungs.

He ran into high laurel hedges through which he had to crawl and then cover the grounds of another villa. Beyond that was a vast no-man's shrubland of gorse and brush that tore and plucked at him and reminded him of the aches and pains of his bruised hands. He could be little more lacerated than he was already after his fight with Leach and it had been a sign of Chieko's distress that she hadn't remarked on it.

The boundaries of the Miyoto estate were difficult to define. Bustillo had found this when he'd first reconnoitred with Nikki. The east side, which he was approaching, was roughly staked out at long intervals with prefabricated concrete posts. It wasn't until he saw the flashing lights suddenly close up as he emerged from a dense thicket that he realised he must have slipped over the boundary without realising it. He'd been making so much noise himself that he'd failed to hear the racket ahead of him.

At first all he could see were torch lights, five of them roughly in line, probing the grounds. He couldn't see the men holding them but he could hear them striking through the bushes like beaters on a tiger hunt. They had presumably worked their way up and were now nearing the villa which had all its lights on. One of his own alarms rattled in the night. Someone swore, there was more prolonged rattling and Bustillo guessed that they were dismantling the cans as they found them. The nearest man to him was only fifty feet away and his torch swept towards where Bustillo crouched.

Bustillo dropped flat before the beam reached him and pushed himself backwards towards the boundary. He kept going as the beam bobbed nearer. When it veered he risked rising and hurried back to a safer distance. The search had more than an element of panic about it. They were desperate, didn't know where he was. As the line moved above him, always approaching the villa, he was able to move into the grounds with little risk. The assumption was almost his downfall.

A big, fat figure was coming up the rise just below and some twenty feet ahead of Bustillo who was lucky to catch sight of the silhouette in a moon patch. And then he was gone, making remarkably little noise for such a big man. The dull light had briefly reflected on a bald pate. He carried no torch and was moving slowly, acting as sweeper for those ahead of him. Without knowing it, it was Bustillo's first glimpse of Susumu. Bustillo froze, too late to duck. After he'd lost sight of him he heard the soft tread of the big man which was almost lost in the noise of his colleagues further up.

Bustillo waited more cautiously now. The men reached the villa at intervals and doused their lamps as they stood in the wide porch. Bustillo kept well to the flank and started to climb towards them. He stopped at a point where he had the villa almost completely in sight. The men were still grouped and were waiting for the big man who had taken to the drive for the final stages. When he joined them they clustered round as if he was giving directions. Bustillo wasn't close enough to hear and he was reluctant to edge nearer. He counted them. Nine. Including the big, bald-headed man. Probably more at the gates. He recognised none of them. In spite of the distance he was satisfied that the Miyotos weren't there.

One man went back inside and all but one of the lights were switched off. The hall light. Bustillo remembered that it was the one light he himself had left on. They were trying to leave things as they had been. It was almost impossible for him to see them now; just the odd passing shape across the glass inset of the front door. An untidy sound of soft footfalls on the drive made it clear that they were going down towards the gates, presumably to where they'd left the cars.

Bustillo waited until they were well below him before he moved towards the villa. Apart from the general danger he had an unease that he couldn't explain: the feeling one has when convinced that something terrible has happened after a bad dream. His alarm grew as he neared the villa, bordering on terror. It was something that overrode the strong fears he held for himself.

He approached the villa from the rear working his way round to the side of the garage. He stopped there. Below him a car engine started up, then a second one. Both cars pulled away with no great speed. They seemed to be going away from Kyoto. Then they faded and he couldn't be sure whether they'd faded behind high ground or had stopped. He continued on to the garage entrance and put his head round the corner.

The Miyotos' car was back in its box. Please God no. Bustillo entered the garage to make sure. It was the car all right. The one that Tadashi and Nikki had used. Sweet Jesus. He now knew the cause of his terror.

15

Bustillo fought down the urge to rush into the villa. How far was the tragedy of the night to stretch? He crept round the back again. Of the three outer doors there was only one that opened soundlessly and that was the kitchen door. When he tried it was locked. He was letting anxiety rule his head. He'd locked it himself and still had the keys. Cool it for Chrissake. With Leach's gun in his hand he dropped to all fours and pushed the door back.

It was pitch dark but he'd memorised the kitchen layout perfectly. He crept in and closed the door. At the dining room door he waited, listened, opened it a fraction, held his breath and strained to hear breathing. Nothing. Still dark. It wasn't until he crossed the wide lounge that the first light crept through and that was only a strip from under the door opening on to the hall.

He waited for some time in the lounge. There was absolutely no sound of life and it worried him sick. His inclination was to go to the bedroom he and Nikki had used, but first things first. The crucial moment was in depressing the hall door handle and in pulling the door open an inch. He kept back against the wall, craning forward only slightly to peer through the slit.

A fair part of the hall was visible but the front door was out of sight. In the far corner of the hall was a closet, the door of which was slightly open with no light on inside.

As Bustillo pulled his own door wider more light flooded in. He stepped out feeling as though he was on stage, spotlighted. He had to cross the door gap to reach the closet side of the hall. Once across he felt less exposed. He crabcrawled along the wall until he reached the door then leaned forward a little to study the narrow black gap. He stepped softly out in front of the door and with fractional hesitation crashed it back with his foot. His own shadow coursed ahead of him and fell across another sitting on the closed toilet seat. A startled face peered up. Almost simultaneously a gun was raised but Bustillo fired on reflex. The sitting form crashed back then slowly forward as if bowing to defeat. His gun was still in his hand as he hit the floor.

Taking no chances Bustillo crashed his foot down on the gun hand while twisting round, his own gun sweeping the hall. No one came. The crashing back of the door and the falling victim had made more noise than his own shot. There was no response under his foot. He removed the man's gun quickly, bent down with his own pistol against the close cropped head, and felt for the pulse. He turned the body over with a heave of his foot. The close range shot had been enough.

Bustillo picked up the gun, put it in his pocket. He stared reflectively at the corpse, aware now of his total commitment. In the closet he found the man's torch and at last he had a useful tool. They had expected him to return normally by the front door. Which indicated that Nikki's car was already back by the time the others arrived. He recalled hearing the first car a few minutes before the other two.

He went up the stairs taking the view that as there was one trap there might be more. He searched each room keeping the torch low and leaving their own bedroom until last. No sign of anyone, not even of a struggle. He gazed at their bedroom door for a long time. He was aware of just standing there staring at the white wood. He didn't want to open it. When he did he pushed it and stood still. The room faced the back of the house so he was less careful as he directed the beam across the floor to the bed where it hovered along the untidy ridge of blankets. With a quick jerk he raised the beam, pointing it as he would a gun and striking his target first time.

Nikki's mouth was open. So were her eyes. The beam shone straight into them but they did not blink. Her lips were twisted as if she'd had a spasm but her days of suffering were over. One arm was stretched out over the sheet, fingers half curled as though she was reaching for him.

Bustillo lowered the torch and leaned against the door jamb leaving Nikki in darkness. It was hard to swallow and his eyes pricked. He didn't want to go in. Yet he had to. It wasn't that he'd been in love with her. Nor she with him for that matter. They had found a need, a bond, a sympathy and understanding that, when you're at the bottom of the pit, couldn't be assessed in emotional wealth. They had belonged in a different sense, even detaching the physical. Both had really known it to be transitory. Both had known they would never forget their joint cry of anguish. She had needed him much more than he had needed her. And she was dead because of him. Why had she returned? And where was Tadashi?

At last Bustillo stepped into the room and drew the curtains. He accepted the risk of switching on the lights. It didn't seem to matter. Nikki was largely under the blankets. They'd made the mistake of putting a nightgown on her. Although she possessed them she never wore them. It had been a joke with her. Why waste time in taking it off? Whatever she'd been she'd paid for it with the final price high. Her syringe was by her bedside table. It was the first indication of how she had been murdered. Nikki always used the bathroom for a shot. It was the one self-conscious habit she'd had.

Bustillo had the terrible sensation that if he pulled back the bedclothes he would find signs of torture on her body. She wouldn't have wanted him to see them. He made it his excuse for not looking.

To guess what had happened was fairly easy. She'd come back for some reason. Probably for nothing more than to be with him. And when the men had arrived she'd paid the price for his absence. She couldn't have told them where he was for she had not known. Then the threat of an overdose of heroin. And the final shot out of chagrin and malice. That it showed an increasing frustration and desperation from those who hunted him hadn't helped Nikki one bit.

In death she looked younger. Bustillo dropped to his knees and cradled her head in his arms. He wanted to express his sorrow not only for her actual death but for her living death whatever its causes. Nikki had been destined to die harshly. She could not have expected this.

The agonising sorrow in him eroded into blazing anger as he stroked her face and closed her eyes for the last time. Poor Nikki. The wasted life of a rich girl who couldn't cope, whose family allowed her to perish. It might have happened to him. He'd been too strong for the drug scene but there were other methods of debauchery. He'd balanced on a perilous rope for a long time. Nikki hadn't pulled him down; he'd failed to pull her up. He rose, bent over and kissed her forehead. "When are you going to stop running, Jimbo?" Her accusation came back to him. He could hear her still. Taking the hand that was outside the sheets he squeezed it. "Now, Nikki," he murmured. "Now. I'll pay my debt." His anger was intense but it showed only in the ferocity with which he gripped her hand. Through the anger filtered alarm. Tadashi.

Bustillo switched off the light, pulled back the curtains and ran down the stairs to the telephone. He pulled out the piece of paper Tadashi had given him, had a brief but vivid argument with the night porter at the small hotel before Tadashi's tired voice came on the line.

"Wake up and get out of there damn quick, Tashi. I'm calling from the villa. Nikki came back here. I suppose she felt lonely in a bed on her own. I wasn't here and they've killed her. But she probably told them where you are before she died. They'd have grilled her for sure. They'll come for you because they want me. Now move, for Chrissake move."

★   ★   ★

Graham Leach waited until Bustillo had given up his search before painfully working his way down the rockery again. His jaw was a massive ache and he thought it was broken. He didn't feel the cold as he resumed rubbing his tie against the sharpest rock. His whole mind and body were numb yet there was an ice-cold corner of reasoning that told him there was still a chance. Bustillo had his problems. On the run from the C.I.A. he could hardly use officialdom. Most officialdom, anyway.

The tie finally came loose because it was silk and the knot slipped as he rubbed. Just a few seconds later he was running through the grounds towards the gates. He had heard Bustillo return to the villa and guessed he'd had a spell by the car. When he reached the car himself, he unlocked it, sprayed front and rear windows with a de-icing liquid, then slipped into the driver's seat. He didn't switch on. Engine noise was a giveaway. He released the hand brake and freewheeled down the valley road, foot lightly on the brake, headlights dimmed.

He didn't go far, coasting until he saw a drive cut into the overhanging banks to his left. The gates were closed but he was able to freewheel up to them and be completely screened from the road. Out of sight meant temporarily out of danger and gave him a chance to review his position. It couldn't be much worse. He lowered the windows.

Unarmed he had little idea of what to do next. Until he had taken care of Chieko and Bustillo he could not consider returning to the hotel. He had almost finished them. Almost. They wouldn't expect him to try again, not soon. And they were right unless he could somehow arm himself. If he could kill them it shouldn't be too difficult to leave trace of an illicit affair between the two. A lovers' quarrel. One killing the other and the survivor committing suicide. Possibilities clicked through his mind like a calculator. He had a slight regret about Chieko. A really lovely girl but if it was not to be he'd cut his losses. He really didn't see that it would affect his relationship with Chieko's father if it was handled well.

As he sat musing, planning, his pains faded behind a fanaticism of self-justification and an unbalanced ego. He had never been beaten. Never. And a damned squirt of a C.I.A. defector wasn't going to stop him. How could he get a weapon? How? He applied his cold-blooded logic to several plans. He sat there for so long that he was forced, finally, to heed the cold as it crept up his leg and into the pit of his stomach. To help his circulation he left the car and walked up and down the short strip of drive cut into the hill. He was so attuned to crisis, so mentally alert to the need of survival, that the sound of footsteps reached him while some distance away.

Leach stopped pacing and went to the junction of the road. There was no doubt about it. Footsteps. And voices; mainly a man's, low, fairly deep. Surely it couldn't be. He waited calmly, then went back up the cut as they drew nearer. Hugging the bank, face low, he saw Bustillo and Chieko approach slowly, then pass. He was tempted to take Bustillo by surprise but the American had two guns and was strong. But he could follow.

They continued for a further hundred yards, stopped, then turned into another villa entrance. The rest was clear to him. They would rest up until morning and then get transport. He waited long enough to be sure that they were staying which was confirmed by the sound of splintering wood. It was easy to guess what was happening. He went back to his car quietly buoyed up. With the stimulus of knowledge came realisation that there were tools right under his nose. He opened the car boot and removed a tyre lever and the biggest spanner.

He waited then. Surprise would be his biggest asset and it was vital that he applied it at the right time. While he waited a car went past, full beams caressing the greenery, followed by two more some minutes later. He hugged the side of the road ready to dive off it should other vehicles approach.

When he finally sighted the villa in which Bustillo and Chieko were hiding he was coldly anticipant. He did all that Bustillo had done in examining the outside. The broken shutter and window were quite clear in the moonlight. He climbed through finding, as Bustillo had found, that the window was low enough to offer no real problems. Noise was his only enemy just then and he made certain he made none, sacrificing the tyre lever which he left outside because it wouldn't fit in a pocket as the spanner did. A chair was conveniently under the window the other side and he stepped down quietly.

Leach had the spanner in his hand when he eased the other door open. Chieko was sideways to him, pale and staring into space, oblivious it seemed of anything. No sight of Bustillo. He pushed the door a little wider. He couldn't believe what he saw. A gun lay on a side table between himself and Chieko. He stepped through and grabbed the gun before Chieko could move.

*   *   *

The two cars pulled up on high ground north-west of the villa and well within earshot of any vehicle that might turn into the Miyotos'. Susumu climbed out to inspect the isolated spot. When satisfied he issued further instructions to his men, then left three of them, taking two men with him in the other car.

His influence was such that he'd had no difficulty in raising men and cars from Osaka, the big industrial port close to Kyoto, when he'd telephoned from Tokyo. He had chosen numbers rather than a solitary specialist as before because he was short of time and real information. Matters were already well in hand when he flew down to Osaka in his own plane piloted by his diminutive chauffeur Yuzuru. He had refused to fly with the Miyotos for many reasons. At the moment his prestige had slipped and it was important to restore it quickly. A ridiculously commonplace execution had got out of hand. Now it seemed Bustillo was an American defector. It explained some things but not others. His experience warned him that there was another hidden factor.

He now drove fast and expertly through the night, finding the need to handle a car himself for once. It helped restore confidence in his own ability. He coped with the numerous bends and ice patches with mastery. He wanted this resolved before dawn. It had meant taking personal charge which had pros and cons. It

194

wasn't a bad thing to live up to his own reputation in front of men to whom he was already a legend. Provided it didn't happen too frequently. But Nikki Miyoto had been a different proposition. He had no intention of leaving a terrified junkie around to bear witness to his presence.

Killing Nikki had hardened his image with the men and it had also removed a danger. He'd extracted what there was but it had proved to be precious little. There was nothing of the Bushido of the Samurai about Susumu. His codes were different. Failure to him could mean someone else would die to cover it. It was fortunate that the motel where the Miyotos had booked in was en route for the place near Lake Biwa where the journalist Tadashi Fujuda was hiding. The connection between Tadashi and Bustillo puzzled Susumu. There was something going on between the two. The passengers behind Susumu occasionally glanced at the bland, narrow-eyed face but they had the sense to observe his preoccupation and to say nothing.

Twenty minutes after leaving the Villa Susumu was pulling up in front of a Japanese style chalet lying back from the road, the main neon sign of the conglomerate still flaring into the night. Susumu handed the car over to his subordinates with instructions to abduct Tadashi, question him about Bustillo and to dispose of him once they'd extracted what they needed. They were to use a knife or garotte. No noise. It shouldn't be difficult to get Tadashi out from the sort of flea bag he was understood to be in. Report back at the point above the Miyotos' villa. Don't lose a single second. Darkness was needed for the whole operation. It was five a.m.

The car had already gone before Susumu knocked on the chalet door. Kenji opened it, his dark eyes demanding answers almost before Susumu was in the room. Both Miyotos were fully clothed, Fujio as if he was going to a business meeting and Kenji in a thick polo neck. The two beds hadn't been slept in but there were indentations in the bed covers to show that the two men had rested.

Fujio guessed there were complications by the impassiveness of Susumu. There was no air of triumph. But it was Kenji who had to force out the verbal admission.

"Is it done?" Blunt as usual; aggressive too.

Susumu slipped his irritation behind his mask. "No. He wasn't there." His tone implied that the Miyotos' surmise of Bustillo being at the villa was wrong, thus transferring his irritation to Kenji. "Something has happened that no one could foresee," he continued smoothly. "The signs are that Bustillo and your daughter had a fight." He was facing Fujio, aware that the quiet eyes were trying to dissect him. "I'm afraid your daughter is dead. She was dead when we got there and Bustillo had flown."

The silence was absolute. Even Kenji had the grace to lose colour though perhaps not for the right reasons. Fujio sank to the edge of his bed without taking his eyes off Susumu: "What happened ?"

Susumu was quick to see that the question was emotionally loaded. The old boy actually was upset. "How can one be certain ? There's no point in hiding the truth for it must come out eventually. I understand your grief, so forgive me, please. The girl had been maltreated. I don't think that killed her. The bedroom was in a state of confusion and there was a hypodermic syringe on the floor. I examined it and the girl. It is my belief that she died of a drug overdose. It was clear from her arms that she was an addict. Whether it was administered by Bustillo I cannot say. I can only point out that he had obviously treated her brutally and had left. There were empty liquor bottles about the place. Perhaps he was raving drunk. We tidied up as best we could and laid her in bed. I thought you might prefer that. We then searched the grounds for Bustillo."

"The bastard." Kenji was glaring at Susumu, for once not hating him, even feeling a certain sympathy. With schizophrenic ease he conjured up a passing affection for his sister that he'd never possessed while she was alive. "Poor Nikki. She didn't deserve that."

Fujio was still looking at Susumu. "What should we do with her ?"

Susumu shrugged. "When we've fixed Bustillo you could find her in the ordinary way. If she's known to be an addict the police know all about overdoses. It can be kept quiet."

"Are there marks on her ?"

"Other than needle marks ? I'm afraid so. Again if people know she was associating with Bustillo he will take the blame. Dead or alive. We must make it dead."

"When ?" The sneer was back in Kenji's voice, his grief already waning.

Before Susumu could reply Fujio asked, "How do you know Bustillo was there ?"

"Because his things are there and the cases your son described."

"So you think he'll go back for his things ?"

"I think he'll go back because he has nowhere else to go. He can't have gone far. Your car is in the garage so he must be on foot unless he hired a car. With one available that's unlikely. Wherever he is, whatever his reason for being away, I think he will return if only briefly."

"Your men are up there waiting?"

"Some by the road, out of sight, one in the villa." Susumu didn't mention Tadashi. This would raise awkward questions. "I came back only to tell you about your daughter. You would not have thanked me for delaying it."

"No."

Susumu stared speculatively at Fujio.

"I'd like to see Nikki once you have Bustillo."

"Of course. But you can stay here until I bring you news."

"I'd rather come." Fujio stood up, straightening wearily, his eyes bright.

"Isn't it dangerous to expose yourself in this way? You're paying *me* to take the risks."

"You might be right. Perhaps I'm getting too old for galli-vanting."

Kenji said, "Well I'm not. I'm going."

"As you wish. Do you mind if I drive?"

"I've no objection."

Kenji was biting his lip. If Susumu balled it up again he'd deal with it himself. He checked his watch. Daybreak came late these mid-winter mornings but there wasn't that much time left. Even he had to admit to Susumu's driving skills on the run back.

*   *   *

"Where is he, Chieko?"

Chieko stared at the cold-eyed stranger who was her husband and repressed a shiver. It wasn't the gun that made her afraid but the fact that he had lived a lie and deceived her so easily. How could she have missed his cold-bloodedness? Where was the charm so readily there? How could she ever have lain with him? This man had nothing but the fervour of blood lust, of saving his own skin. There was nothing about him that she really recognised from the past. Even his features had hardened, the lips that had smiled so often compressed into uncompromising lines.

"I don't want to hurt you, my darling. Now where is he?"

She projected contempt as she could regality. When the two combined it was formidable. Leach's eyes flickered before the tiny moment of self-doubt was gone. Yet in that short time she had achieved more than anyone else. His presence gave her strength. Although her world had disintegrated and she was being pulled apart in all directions, his threats gave her a resolve to resist. In a strange way she was being held together by his menace because it was something openly to defy. It was the only way she had of expressing herself without resorting to useless verbiage.

"I don't want to hurt you," he repeated.

The effect was to straighten her back, look him in the eye, pour out silent disdain.

Leach shrugged. "All right. We'll wait. He wouldn't leave you here without a promise to return; not our gallant American defector."

The jibe almost provoked her to retort. Her silence of indifference had rattled him. It was more difficult to find self-justification without some form of opposition. He had always been clever with words. She would give him no opportunity to use them. If Bustillo came back she would shout a warning and take the consequences. It would then be over for her.

Leach pulled a chair behind the door and straddled it, arms along the back. Sideways to his wife he watched her profile, chin high, thoughts shielded but attitude calmly defiant. She had always kept her thoughts well hidden. Not, he had to admit, out of deviousness, but in acceptance of him being master. It never occurred to him that they were complete opposites. To accept that was to accept her complete honesty against his total dishonesty. He wasn't dishonest, merely protecting his elected way of life. His reward for serving others was threatened and he saw it as his right to protect.

"We could still make a go of it, Chieko. If only you understood. Your word would be good enough for me. I've always accepted your word."

She turned her head so slowly that it seemed she was in physical pain. Her hauteur was something beyond his reach as she met his gaze. He felt the inseparable distance that had widened between them with all its impact as she conveyed the incredulity of his monstrous suggestion.

"Why don't you speak, you proud bitch?" He had instantly destroyed the frail bridge he had tried to build between them. Then he burned it as it collapsed. "I shall kill you. Bustillo too. You've made it impossible for me now. You realise that. You've done it yourself. Only yourself to blame."

198

He relapsed into silence, wanting to shoot her now, mad that she had found his flaws without uttering a sound. Logic cooled him. He still might have a use for her.

The wait was nerve stretching. Leach became increasingly edgy in the condemning silence of his wife and because he didn't know what was happening. Had he thought torture would have forced Chieko to talk he would have used it but he reluctantly acknowledged that nothing now could break her silence. Yet even she was showing signs of tension and as it was clearly not concern for himself it had to be for Bustillo. His mind went round slotting in possibilities, as calculating as ever but not so confident. Where the hell was Bustillo?

A car went past and he stood up, gun pointing at Chieko. It continued on and the sound was lost. Leach stood for a few more seconds then sat down warily. He stared coldly at Chieko. He wanted to talk but didn't want to lose more face in front of her. She'd die looking composed like that, she was the type. It didn't help him.

Another twenty minutes passed before he heard another car, again climbing the valley road. It too went past. What was going on? Could it have any connection with Bustillo? His logic began to crack under the uncertainties built up by the unnatural silence. His nerve started to go as he felt himself to be in danger. Out of the encroaching confusion came one logical conclusion forced on him by the need for action.

"On your feet. We're going."

Chieko continued to sit. She did so deliberately. She had hoped against hope that her unprotesting acceptance of the situation might finally force him to believe that she wanted him to stay there. Had she immediately conceded to his order he might still think that. At all costs she wanted to get him out before Bustillo returned.

"I won't tell you again. Get up."

She rose reluctantly, putting a hand to her wound.

As long as she could walk that was all that mattered. If she tried to run he'd shoot her.

He climbed through the window first then ordered her through. The spanner was now a nuisance in his side but he wouldn't discard it. Once she was outside he retrieved the tyre lever. He made her walk slightly ahead of him down the drive, a slim willowy figure attractive even in outline. The fact that she didn't hurry convinced him more that she was trying to delay him here. He made her increase her pace. At the bottom they turned left on to the road and she laboured up the gradient until they reached his car.

"Tucked away neatly, isn't it? I saw the two of you go past. Get in."

She climbed in while he put the tools back in the boot. He wiped the windscreen, started the engine, the gun on the shelf near his right hand. He reversed out of the cut then U-turned to go up the road in the direction of the Miyotos' villa. Chieko stared at him in surprise. It was a giveaway. Her first.

Leach smiled thinly. "I thought he might have gone back there. His options, like mine, are rather limited."

Still she said nothing. With luck Bustillo was on his way back to the villa she had just left. They turned into the Miyotos' drive and she wondered what was in his mind. An open approach? Graham? As they wound slowly up towards the villa she noticed that the hall light was on as it had been before. Everything looked the same.

Leach pulled up outside the porch, snapped off the headlamps. He had swung in so that Chieko was nearest the villa. With the butt of the gun he smashed the two interior lights so that when he opened the door the car would be in darkness. He already had one foot on the ground when he said to her, "Get out. Go up to the front door and knock in the usual way. Do it quite slowly. I shall fire if you disobey in any way. And you know that I will."

As Chieko climbed out, so did he. He crouched down to come round the car, approaching her flank as she mounted the steps. He closed in as she knocked on the door, her head level with the opaque glass inset. He came nearer to her but not directly in front of the door. He heard, rather than saw, the slit of mail box open and close. At the first sign of the door opening he was behind Chieko, arm round her neck, gun against her temple.

Bustillo, who had recognised the car, had anticipated trouble even though he hadn't seen Leach. He had swung the door open and backed against the wall going down on one knee.

Leach held Chieko in the open doorway. He didn't move into the hall. Instead he said, "If you don't come out now I'll shoot her through the head."

Chieko said, "He will do it, anyway. Stay there."

"You bitch." Leach tightened his hold so much that she choked over his arm. It was this more than anything that drew Bustillo cautiously forward. One girl had already died because of him.

When he took in the scene there was precious little of Leach to shoot at. Leach was directly behind her, his eyes just above her head, gun at her temple. Leach said, "You've seen enough. Drop your gun or I pull the trigger. Now."

16

SUSUMU WAS BACK ON the ridge watching the villa through night glasses when his two men returned to report that Tadashi had fled. He had taken them away from where Kenji Miyoto was sitting in their car, hunched against the cold. All the signs at the hotel were that Tadashi had left in a hurry. One small drawer of shirts hadn't been packed. Two ties were still on a rack. So he had been warned. By whom and how?

Imponderables like this were beginning to worry him. He had underestimated one big factor but that only because initially he had not known that Bustillo was Warton. This man was used to being on the run. He was a ghost. A shadow. He'd had luck and at the first execution attempt warning from Kenji's big mouth. That sort of luck had to run out.

They all saw the car come up the hill. Dipped headlights. No attempt at concealment. They came to life when it turned into the Miyotos' drive. Susumu issued instructions at once. His men climbed into the cars. Only Susumu remained outside and he was joined by Kenji.

"Bustillo?"

Susumu still had the glasses to his eyes. "It must be. Who else?" From the moon and the distant hall there was a good deal of light for the specialist lens to magnify into a reasonable sighting. Feeling that Kenji wasn't satisfied he added, "Don't worry. I have an expert shot hidden in the hall closet."

Two of his own cars were already coasting down towards the villa entrance, lights and engines off. The crackle of the tyres on the road was eerie as the vehicles dropped from sight.

Susumu's concern increased as he watched. The front door had opened apparently of its own accord and he knew that couldn't be. Just before this he had picked out two figures one no more than the size of a youth. They closed up, one behind the other as the light flooded from the hall. He couldn't see the gun held to Chieko's head but he did see a crouching figure emerge from the side, gun held out. *It wasn't his man.* Was it Bustillo? Susumu felt himself at a complete disadvantage. Damn Kenji. He thought quickly and kept his glasses to his eyes.

"I think it's Bustillo there. And he has help. There are three of them. One small."

"That could be Tadashi Fujuda. The journalist. He's a friend of Bustillo and Nikki." Kenji put his hand out for the glasses but Susumu elected not to notice.

Kenji said scathingly, "What about your man inside? I thought he was supposed to cope with it."

That was also worrying Susumu. He shrugged. "I can't answer you. We must get up there. They are three, we are nine and mobile." He turned to Kenji. "The villa's insured?"

"Naturally. Do I read you right?"

Susumu nodded. "If Bustillo has help we must take all three which changes the situation. We'll have to burn the villa either to kill them or to destroy them after they're dead."

"That means cremating Nikki also."

"I'm afraid so. It's better to leave no trace."

The front door had closed, the two callers having gone inside.

"Let's move." Susumu spoke quietly but he wanted the night over more than any of them. He wanted the job done now, with no delay. There could be no further excuse. Those in the villa were sitting ducks. He would have been much happier had he known of their enmity. The two men climbed into the Miyotos' hired car as another plane from Osaka airport travelled north above them.

*   *   *

"Drop your gun," repeated Leach. Chieko winced as he pushed the muzzle too far into her temple.

Bustillo backed towards the stairs, automatic still levelled.

"Harm her, Leach and you're dead. I guess this is stalemate."

There was little either man could do. If Leach tried a shot at Bustillo he could rely on Chieko to try to spoil his aim.

Bustillo was grinning slightly. "You're gonna get tired before me." He sat on the lower stair without taking his gaze off Leach. With a confidence that ruffled Leach he unscrewed the silencer on his gun. "We seem to have changed weapons. A silencer won't make any difference out here except that I'm more accurate without one."

When Leach didn't reply Bustillo added, "You're thinking that as long as you have Chieko you can back off to the car. The car's no use to you now. You'll never reach the end of the drive. We're all dead, Leach. You, me, Chieko. The moment you drove up the way you did, you alerted at least nine men out there who have been waiting for me to pitch up. You see, you're not the only one who wants me."

"Don't try that, Bustillo. I would have seen them,"

"No. They were beating the grounds when I came back. I was lucky. They retired to the high ground to wait for me." Bustillo jerked a finger. "Upstairs is Nikki Miyoto. You can go up and look. She's dead. Tortured first. By the torpedoes out there· They're professionals, Leach. No qualms. Too good for us."

"I don't believe you."

"No ?" Bustillo rose, noting that Leach took up the first trigger pressure. "Go easy with that thing. I want to show you something." He sidestepped across the hall, eyes on Leach, ready to shoot straight through Chieko to get at Leach if he shot her through the head. Leach swivelled with Chieko as Bustillo moved. Bustillo flipped open the closet door and stood aside. Leach's eyes narrowed as he saw the corpse.

"*He* was waiting for me to return as well. Do you believe me now ?"

Leach didn't answer. He wasn't sure, he didn't understand the new development.

Bustillo said. "We're running out of time. You'd better make up your mind."

Leach, suspecting some sort of trap, still didn't move.

"Okay. You still don't believe me. Will you believe Chieko ? Has *she* ever lied to you ?"

"Is it true ?" Leach almost snarled the words into her ear. He relaxed his hold very slightly for her to speak.

"Yes it's true. I was told about them in the other villa."

"Didn't you hear the cars go past earlier on ?" Bustillo could see that he was almost there.

Leach remembered. "What are you suggesting?"

"I'm telling you that we're landed with each other whether we like it or not. With three of us there's just an outside chance we might hold them off. Singly we're dead. They'll already be moving into position. They'll have covered the villa, back and front."

"Are you saying we must defend together?"

"Take it or leave it. It's your only chance."

"Good God, we'd never trust each other."

"That's right. But if one of us shoots the other in the back he'd be committing suicide. Our only chance is to hold out until it's light, when the road becomes more active. Even that may not save us but it's the only chance we've got."

"And after? If we survive?"

"You don't need me to answer that. Back to square one. But at least we know what we're up against."

"Put your gun away."

"You too."

Neither man made a move. Leach said, "Don't you see how it will be? We can't even get that far."

"Listen, Leach. I'm gonna take a chance because I know we haven't a hope in hell if I don't and because I think there's little chance anyway. I'm lowering my gun. I'm not putting it away, because we'll need it. If you kill one of us you'll have to kill the other. That will leave you on your own against at least nine hired guns whose one aim is to finish whoever is in here. Figure it out." He stretched out for the telephone on a console-table. "They've cut the phone already. Which is maybe just as well because the police mean big trouble for both of us, especially you with me here and two stiffs in the house. You'd better get wise." Bustillo lowered his gun.

Leach stayed where he was, then he released Chieko who stepped aside rubbing her throat. Leach lowered his gun to point at Bustillo's chest. Chieko froze, afraid that the slightest move might provoke her husband to fire. Bustillo didn't move a muscle. He'd taken a gamble but it was all a gamble anyway. Leach was a calculator, he let him do his calculating. His impulse was to prepare to throw himself sideways but even the slightest suggestion that he might could make Leach squeeze the trigger. There was a moment when he thought it was all up, that he'd taken a ridiculous chance, and he glanced towards Chieko in apology. A reflection of light touched the glass panel in the front door and it was the final argument for Leach. Someone out there had been careless with a torch. "What do we do?" Self-survival had taken another turn. He lowered his arm.

Bustillo immediately took his spare gun from his waistband and handed it to Chieko. He could see that Leach was about to panic at the new, unexpected threat so he bawled out, "Don't scare, for Chrissake. We can't afford passengers and if Chieko can poop off now and then they won't know that she can't hit a barn. Now, all the lights on upstairs. All lights off down here. Chieko, you stay here."

The two men dashed upstairs. Sight of Nikki further convinced Leach of a temporary truce but he was already planning survival if they lasted out the siege. They switched on every light there was, keeping below window level as they sped from room to room. Downstairs again Chieko had already turned off the hall light and apart from a spillage from upstairs into the hall, the ground floor was in darkness.

The effect of the upper rooms being illuminated was to cast an oblique canopy of light down to ground level making it difficult to detect detail on the shadowed ground floor. It also threw back the darkness making movement within the immediate light fringe more easily noticeable. It was a small, pathetic, early warning system of anyone approaching. After a brief argument Bustillo took guard at the rear of the house, while Chieko and Leach watched the bigger window space at the front. Leach had made it clear that he must be with one of them at all times. He would not trust them together while he was elsewhere. It was a most unlikely truce that couldn't survive but which Leach would follow just as long as it suited him.

Bustillo scrambled into the kitchen and opened the tool drawer. He had to feel for tools; hammer, screwdriver in lieu of chisel. By touch he found the joins in the kitchen floor tiles and started to chip them up.

"What the blazes are you doing?"

Bustillo didn't stop. "You'd better learn to trust me for the duration, Leach, or we might as well surrender now. Get back to your window."

"I'd be mad to trust you, Bustillo. I asked what are you doing?"

"I've got to get under the house to the garage. There's stuff there we can use."

"You're not going."

"Then you'd better shoot me now. I've got my back turned."

"We'll go together."

Bustillo had raised a string of tiles slinging them aside. "And leave the villa empty? Just with Chieko? They'd swarm over us. It's no safer under the place than in it." He was now working on the floorboards. "Okay," he said suddenly as if capitulating, "you go. You get to the garage and I'll tell you what you've got to get and what to do with it. It's risky but I guess we're all at risk anyway. Meanwhile help me up with these boards." He was levering with the pane of the hammer. "Get your fingers under this and pull." The board came back, the wood creaking, the nails screeching as they bent. "Now the others."

Between them they made enough gap for a man to drop through. They stared at each other across the gap, the cold air coming up at them like a blast freezer; two dark shapes with slight luminosity in the eyes.

"Are you going or am I?"

"How long will you be?"

"As long as it takes. If I don't come back don't kid yourself I've escaped. There'll be just the two of you then. And they won't let you off the hook, Leach. No witnesses. So you'd better operate from the rear while I'm gone and make sure I'm covered." As Bustillo swung his legs into the gap Leach put a restraining hand out, still not really satisfied. Bustillo pushed it away. "Do you think I'd leave Chieko with you from choice? Do you know what she's suffering?" He lowered himself to find that here at the rear of the villa the drop was only three feet. He scuttled away like a rat.

Bustillo paused by one of the wooden supports under the villa to get his breath back. He peered out into the night. They were out there somewhere waiting for an order to move in. It would be co-ordinated. He guessed they'd have at least one man at each corner ready to pick anyone off who left the villa.

When he belly-crawled down towards the garage doors his nape was prickling. Occasionally he heard movement; they seemed to be very near but direction and distance were tricky at night. He wriggled on. On reaching the front of the villa he felt on show, the floorboards now high above him due to the slope. The garage was slightly detached from the house, its base dug into the hill. It was only a few feet away but completely exposed.

Bustillo flattened, raised his head just sufficiently to get direction. To his left a figure broke cover, raced, crouched, across the open ground and disappeared into the garage. Bustillo could have fired but he held back deliberately.

He crawled towards the garage, heading towards its blank wall instead of directly for the entrance. He reached it and rose, flat against the wall edging slowly towards the doors. Bustillo was three feet from the entrance when the figure came hustling out and passed straight in front of him. Bustillo pushed himself against the wall and the man didn't see him as he headed towards the spot Bustillo had just left. The man was half crouching, carrying a bundle under one arm and dangling a can from the other. It was impossible, in the bad light, to get precise detail, but he passed close enough for Bustillo to note the essentials and to be dismayed.

The man was lost to sight under the villa but Bustillo heard the odd movement and it was enough to send him hurrying back. The crawl was painfully slow. His feeling of sickness was not from effort but the certainty of what was about to happen. Yet he couldn't speed up without revealing himself.

The murk under the villa was almost Stygian. Bustillo couldn't see the man but he homed on the faint sounds of him. He smelled petrol and risked rising to a crouch and moving faster. Now he could just make out a shape, low down, noticeable as it moved. He dare not fire with petrol about and the fumes were stronger as he neared. He rushed forward as quietly as he could but not quiet enough. The man turned, intuitively knew that it wasn't a colleague, and pulled out his gun.

Bustillo still a few feet off whispered urgently: "You fire that thing and we both go up." The petrol fumes, trapped under the villa, were pungent now. A spark would do it. As the man realised the truth of it Bustillo dived tucking his head in as a pistol butt swung down at him. They rolled and as they did Bustillo guessed the man was reaching for a knife. As his hands closed on him Bustillo was full of a rage that was not for himself. He released his grip when he was under the man who mistook the move and pulled at his waistband. With one less hand to deal with for a second or two Bustillo grabbed the throat with both hands and squeezed with everything he had. There wasn't even a gurgle. Fingers tore at his hands, the knife forgotten, and tried to pull back his little fingers to break the hold but there was nothing that could.

After the man was dead Bustillo still held on. He shook the body with terrier fury and the head rolled aimlessly on the shoulders. "That's for Nikki Miyoto, you bastard." He flung the body down and groped around not daring to use his torch. He found the petrol can, the cap was missing and he couldn't locate it. The strong smell pulled him to a pile of waste rags that had been brought from the garage and soaked. Leaving them there he dragged the corpse by the collar to the garage side of the villa.

They'd see him come out, a shape no more, but would they recognise him? He went across the open ground as fast as he could still dragging the body. Inside the garage he was safe for the moment. With difficulty he raised the body on to the driver's seat of Nikki's car, groped about the garage until he found the second gas can and threw it onto the back seat. He found some more waste but he was fighting every passing second now. He opened the gas cap on the car.

Bustillo dashed back openly under the house. He kept very low but there was no reason for the moment why those watching shouldn't think he was their own man. Time would give him away, not recognition. He climbed through to find Leach bending over the hole.

"You're supposed to be on look-out, you bastard."

Leach didn't help him through. "I heard a rumpus. Sounded like a fight."

"It *was* a fight. They're one less and were about to about to fire the house, pick us off as we came out. Get Chieko, we're moving out."

"Where?"

Bustillo rammed his gun into Leach's throat. "Get her, you stupid bastard, or I'll blow your head off now and take my chances. I'll be waiting underneath." He dropped through the hole again, dashed to the centre, groped for the can and swilled more petrol over the waste, spreading it out as far as he could. He ran back to the hole to help the others.

Leach came hurrying back with Chieko. He came down first, still suspicious of every move Bustillo made. Bustillo helped Chieko down, careful not to touch her waist where the bullet had sliced. He could barely see her. "You all right?" She felt cold. He sensed her nod. She whispered, "Do I really have to have this thing?"

"The gun? It might be useful, believe me." He took them to the spot opposite the garage. "You two crawl across now. I'll join you."

They started off and he was satisfied when he lost sight of them in the dark. He forced himself to wait, to give them time, but every second was against them. He hustled back under the villa, found the waste, the concentration of smell impossible to miss, unwound a stretch and pulled it with him as he backed towards the garage. Far enough. He dropped the end streamer of the waste, backed a few feet, lit a match and then tossed it. The sudden explosion of light and flame blinded him. He turned and ran for the garage keeping his face averted knowing they could see him now. His face was seared and his direction was largely instinctive.

Reaching the garage he dived in, rubbing his eyes, praying for his sight to return. It came slowly. Leach and Chieko had retreated to the rear. Fine. He looked out. They'd be watching out there. Wondering. He edged towards the entrance, lay flat and gazed towards the villa. It had erupted like a volcano. The flames shot upwards and out as the petrol soaked waste caught and spread. It was unbelievably awesome. Only moments later the can exploded with an enormous roar and the flames poured out like molten fury, licking and spreading and devouring the wood. The wind, thank God, was blowing away from the garage.

Bustillo was surprised by the sheer speed of it. It caught and spread as he watched. His eyes were seared, the heat already unbearable. He eased back a little. What impressed him most was the noise level. Roar after roar filled the air as floorboards, walls, ceilings caught and burned as if they'd been in the middle of a drought, ready tinder, instead of a frost laden winter. He squatted, watching the huge flames tonguing the upper windows, the electric lights fading against the greedy red glare that showed up most of the grounds. He took his gaze from the searing fire and looked out. The whole shrubbery had turned red, flickering and changing, and forming moving shapes and shadows as if the grounds themselves were alight with humanised shrubs pulling on gigantic cigars that glowed and receded and pulsated at the whim of a fickle breeze. And from this erratic, ever moving glow stepped armed men. Bustillo didn't doubt that there'd be more behind. They stood in the open grounds, guns high, waiting to execute anyone running from the frightening blaze. He called back softly, "Come on, Leach. Chieko, stay where you are."

Leach came forward cautiously, curious to see the blaze now roaring at its highest level. He still put first things first. "There's no need," he said, looking out. "No one could survive that. They'll think we're dead."

"They'll have expected *someone* to make a run for it and must be puzzled by now. We've got to take them before they know we're around."

The floors of the villa had started to cave in. The cracking, crying agony of collapsing boards filled the night. Something sounded like a human scream, and, with luck, Bustillo hoped that was what it would be taken for. "There are three on show," he said. "Take them while the noise level's high. Come on, Leach, it's not over."

Bustillo made sure that attention was on the villa then ran obliquely away from the garage and the flames with Leach on his tail. They dived into the shrubs and wasted no time circling through them to come up behind two men who were waiting at the nearest corner of the villa. The flames threw them up in a fiery, dancing silhouette, jigging on the drive. From the front, Bustillo could see that the lower windows had already caved in, the porch was a raging mass and just behind it the once white front door was a black, blistering, cringing object writhing and shrinking in its own destruction. Incredibly the lights in the front upper window were still on although the roof above them was curling at its ends. Then they went out and glass splintered, then broke and melted out of sight. The noise of the inferno was difficult to understand. Apart from the roar of the flames the villa itself was screaming an agonising protest. Leach's car miraculously still stood in front of the house as if it had changed colour to a psychedelic pattern as the paintwork bubbled and popped.

"This is far enough." Bustillo stopped on the fringe of the clearing. "Two this corner. One on that. The other two corners will be covered. And there are sure to be some between us and the gates. You take the one on the left. I'll take the other one. Don't miss." He had his mouth close to Leach's ear yet had to raise his voice to make himself heard.

The range was about thirty feet. They were kneeling. They aimed and fired almost simultaneously, the crack of the shots lost in the general uproar. Bustillo had only to recall Nikki to swallow his qualms at shooting someone from the back. He dropped his man who fell to his knees, then forward. Leach missed. The man he had aimed at saw his colleague collapse. He'd probably felt the wind of a bullet for he swung round as Bustillo fired again while Leach seemed paralysed. The man's right leg buckled and he loosed off a couple of wild shots into the shrubs as he fell.

Bustillo fired once more and the man collapsed. He still wasn't dead, for suddenly he was screaming out both in agony and to attract attention.

"Back to the garage quick." Bustillo was quietly furious at Leach who pulled at his arm.

"We can get down to their cars."

"You think they've left them unguarded with the keys in?" Bustillo grabbed Leach by the shoulder, eyes blazing. "What are you figuring on? Killing me on the way down and leaving Chieko to *them*." He doubled up and ran back keeping just behind the shrub line, knowing that Leach would have to follow. When he was level with the garage he stopped. The flames were so high now that they'd turned the dark sky to a pink canopy with black belching smoke shooting up like a dark rolling pastel washed fantasy. Leach came panting up. Bustillo reasoned that the moment Leach considered the odds were in his favour to escape alone he would have to watch his back and Chieko's too.

The man stationed at the far corner of the villa was running across its front to where his two colleagues lay. Bustillo and Leach chose the moment to rush across the open ground and dive into the garage. They remained panting just inside the entrance. Chieko came from the rear to join them. In the reflected light Bustillo thought she looked ill, the red glow catching her cheek bones making her appear hollow eyed.

"You okay?"

She shuddered. "There's a man in the car."

Bustillo turned. The corpse had fallen sideways, lifeless face pressed up against the window. "He won't hurt you. We got two more."

"Yes, and they now know that we weren't in the villa," snapped Leach.

"They were on the point of believing that anyway. They must know that we weren't gonna stay to fry."

"All we've done is to trap ourselves in here."

"Don't bet on it. They're three short. Hold it." He held up a hand and crept up to the doorway.

Men were gathering on the fringe of the drive. Two gunmen were quietly circling ready to blast at anything that moved in the shrubs. There was a fat man, the reflection of the fire flickering on his bald head; he held a gun. Another man hurried towards the two who were shot, picked up their guns, apparently made certain that one was dead and then dragged the injured man back to the fringe of garden. Kenji Miyoto. Bustillo was sure of it.

Leach was on the opposite side of the doorway, ever calculating. He had to agree with Bustillo; there would certainly be men at the gates. They were all out of effective pistol range.

Bustillo was puzzled. Something was wrong or they wouldn't be hanging about like that. The fat guy was now conferring with Kenji, their faces flickering pink in a glare that had now passed its peak but was still strong. Bustillo didn't risk putting his head round the door, but the villa was beginning to break up, fall in on itself. The rending, crashing of burned timbers carried in the valley. Surely dawn couldn't be far off. He checked his watch, holding it close to his eyes. "What time have you got?" His own showed ten after seven.

Leach checked. "A quarter past seven."

Near enough. It would begin to get light by eight.

The short conference ended and the men fanned out and advanced slowly on the garage, Kenji and the fat man hanging behind the other three. Goddam, the injured guy must have seen them come here. "Chieko," Bustillo looked over his shoulder at her. She was hugging herself. With the heat from the villa it couldn't be from cold. "We're going to need you now. When I tell you to fire just point the thing and pull the trigger. They know we're here."

Leach said nothing as though he'd long accepted that he'd lost proprietary rights to his wife. He didn't even glance at her.

The gunmen stopped at a safe distance from the garage. They were well spread, the two flanks so separated that Bustillo and Leach were looking in almost opposite directions. Bustillo had half an eye on the fat one. From this distance the face was familiar then he recognised it from the old days when he'd been stationed in Japan. Susumu Takana. The Miyotos had really gone for the big time. Susumu didn't come cheap, and it spoke loads for the importance they attached to himself that he was operating personally.

It was Susumu who called out in English, "Bustillo, you were seen going in there. Two of you. Perhaps the third too. You can come out without your weapons or we can seal you off. Perhaps start a little fire at the entrance, eh? How do you want it, quick or slow?"

Bustillo opened the rear door of the car and splashed more petrol over the seat and the dead body. He closed all doors and windows with the exception of one rear window. "Get to the back of the car you two. Push when I say." He went to the entrance but remained far back to be out of sight. He bawled out, "Kenji. Did you know Susumu's hoods killed Nikki?" Immediately two shots were fired at him, one hitting the car, the other chipping above his head. He got down. "They tortured her. To find out where I was. Then they gave her an overdose. Did you know? Before he'd finished a barrage of shots screamed into the garage one holing the windscreen, another a whining richochet off the metal body.

"Push. Push."

The car began to move forward. Leach and Chieko safe behind it, Bustillo at the side getting purchase by the open window. A fusillade of shots pumped at them, most of them hitting the car. Bustillo, the only one exposed, kept close to the body, straining to keep the car moving. It tipped on to the slope of the drive. "Get in the shrubs as she rolls."

The car gathered momentum. When it was rolling of its own accord Bustillo ran a few feet beside it and fired through the open window. The flash ignited the vapour at once, the whole interior bursting into a mass of flame. Bustillo threw himself flat as the car gathered speed. Kenji and Susumu had to jump aside as it raced past and crashed into a tree its rear wheels lifting on impact. Two of the doors burst open, flames cascaded down and started on the tyres. The breeze was helpful, fanned flame over the open, half empty tank, caught the vapour and a sheet of solid flame burst up like a gusher before the tank exploded and flaming petrol spurted in all directions, creeping down the hill.

In spite of themselves the gunmen were attracted to the car. They saw a man being cremated inside it and were mesmerised for the few seconds Bustillo needed to join the others. As he rolled towards the shrubs he knew that all he'd done was to set them free from the garage. The gunman who had gone to the far side of the garage loosed off a couple of shots as Bustillo rolled past him and then crumpled as Leach shot him from the cover of the shrubs.

Bustillo crashed through the greenery and got to his knees. "Thanks," he said.

"I was hardly doing it for you, Bustillo. Let's get down the hill."

It was not to be so easy. Under a lashing from Susumu's tongue the other two gunmen were racing forward firing where the trio had entered and wildly missing because they had moved. "Now," growled Bustillo. Leach sensed it too. The two men pumped away and another gunman fell. The last one turned and skidded then ran back for cover. There were still four of them in sight but out of range.

Susumu was too experienced to try a frontal attack himself. His image had been shattered in front of his men yet he still managed outwardly to hold it. It was difficult with Kenji jibing him at every turn. If it would have helped he'd have shot Kenji then if only to relieve the tension building up in his huge frame. "We'd better get down to the gates. They can't get out, I've reinforced down there."

"Can't they?" snarled Kenji. "They've made rings round you. Bustillo has held the initiative all along, beaten you at every turn." He swept an arm round at the casualties. "Look at them. They couldn't kill a fly in winter. One in the villa. Another in the car. Two dead out here and one wounded. What do they do when they're not firing at shadows?"

"Bustillo still has to get out," rapped Susumu mildly. "There is nowhere to run to at the rear from what you say. Whatever they do they must try for the road."

"They're probably down there already."

"Then they will have a surprise."

Susumu raised his gun. "One thing stops me from killing you now, Kenji; your signature. You're good at talking. Let's see what you're really like. Now down to the gates."

Bustillo, Leach and Chieko had been watching out of earshot. They had stayed because they wanted to see what developed, how they might combat it. It was obvious that there was an argument between Kenji and Susumu and it was too good a chance to miss. Bustillo broke cover and raced round the edge of the drive. Kenji was backing off from Susumu who had started down the drive. Bustillo said softly: "Drop it or you're dead."

Kenji swung round with a strange expression, in the still formidable but dissipating fire glow. Wild-eyed, Kenji was too late to raise his gun. He looked back but Susumu had disappeared, expecting him to follow. "Just drop it," repeated Bustillo. "You're our passport out of here." Leach and Chieko were padding up behind him. As Kenji dropped his gun Chieko screamed, Bustillo spun round sensing the danger too late as Leach fired at point-blank range. Bustillo clutched his stomach and collapsed. Leach swung round to aim at Chieko who held a wavering gun in front of her as she tried to pull the trigger. When she did the shot went wide but she kept firing, unable to stop.

None of the shots hit him but Leach had to duck down and back off and it spoiled his own aim as he fired back at his wife. Chieko didn't move, standing there, the empty gun clicking repeatedly, tears streaming down her face. Ironically it was Kenji who saved her. With Bustillo out he took heart, retrieved his gun and fired at Leach's back. Leach took the shot in the leg, stumbled, fired back at the retreating Kenji who was bawling to Susumu that Bustillo was hit. When Leach looked round Chieko had gone. He looked down at Bustillo who lay absolutely still, blood oozing through his fingers as Susumu came panting to the edge of the drive to watch.

Leach wondered how many rounds he had left? Not more than one or two. He could spare one. He shot Bustillo as he lay there then limped painfully to his blistered car that was still outside the villa. When he touched it, it was hot. Red-hot timbers fell across it as he opened the door with a handkerchief. He looked back. To the east a series of lights were slicing the sky as they took the undulations of the road. Susumu had already seen them and was hurrying down the slope as Leach climbed into the car.

The heat inside was unbearable. Leach had to use his handkerchief to open all the windows as the sweat poured off him, saturating his clothes. Only desperation made him suffer the blistering of his legs from seats that were red hot. He turned the key and it was a signal for the fuel cap to blow off under the extreme pressure of vaporising petrol building up due to the extreme heat in the tank. Falling sparks were enough to do the rest. The flame jet belched and Leach knew that he'd better get out before the tank exploded. Under the strain of heat and fear he half fainted, falling sideways on to the drive as the tank blew. He retained sufficient sense to roll as the petrol flared towards him. There came a moment when he had almost reached the inert Bustillo, when he passed out.

It was the moment for Chieko to reappear. She stood for a second looking down the hill at the approaching lights, turned to look at Leach, moved towards him then veered towards Bustillo. The fireglow made red rivulets of her drying tears but action forced back her despair. She cried silently as she tried to turn Bustillo over, not sure whether she should or not. Then she cradled his juddering body as the lights drew nearer.

*   *   *

Because of the haste to escape and the detour forced on them by

the approaching police cars, Susumu and Kenji did not arrive at
the motel until a good hour after dawn. During that time they had
hardly spoken. Susumu's quiet complacency after dispersing his
men had fed Kenji's dissatisfaction about the whole thing. Initially
it had taken both men time to recover their breaths after the mad
dash down the hill followed by Susumu's expert driving without
lights for some distance on winding roads. This expertise was all
Kenji grudgingly conceded to the fat gangster. And perversely,
even that concession added to his anger. By the time they walked
in on Fujio, Kenji was seething.

Fujio was sitting on the side of a bed, almost as they had left
him. He was staring fixedly, raising his gaze only as Susumu spoke.
"The mission is complete."

"In spite of your handling." Kenji was verging on the reckless
ready for open war. He threw his gun on to a bed. "We must get
rid of that."

"Is Bustillo dead?" Fujio climbed unsteadily to his feet as if he'd
been sitting too long.

"He's dead."

"How would you know? You didn't shoot him," Kenji flared,
no longer caring about control.

Susumu kept his temper. "You'd better keep your voice down.
There are other cabins. I went back. The stranger shot Bustillo
while he lay there."

"Stranger?" Fujio didn't understand. He was drawn and looked
his age.

"Someone was with Bustillo. They must have had their differences. The stranger shot Bustillo twice."

"And *I* wounded the stranger." Kenji couldn't resist the boast.

Fujio was bewildered. "I don't understand. Is this man still
alive?"

Susumu expanded, as if to a child. "Don't you see? It doesn't
involve us. Bustillo was shot by a man who will be caught by the
police. Maybe he's dead, I don't know. I heard his car explode.
But anyway they'll find his gun and it was *that* gun that killed
Bustillo. We are all off the hook."

"You don't know who he is?"

"No. Nor would he know us. If he survived. We must get
back to Tokyo. The police will contact you there about the villa
burning down."

It was almost too much for Fujio. "The villa? With Nikki in
it?" He turned to Kenji. "Did you see her first?"

217

Kenji ejected his spite before thinking. It was a blow at Susumu. "He killed her. Not Bustillo. He tortured her first."

Susumu went white with anger. He pulled his gun and Kenji realised that he had spoken stupidly and that his own gun was out of reach; he dare not go for it. The two men faced each other, hate no longer disguised but the experienced Susumu fought for control knowing that killing Kenji could be disastrous. Sweat trickled down his putty puffed face as he gradually lowered his hand.

Kenji was just beginning to breathe again when the roar of a shot shattered the dreadful silence that had fallen between them. He watched Susumu jerk, his eyes roll, then, rooted by fascination, he saw the knees bend outwards as the body began to sag. Kenji turned in horror to see his father holding his own gun. It fired again before he could move, the roaring echoes bouncing round the small room like a ragged volley. By the time he'd grabbed Fujio's gun hand it was over. Susumu had sunk in an ungainly heap that was obscenely spreading over the floor.

"You fool. Oh God, Papa, you've blown it."

Fujio wasn't listening, unaware that the gun was being taken from him. There was a quiet dignity about him, a resignation as his back straightened.

"Let's get out of here quick. Move, Papa, please. Get your things."

Fujio focused. "Do you imagine no one heard the shots?" An expression of relief touched his features as they softened. He looked down at the now still Susumu. "It's too late, Kenji. It was too late from the time you decided Bustillo must die. Nikki's gone. Horribly. It is our turn to atone."

*　　　*　　　*

"You look beautiful."

"Thank you. And you've lost weight. It is better for you."

The spring blossom was scattered in soft splashes through the park, the trees green and rich. The Gold Pavilion showed its twin in a perfect reflection on the placid lake. The paths round it were loosely full of people.

"You're going a little too fast for me."

"I'm sorry." Chieko checked her pace. "It is painful still?"

Bustillo grinned. "I can't get used to this damned stick; but it helps take pressure off the leg which in turn eases my back. I'm not complaining."

"I know you're not. I've never heard you complain."

Bustillo hobbled beside her. "Then you should stick around, you're really missing something."

Chieko smiled faintly. She looked splendid in a pale blue and ivory patterned kimono. They walked in silence for a while. They reached strands of wire to keep people back from the shrine but different in that hundreds of small pieces of paper were twisted round each strand forming paper barbs.

"You know what they are?"

Bustillo nodded. "People write a prayer and twist them on hoping they'll be answered."

"Yes. Did you know I did one for you?"

He was touched. Memory came back strongly. He wanted to ask her but she anticipated him.

"Yes. I did one for Graham too. Perhaps he needed it more than anyone."

"You sure you want to talk about it?"

"It is easier now. I cannot run away from it."

"No. The British expect to extradite him any moment. These things drag on. It must be difficult for you."

"For you too. What is happening?"

He hedged. "I want to recover from those two slugs first. One was not too much trouble but the other played up a nerve at my back. Almost went clean through. They say it will heal in time, that I can discard my stick, but I guess you know what doctors are like."

"Are they taking you back to America?"

"No. Officially I don't exist. The British were very good about it. Put up a strong case to my own people. With the help of your Police and British Intelligence, the C.I.A. have been allowed to interview your husband. I'm afraid they'll keep at it once he's back in London. He's a lot to answer for." He looked down at her to see how she was taking it. Her piled up jet hair was just above his shoulder. "Anyway, you were right back there that night in the villa. His capture has helped me. The C.I.A. will eventually get more from him than they figure I might have given the Cubans. He is a much bigger fish. I'm sorry you were right but that's the way it is."

Chieko was quite composed but she didn't reply.

"Then your own people were helpful when I made a statement about the Miyotos. I guessed they're *really* finished. Their empire is already folding."

"It is tragic for Japan."

He took her arm lightly to reassure her. "Every country has its big corruption scandals. The British had Poulson. We had Watergate. The French had the big wine racket. You're landed with the Miyotos. They deserve whatever they get." He looked at the sky, reflectively thinking how similar in colour it was to the frail motif on her kimono. "My escaping from Cuba helped my case too. We've come to an agreement that I'll not publicly divulge my reasons for leaving the C.I.A. So I remain Jimmy Bustillo. No one knows what happened to Warton."

"Will you go back there?" They had continued walking.

"The States? That's more difficult. I'd like to stay here in Japan. I was always happy here."

Chieko nodded, pleased. "Am I going too fast?"

"No. The old third leg is doing its stuff."

"Did you *love* Nikki Miyoto?"

He stopped, looked down. "Not in the way I think you mean. We both needed each other. We knew a little of what the other was suffering. Nikki deserved better. She had it rough right to the end."

"You're a very compassionate man."

"Ask my old bosses and they'll call it weakness. I guess it's the way I am. Soft."

Chieko laughed spontaneously, hand flying to her mouth.

"What have I said?"

"I'm sorry. It's really nothing to laugh about. But if I didn't laugh then I would cry and I've done enough of that to last a long time. I was thinking of how soft you were *that* night. Our newspapers hailed you as a hero in breaking Susumu."

Bustillo grinned widely. "I guess that helped my case too. That was quite a night. We were lucky Tadashi routed the police out."

"I have much to thank you for."

"I should have thought the opposite."

"A fool's paradise is of no use to anyone."

"I guess you're right. Are you hungry?"

"Would you like a taste of old Japan?"

"Aren't we in it?"

"To eat?"

"Sure."

"There is a small hotel near Kyoto called the Tawaraya. It has its own gardens and they are beautiful. I will take you there. It is easy to forget in such a place. Easy to be compassionate and a fool. It is nearly nine hundred years old. Will you step back in time with me?"

"I already have, Chieko."